BET ON IT

AN AGE GAP, BILLIONAIRE, OFFICE ROMANCE

HIGH STAKES

AJME WILLIAMS

ALSO BY AJME WILLIAMS

Ajme Williams writes emotional, angsty contemporary romance. All her books can be enjoyed as full length, standalone romances and are FREE to read in Kindle Unlimited .

Books do not have to be read in order.

Billionaire Secrets
Twin Secrets | Just A Sham | Let's Start Over | The Baby Contract | Too Complicated

Heart of Hope Series
Our Last Chance | An Irish Affair | So Wrong | Imperfect Love | Eight Long Years | Friends to Lovers | The One and Only | Best Friend's Brother | Maybe It's Fate | Gone Too Far | Christmas with Brother's Best Friend | Fighting for US | Against All Odds | Hoping to Score | Thankful for Us | The Vegas Bluff | 365 Days | Meant to Be

The Why Choose Haremland
Protecting Their Princess | Protecting Her Secret | Unwrapping Their Christmas Present

Dominant Bosses
His Rules | His Desires | His Needs | His Punishments | His Secret

Strong Brothers
Say Yes to Love | Giving In to Love | Wrong to Love You | Hate to Love You

Fake Marriage Series
Accidental Love | Accidental Baby | Accidental Affair | Accidental Meeting | Accidental Daddy

Irresistible Billionaires
Admit You Miss Me | Admit You Love Me | Admit You Want Me | Admit You Need Me

Check out Ajme's full Amazon catalogue here.

Join her VIP NL here.

DESCRIPTION

Being a billionaire had become boring until a stranger showed up to a conference and spiced things up...

Curvy, sassy, and dangerously younger than me...

Analyn was everything that a former hockey player needed to stay away from.
I was used to women falling all over me.
But Analyn's pretty mouth that never shut up was still tempting.
Especially when I made a bet that she couldn't resist.

Analyn had no idea she was setting herself up for failure.
Little Miss Sassy came back to me, this time looking for a job.
And I knew it was my turn again to suggest a wager.

Our one-night stand had to be forgotten.
But I couldn't *not* notice that cute pencil skirt she'd wear to the office.

All eyes were on me... on *us.*

And my eyes were on the only woman I could *bet* would never
trust me.
Or would she?

PROLOGUE

Analyn

Men are scum. Especially Chase Tolliver, the man I was sure was going to propose to me. I was right. Oh, did he ever propose to me. Except it wasn't marriage. It was an open relationship.

As it turned out, we'd been in an open relationship practically since we started dating. I just hadn't known it.

When he'd suggested the new arrangement, we were at a fancy restaurant in Chicago, my heart beating a million miles a minute, at first in joy and then in shock. Did he really mean that he wanted an open relationship? Did it go both ways?

I pointed toward a handsome man sitting at another table and asked, "So if I wanted to sleep with him, you'd be all right with that?"

He gave me an affable smile. "Sure. That's the point, isn't it?"

I wasn't sure what hurt more—that he didn't feel sex should be monogamous or that there was no sign of jealousy at the idea of my sleeping with another man. Both were bad. Both indicated that I wasn't in the type of relationship I wanted.

"And what if I didn't want that?" I'd asked him.

He didn't say anything at first, but that pause told me everything I needed to know. He hadn't been faithful while we dated. He wouldn't be faithful in a marriage. A marriage he hadn't even proposed. Chase wasn't the man for me, after all.

I put my napkin on the table. "Let me save you the trouble. You're welcome to screw around with all the women you want, but when you need a plus-one or a girlfriend, don't call me."

I stood and walked away from the table to leave the restaurant. When he didn't call after me, I began to wonder if my reaction was exactly what he wanted. He'd set me up to break up with him so he wouldn't have to break up with me. Coward.

Men are scum and cowards.

The best way to get over a breakup is to spend time with your best friend. Unfortunately for me, my best friend lived in Las Vegas while I was in Chicago. No worries. I simply packed a bag and hopped a plane and was now spending a week with my best friend, Betts. In the few days I'd been there, we had done all the things required to get over a man, which involved copious amounts of ice cream and wine. We were having such a great time, she invited me to be her roommate if I wanted to move to Las Vegas. I was seriously considering that idea.

Unfortunately, tonight Betts was on a date with her boyfriend, Paul. They had an on-again-off-again relationship that had been off when I arrived, but then he called earlier tonight, and it appeared that they were on again.

She felt bad leaving me at her place alone while she made up with Paul, but I assured her that it was okay. I wanted her to be happy, and if Paul was the guy who was going to make her happy, then she needed to see him.

After she got all dressed up and headed out to meet Paul, I putzed around her condo for a little bit, but I didn't like being alone. I started to think about Chase, and instead of thinking what an asshole he was, I got down on myself.

What was wrong with me that I wasn't enough? I determined the best way to combat self-pity was to go out and live it up. I was in Las Vegas, Sin City, after all.

There had to be a reason the motto of Las Vegas was, "What happens in Vegas stays in Vegas." Surely, that meant I could let go of my inhibitions in an effort to forget Chase and not worry about any ramifications. That sure sounded better than hanging around Betts's condo feeling sorry for myself.

I did a quick Google search looking for the best places to go that weren't about gambling, or at least only about gambling. In Las Vegas, I swear there were slot machines in the bathrooms. But I didn't have any money to lose, so I just wanted a nice club where I could drink and let my hair down.

I decided on the Golden Oasis. According to Yelp, it was the coolest club because it included tech features like holograms with famous celebrities of Hollywood's golden era. I dressed for a night at a club, which included a red dress that clung to my ample curves, styling my long, dark hair into thick waves, and putting on enough makeup to suggest I was interested without being trampy.

I studied the result in the full-length mirror in the guest room of Betts's condo. "Eat your heart out, Chase."

I ordered a rideshare that dropped me off in front of the club. I walked in and was pleased to see that it was as cool as the Yelp reviewers and images had made it seem. On one wall, a hologram of Marilyn Monroe in her iconic stand over a vent moved until air blew her dress out. A few drunk men joked around like they were trying to look up her dress. Women took selfies of themselves modeling the same stance as Marilyn.

The drunk men notwithstanding, the place had a young, hip, yet sophisticated vibe. I patted myself on the shoulder for making a good choice.

I made my way to the bar, taking a seat on the stool. I should have ordered something exotic, but I couldn't think of anything offhand so I started with a plain white wine.

As I drank, I watched the activities in the club. A crowd filled the dance floor, where new arrangements of old standards played. More holograms of Hollywood's shining stars shimmered among the dancers.

I finished my wine and ordered a cocktail that included cranberry juice and vodka and continued to watch the crowd. I could tell the people who were single, looking for a good time, apart from those who were couples.

Couples just had a vibe about them. It was like I could see the bond between their hearts. The more I thought about it, Chase and I didn't have that bond. I thought we had true love, but clearly, we didn't. It was time I stopped grieving over losing something I didn't have.

What better way to forget one man than by spending time with another one?

I didn't know where that thought came from, but after a glass of wine and a cocktail, it made perfect sense. A titillating thrill shimmered through me at the idea of meeting a stranger in a bar. Betts would probably be worried, because neither she nor I was the type to go clubbing and hook up with men.

Did I want to hook up? No, I told myself. But I wouldn't mind having a man notice me. Or pay attention to me. I could enjoy the company of a man without it ending up as a hookup, right?

I scanned the bar looking for someone with the potential of enjoying an evening of drinking and maybe dancing. There were many men to choose from, but some I dismissed off the bat, like the ones trying to look up Marilyn's dress. Sure, I'd like to spend my evening with someone handsome and sexy, but it would be nice if they had a little substance as well.

My gaze settled on a man sitting at the end of the bar looking bored and maybe disgruntled. Like his life hadn't turned out the way he thought it would. *Welcome to the club, buddy.*

He appeared older than me, maybe in his mid-forties, but he was definitely handsome. He was the epitome of distinguished, with short brown hair with a little pepper of gray, lines along his eyes that hinted at wisdom or experience, and a strong, chiseled jaw. He wore a T-shirt that showed muscle definition a man half his age would envy. I decided he was the perfect one for me to make friends with tonight.

I made a beeline toward him, taking a seat in the stool next to him. "Can I buy you a drink? And before you say no, or yes, I just want you to know the only reason I'm over here talking to you is because you look like you're alone, and so am I, and I'm looking for someone to have a good time with tonight."

His head turned, showing pale blue eyes that made me think of a meadow stream. His arched brow suggested he thought I was a lunatic.

Only then did I realize how he could take my words.

I gave my head a quick shake. "I mean a good time as in having drinks and talking and dancing. You look like you could benefit from having your mind taken off whatever it is you're ruminating over. And I'm here to forget a man, whose name will never cross my lips again."

I half expected him to get off the stool and walk away without a word. Instead, he tilted his head to the side. "What makes you think I was going to say no?"

His question took me off guard, mostly because I expected him to respond to my bad attempt to buy him a drink.

I shrugged. "I don't know. I've never actually gone to a bar and talked to a stranger. You might think I'm crazy. I'm not, unless approaching a stranger in a bar is crazy."

His lips twitched upward. "Sometimes, crazy is a good thing. Makes life interesting."

I nodded.

"I could use something interesting in my life right about now." He held up his hand toward the bartender. "Josh."

Yay. It was working.

The bartender headed over to us. "What can I get you?"

My new friend looked at me. "What would you like?"

"I'm buying, remember? What do you want?"

He flashed a grin, revealing a dimple, and holy cow, he really was handsome. He turned to Josh. "I'll have a bourbon and water."

"And I'll have another one of those cranberry vodka things."

Josh went to fix our drinks.

"You must come here a lot if you know the bartender's name," I said.

"I come here enough. It's not really my ambiance, but the owners run a good club. I know one of them and have been bugging him to open one like this but with a sports theme."

I frowned. "Aren't there a lot of sports bars?"

"Yes, but I mean like this with the holograms. Imagine being able to sit with a hologram of Babe Ruth or Wayne Gretzky."

"Wayne who?"

He closed his eyes and shook his head.

I felt a little dumb not knowing who this Wayne guy was.

Finally, he opened his eyes, his baby blues showing humor. "Wayne Gretzky, probably the single best hockey player ever."

"I'm sorry, I don't know hockey."

He sighed, like he'd heard that more than once. "The point is a place where fans can come and be with their all-time favorite sports giants." Movement caught his eye, and he raised his hand again. "As a matter of fact . . ."

A couple approached him at the bar. "Hey, Max, Amelia." He turned to me. "This is . . .?" He laughed sheepishly. "I'm sorry, I haven't gotten your name."

"Analyn."

"This is Analyn. She might be crazy, but in a good way."

The heat of a blush came to my cheeks, but I extended my hand to the man and woman.

"This is Max Clarke and his wife, Amelia. They own this place."

"Nice to meet you." I'd never met the owner of anything. In movies, it always seemed like knowing the owner, or the owner knowing you, meant you were a big deal. I wondered who my new friend was.

Max laughed. "We were having dinner when we realized that the kids were over with Amelia's brother and his wife and decided that we would have a night on the town. In fact, we're talking about maybe getting a suite at a local casino."

"Not just any suite," Amelia said, waggling her brows at her husband. "The suite that started it all."

I watched them with envy, wondering why I hadn't been able to have that sort of relationship with Chase. I didn't know Max and Amelia, or about the suite that started it all, but in the few seconds I'd been with them, I knew that they had something special.

"Well, don't let me keep you from your night on the town," my drinking buddy said.

"You have a good evening. Both of you. It's nice to meet you, Analyn." Max turned his attention to my new friend. "And the next time my brother Sam is in town, we'll get together and talk about that sports bar idea of yours."

"Sounds great."

As Max and Amelia walked off, Josh, the bartender, served our drinks.

I held up my drink to click with his, but first . . . "I think you should tell me your name, and then we can cheers."

He held up his bourbon and water. "I'm Reed."

"Here's to crazy, new, interesting friends."

"Cheers to that."

We clicked our glasses and sipped, and then we started talking about anything and everything. Well, maybe not everything. We didn't talk about work, or even much about our personal lives short of telling him about my ex and his desire for an open relationship.

Reed showed the right amount of disgust at the idea. "I don't think I'll ever understand that. If you find somebody you want to be with, it seems to me you need to hold on tight and not let anything get in the way."

I studied him. "Have you ever had that?" I wondered if he was divorced or widowed. He couldn't be married and believe in monogamy unless he was playing me and his reaction was all an act. I sipped my drink and pushed that thought away. It didn't matter. We were in Vegas, and once I went home to Chicago, it wouldn't matter.

He shook his head. "I haven't had much luck in that department."

I must have gaped because he laughed. "Why does that surprise you?"

"Because of all this." I made a motion toward his face and the hard planes of his chest etched in the fabric of his T-shirt.

He shrugged. "I suppose I'm looking for somebody who wants a little bit more than this."

I nodded. "I hear you. Well, actually, I don't because I don't have this . . ." I made a motion to my own body. Don't get me wrong, I don't think I'm unattractive, but I'm no super model.

He frowned. "What do you mean, you don't have this?" He motioned to me. "If you weren't here sitting with me, any one of the single men—hell, maybe even some of the married men—would be coming over here to make your acquaintance."

I shook my head as I sipped my drink. "That's nice of you to say, but I doubt it."

"I bet you that if I left, there would be a man, several probably, who'd show up. Whereas I've come here plenty and never had a woman hit on me."

"I did . . . hit on you . . . I mean . . . well . . ." God. Why did everything I say suggest I wanted to have sex with him? I let out a sigh.

"Perhaps we'll have to agree to disagree because I don't really want to take that bet."

I went all warm inside as I took his words to mean he was enjoying my company, awkward as it was. "I guess it just goes to show that there's much more that goes into a relationship than just attraction."

He held up his bourbon. "I'll cheers to that, too."

We continued talking and drinking. I wasn't drunk, but the inhibitions were down, the music was pumping, and I could feel it vibrating in my blood. "Do you happen to dance, Reed?"

He shook his head. "Not very well."

"Me neither."

"I don't believe it."

"I bet you're better than me," I said, playing off the "bet" he'd made earlier.

He grinned, and for a minute, I was blindsided. "I'll take that bet." He stood, and I was able to note that he was tall. Tall and broad, like a football player. He held his hand out to me. I placed my hand in his, and it was large like the rest of him. I had a moment to remember the adage about a man's hands being reflective of the size of his package. I let out a giggle and immediately tried to take it back. How mortifying.

"What's so funny?"

I shook my head. "Nothing. I was just noting the size of your hands."

His eyes narrowed, and I swore there was a wicked feral quality to it. "It's true, you know, about hand size."

All my girly bits flared to life. "No, I wouldn't know."

The music was a fast rhythmic beat, but he put his hand on my hip to keep me close to him as we danced on the crowded dance floor. I might have thought he'd respond to my comment and was a little disappointed he hadn't. I reminded myself that I didn't want this to be more than a night of drinks, dancing, and scintillating conversation.

He was right. He wasn't a great dancer, but neither was I. Neither of us cared as we allowed our bodies to move to the beat. I felt free and uninhibited. I wasn't worried about what others thought. I just let go and lived in the moment. It was the most fun I'd had in a long, long time. In fact, I'm not sure I ever had so much fun with Chase.

The song ended and the DJ came on. "Time for the true Mr. Blue Eyes himself." A hologram of Frank Sinatra appeared near the stage. The music swelled, and the hologram sang *Strangers in the Night*.

My chest filled with a strange sensation as the words of the song mixed with Reed pulling me close. "Shall we keep dancing?"

"Yes, please." I didn't want the night to end. I felt like Cinderella, afraid of the clock hitting midnight and this wondrous night coming to an end.

"I suppose we haven't resolved the bet. I'm pretty sure I've lost."

I shook my head. "I think it's a tie."

He laughed as he pulled me to him for the slower dance. As we moved, our bodies drew closer until I was flush against him. My hand settled on the hard, warm plane of his chest. Lower, I felt something else hard. Something that proved the point about large hands. I looked up at him.

He gave me a sheepish smile. "You'll have to excuse my friend."

Arousal rushed through my body. I wanted to strip this man down and drag my tongue over every inch of him. It was unsettling and exciting, and I laughed, feeling a little bit giddy about it all.

He leaned his head closer, his lips just along my ear. "If you had any interest in seeing the proof about hand size, I'd be happy to show you."

I'm pretty sure I groaned. Not a groan of dismay, but a groan like I was about to orgasm right there on the dance floor.

I wasn't a prude, but neither was I a woman who normally went home with strange men for a hookup. But the bartender, Josh, knew him. And the owner, Max Clarke, and his wife knew him. That had to mean he was an okay guy, right?

Plus Josh, Max, and his wife knew he was talking to me. If I turned up dead, they'd be able to tell the police I was with him. God, I watched too much true crime TV.

I pushed that away and reminded myself that I was here tonight to live life out loud and not worry about ramifications, of which there would be none because this was Vegas, baby.

"Your hands are impressive," I said with a sexual bravado I'd never felt before.

His hand slid down to my ass, tugging me a little bit closer, letting me feel the steely length behind the zipper of his jeans. "How about we find a place more private to dance?"

The next moments were a blur as we left the club and entered one of the nearby casino hotels where Reed had a room. Then we were in the elevator, where he pressed me against the wall, his hard length teasing me and his lips giving me a searing kiss that almost had me orgasming right then and there.

Our hands were all over each other's body as the doors of the elevator opened, and we managed to make our way into the hall and toward the room that he'd rented.

By the time we entered the room, he had lifted my dress so that when the door closed behind us, he'd slipped his fingers into my panties and yanked them down. Thank God I went with the lacy red thong.

Then he dropped to his knees, lifting my leg over his shoulder. His hands ran along my thighs as he looked up at me. "I hope you don't mind my putting off showing you the proof of my size. If I don't go down on you now, I'm going to go fucking mad."

"Okay," I squeaked as the intensity of his eyes and the hoarseness of his voice stole my breath. He was like a fantasy come true.

The minute his tongue slid through my folds, my world tilted on its axis. His tongue was hot and wet and oh, so very talented.

I gripped the door handle to keep me from tumbling over. My hips gyrated, and the one leg I was standing on trembled.

His tongue licked, flicked, and sucked and at one point, dipped inside me.

"Oh, my God."

His lips moved away, sucking on the inside of my thigh.

I whimpered, wanting him back on my clit. "Don't stop."

He looked up at me again. "I'm not stopping. You taste so fucking good, I don't want it to end too fast."

Yeah, no. I couldn't wait. Maybe his other women could hold off, but I'd never needed to come so badly in my life. "I'm sorry. I need to come."

He gave me a sweet smile. "Don't be sorry. If you need to come, then I'll make you come."

Then his mouth was on me again, and holy smokes, I felt like I was on a runaway freight train about to fly off a cliff, but in a good way. He inserted a finger inside me, and his lips wrapped around my clit. The two of them working together shot me off to the stratosphere. My entire body went rigid and then shuddered as wave after wave of pleasure rolled through me.

He made an "mmm" sound, as if he were having a sweet dessert. Then he slowly stood, his immense body blocking me in. He brought one hand in front of me, holding it in front of my face, splaying his fingers wide. "Are you ready to experience the proof about hand size?"

I nodded because I still was unable to form words. He took my hand, bringing it up to his lips and kissing it and then pulling it down, pressing it over his hard shaft.

I looked into his eyes, finding my voice. "I'm going to need more proof than that." I found my strength next, pushing him away from the door and toward the bed, knocking him back until he was lying on the mattress.

I did a striptease, feeling wanton and sexy and at the same time safe. His eyes flashed with wild passion as my dress dropped to the floor along with my bra.

"So fucking sexy."

I crawled over him, straddling his thighs as I unbuckled his belt and then undid the button and zipper of his jeans. I tugged and tugged at his jeans and boxers until his dick sprang free. The rumor about hand and dick size was true, and then some.

1

Reed—one month later.

I really shouldn't complain. How many men in the world could make money hand over fist in business while spending the morning in their office drinking coffee and watching the hockey highlights from last night's game?

I bet there were many who couldn't, yet here I was, sitting at my desk while I watched the home team star player, Bo Tyler, score two goals on the big-screen TV in my office. I justified having the TV because as CEO of a billion-dollar daily fantasy sports site, I needed to know what was going on in sports. It was a fucking fantastic excuse to watch TV.

At the end of the game highlights, the commentators switched to showing Bo's after-game antics in which he was caught celebrating his success by getting drunk and sneaking onto a golf course to play drunken golf with glow-in-the-dark golf balls.

I shook my head as I watched him get escorted off the course by the golf club's security. I smiled wryly, wondering how my best friend,

Pierce Jackson, coach of Bo's hockey team, was faring this morning. He had to be happy about winning the game, but he wasn't going to be thrilled about Bo's nocturnal golfing habit.

I clicked off the TV, tossing the remote on my desk. As I looked at all the paperwork scattered on it, I had to remind myself again how lucky I was. As the owner of the number-one daily fantasy sports company, I made more money than I could ever spend in my lifetime.

My kids—hell, my grandkids—probably wouldn't be able to spend it all. Not that I had kids or grandkids because I didn't and it was unlikely I ever would.

My dating life was shit.

I was a forty-five-year-old ex-hockey-star turned billionaire who couldn't find a woman who would stick. And it wasn't from a lack of trying.

During my hockey days, I didn't date. I hooked up. But once my business hit a million dollars in net worth not long after I started when I was forced to retire from hockey, I decided I'd find someone to share my newfound wealth. But every woman I dated dropped off the radar after a few dates. It was annoying, although today, I couldn't remember much about any of them, except for one.

Analyn.

Ever since that night a month ago, she had become my fantasy sex sport, starring in my dreams and my daytime jerk-offs. I couldn't quite pinpoint what it was about her that stuck with me, compared to the other women I had dated.

Yes, she was beautiful and sexy, but so were the other women. There was something sweet and vivacious about Analyn. There was an authenticity about her that was refreshing. She said what she thought and didn't act with any guile or pretense.

When she'd first come to sit next to me at the bar, I wasn't sure what to think. To be honest, I wasn't in the mood to be picked up by a woman. I went to the bar to lament, as had become my habit, on how boring my life had become. I wasn't sure I had ever gotten over the fact that my hockey career came to an end earlier than I would've liked due to an injury. Now I was a billionaire with the world at my feet, but I was alone and bored out of my gourd by life.

Sometimes, I thought I should have gone into coaching, like Pierce had. But at the time, I didn't think I could handle watching all the players on the ice and not be able to skate with them. Hockey had been my dream, and then my life, and then it had all come to an end.

Of course, I understood what a whiner complaining about my charmed life made me. When I quit playing hockey and started my business, my dissatisfaction only continued to grow. I thought maybe if I were to find a good woman and have a family, that would be the answer. As it turned out, finding a good woman wasn't so easy.

Now, over ten years since my forced retirement from hockey, I was still unmarried and childless. There must be something wrong with me that after a few dates, the women would disappear. It took Analyn one night. I woke up the day after having the most amazing sex I'd had in a long time, maybe ever, ready to fuck like rabbits again, only to find the bed empty. The disappointment was acute.

But it wasn't just that there wasn't going to be any more sex with her that bothered me. I really enjoyed her company. I would've liked to have seen her again. I was aware that she was from Chicago, but maybe I could have flown out to visit her or flown her here to visit me. On the one hand, it seemed like a lot of work to date a woman long-distance, but since she was the first woman in a long, long time to get me out of my funk, it would've been worth it. Imagine the phone sex!

But it wasn't to be. Not only had she left while I was sleeping, but there was no note. I wondered what happened when she woke up next to me. Had she regretted it? Had I done something to offend her? Maybe in the early morning light, without the haze of alcohol, she realized how much older I was than her. I had to be at least twenty years her senior, practically old enough to be her father. I shook my head free of that thought because it was disturbing.

The intercom on my desk buzzed, pulling me out from my ruminations. I poked the button. "Yes, Catherine?"

"I just want to remind you that you're interviewing for the new social media marketing manager today. The first candidate is in twenty minutes. Would you like me to bring in the file for the applicant now?"

I scraped my hand over my face. Sometimes, I really hated my job. "No. I'll look at it when it's time."

"Very well."

The line clicked off, and it occurred to me that Catherine often spoke to me in a tone that made me feel like she was disappointed in me. Considering I was a billionaire who spent his day whining, I couldn't blame her.

A few moments later, there was a knock at my door, and Catherine poked her head in. "I brought you some coffee. It sounded like you could use it."

That was the other thing about Catherine. She was fucking efficient. She was so good, it was probably why I found my work boring. She could anticipate anything, so I very rarely had to deal with any sort of crisis. Everything at work ran smoothly, almost like I didn't even need to be here. There was a thought.

"Thank you. I appreciate that."

She walked around my desk to stand next to me as she set the mug on the blotter. She rested her hip on the desk and smiled down at me. She was a professional, and at the same time, we'd been working together long enough that there was a familiarity between us. I wouldn't say we were friends, but we definitely had a connection that made us work together well.

"I suppose you caught the news footage of Bo last night," she said.

I picked up the mug, taking a sip of the hot, dark brew. Another thing that Catherine excelled at was coffee. "I did. I imagine Pierce is having a conniption fit."

She laughed. "No doubt." She tilted her head to the side. "Were you like Bo when you were playing?"

"No." Not even a little bit. I had dreamt of playing professional hockey my entire life, so when I finally made it, I was focused on staying there. That wasn't to say I didn't sow my oats and party. I just didn't do it to the level that Bo Tyler was able to do it. Bo got away with it because he was so fucking good on the ice. It was possible he'd surpass Gretzky as the greatest of all time.

Catherine gave my shoulder a light push with her perfectly mani- cured hand. "Oh, come on. You can tell me."

I shook my head. "Nope. I was living the dream back then. I wasn't going to fuck it up, no way, no how." I supposed it wasn't good to use the F-word in front of my administrative assistant, but she didn't seem to care. In fact, I think a part of her appreciated that while we had a professional relationship, around her, I could be myself.

She laughed and then straightened from my desk. "Well, I'll give you a few minutes. I'll let you know when your appointment is here."

"Thank you, Catherine."

I watched as she left, reminding myself how lucky I was. I had an extremely successful company, in part because my administrative assistant was the epitome of efficiency. She was smart and clever, and when she needed to be, she was the best damn gatekeeper any CEO could have. I had friends that asked whether I'd ever fucked her on my desk because she was also attractive. The answer was no, I never had, and in fact, I had never thought about it.

Catherine had a lot of things going for her, but I didn't feel sexu- ally or emotionally attracted to her. The truth was, while I occasion- ally might have been sexually attracted to a woman, I had never been emotionally attracted or felt a pull beyond my dick for any woman except Analyn. And goddammit! Now I was thinking about her again. Maybe I needed to go out and get laid to get her out of my mind. With my luck, I'd fantasize about her, maybe even say her name while I came, ruining it with the woman I was with.

I forced myself to focus on work, pulling up recent data files to see how well the company was doing. There was a time when looking at my numbers gave me a thrill. Today it was more of the same.

A few moments later, Catherine knocked at my door again.

"Your appointment is here. I've put her down in the conference room."

I nodded and stood, putting on my coat and straightening the tie I'd loosened when I'd arrived. I felt like a dead man walking as I exited my office, which again made me feel pathetic considering how fortunate I was in my life.

I walked with Catherine down the hall to the conference room. Catherine entered first, and I followed behind.

I stopped short when I saw the curvaceous dark-haired woman standing next to the conference table. Holy fuck, it was Analyn.

Her eyes rounded as recognition came. Well, at least she remembered me. The way she had left, I wondered if she would. I had spent that night getting to know every inch of that woman and knew that I would never, ever forget her.

"Analyn Watts, this is Mr. Hampton, the CEO of Dream Team." Catherine handed me the folder with Analyn's application. "Mr. Hampton, this is Analyn Watts."

Watts. We hadn't shared our last names a month ago. I'd cursed that since I couldn't find her, but then I realized that had been the point. She hadn't wanted to be found.

"Would you like me to get you another cup of coffee? Ms. Watts has already declined one."

My gaze stayed on Analyn as dueling emotions ran through me. On the one hand, I felt hope. Here was the woman I couldn't get out of my mind. Maybe I'd be able to see her again.

But another part of me had a growing anger at the way she had left after that spectacular night we'd had. It was stupid of me to be pissed off. It'd been a hookup. There had been nothing about that night to suggest that it was any more than that. But by the time I was drifting to sleep that night, I knew I wanted more than a hookup, but she had taken off without a word, taking away that opportunity.

"No, thank you, Catherine. That'll be all for now."

Catherine left the room, shutting the door, leaving me alone with Analyn. I had so many questions that I wanted to ask her and none had to do with the job. I reminded myself that she was expecting a job interview, which had me wondering why she was here. Had she lied to me about being from Chicago?

I motioned to the chair in front of her. "Have a seat, Ms. Watts." I had to be professional, and if she thought maybe I didn't remember her, that would be okay too. Petty, I know.

She stared at me, and for a moment I thought she was going to leave. I arched a brow, in my mind, challenging her, asking her if she was going to bolt again. She let out a sigh, as if she was resigned to the moment. For some reason, that angered me more.

She pulled out the chair and sat down.

I sat in my chair, opening the file. "Let's start by having you tell me, have you ever walked out on anyone?"

2

Analyn

Oh. My. God.

What were the odds that I would run into Reed again?

Well, maybe it wasn't so unusual. I now lived in Las Vegas after taking up Betts on her offer to be her roommate. I suppose the chance was always there that I'd run into him.

To be honest, deep down, I hoped I would. But not at a job interview. How could I be interviewed by the man who'd done such delicious things with his mouth all over my body just a month ago?

Looking at him now made my body heat to the point I worried my skin was turning a rosy pink. How could I think about Instagram and TikTok while my body was remembering the way it felt when he slid inside me and made me orgasm until it felt like my head exploded?

But then something even worse happened. It appeared he didn't remember me. How mortifying was that? At the same time, it gave me some ease that he wasn't thinking about all the delicious things he did to me. To him, I was just another job applicant.

Of course, I'd be in this situation. Ever since I walked out on the boyfriend whose name I refused to utter, my luck had tanked. The only exception was the night I spent with Reed, but ever since then, I've had one bout of bad luck after another.

This morning, it was that my alarm didn't go off, so I overslept. Because I slept in and I didn't prepare everything last night, I didn't have time to iron my shirt, so it was wrinkled. I'm sure I looked like I'd slept in my car. Then there was the run I got in my only pair of pantyhose. And now this. I walked in to find my potential boss was the man I picked up in a bar a month ago. Thank God he didn't remember me, because what sort of woman did he think I was to have picked him up like that?

I watched him, noting that he didn't smile or seem very welcoming. It reminded me of how he looked when I saw him in the club.

He motioned for me to sit, so I took the seat while he opened the folder, presumably with my application. Would he recognize my name? We didn't give last names when we met. Was Analyn so unusual that he'd figure out who I was?

He looked up at me, his pale blue eyes pinning me with a stare. "Have you ever walked out on anyone?"

I blinked, wondering what kind of question that was. It was only then that I realized he did remember me. And whatever his memory was, it wasn't a good one.

"I . . . uh . . ." Stammering wasn't a very good way to open an interview, but what were the odds I would get hired, anyway? "I've always been very committed to my jobs." I didn't know what the hell to say. After all, I had quit my job in order to move out here. I didn't regret it, but I had the feeling that not regretting walking out on him was a bad answer.

He tapped my resume with his finger as he continued to scrutinize me. "Do you ever regret any of your decisions?"

Right then, I regretted applying for this job. I was beginning to regret moving to Las Vegas.

Why was he so peeved at me? We had a one-night stand. A hookup. We had fun and then it was over. I didn't linger or cling to him wanting more, even though when I woke the next morning, it was all I could do to drag myself out of bed since I did want more.

But I was a little shocked that I had spent the night with him because it wasn't something I normally did. Plus, I wanted to get back to Betts's house before she found out that I had been out all night. I didn't regret what I had done, but it wasn't something I was going to do again, and it wasn't like either of us had made any sort of commitment. So why was he mad at me? Was he mad at me? Maybe he was like this all the time.

Feeling confused and knowing that I couldn't work for a man who'd seen me naked, I decided to cut my losses. I got the feeling I wasn't going to be hired, anyway.

I calmly stood up. "Thank you for your time Re . . . Mr. Hampton, but I don't think I'm going to be a very good fit. I do appreciate your taking the time for the interview." For a moment, I waited for him to say something. The longer I stood there, I realized I wanted him to say something, but he just continued to watch me with those pale blue eyes.

"Thank you again." I hurried to the door and to the elevator, heading to the ground floor of the building. It wasn't until I was outside that I let myself breathe. But with that breath also came the crush of disappointment.

I had really thought this was the perfect job for me. I had a degree in marketing, and then in Chicago I'd spent the last four years working my way up to better positions. This one in Las Vegas, a social media marketing director, was right up my alley. I knew all the concepts of marketing, but my superpower was the ability to take a company and turn their message into interesting videos and images that made an impression on viewers.

While I didn't know a whole lot about sports, over the last week, ever since I applied for the position, I was learning everything I could about sports and online gambling. Not only did I research this company, but his competitors as well. I looked at all their social media followings and identified areas that could be enhanced and new ideas that I thought could go viral for them. But all that was washed away.

I should have stayed home that night and this wouldn't have happened.

Even as I thought that, I didn't really believe it. I couldn't regret my night with Reed. In fact, part of why I decided to move was because of that night.

But I needed to accept that this perfect job wasn't to be. It was a disappointment not just because I felt it was a step up in my career, but also because having a job would make it easier to find my own place.

Betts had invited me to be her roommate, and I had come with enough in my savings to share in the rent and utilities. But it was clear that she was expecting Paul to pop the question to her anytime now, in which case she'd either move out to live with him or he'd come to live with her.

I suppose if she went to live with Paul, I could take over the lease on her condo, but I definitely needed a well-paying job to be able to afford it on my own.

God, why did the CEO of the company have to be the man I'd picked up last month? I knew why. It was my rotten luck.

I headed to the parking garage, and once inside my car, I texted Betts letting her know that I was on the way home with ice cream and wine. She sent back a sad emoji. Maybe I needed to take my meager savings and start investing in ice cream and wine, since it appeared they were going to feature predominantly in my life.

As I drove back to Betts's place, I began to rethink this move to Las Vegas. I read somewhere that huge decisions shouldn't be made after a loss. I suppose the thought was that big decisions, particularly ones involving moving, could be a form of running away. At the time I made the decision to leave Chicago and moved to Las Vegas, I truly believed that I was running toward something. I was moving past the life I thought I was going to have with my ex and reaching for a new future.

But maybe I had been running away. Either way, it was too late now. I was here, and until I got a job and made some more money, I didn't have the resources to move back.

After picking up the wine and ice cream, I arrived back at Betts's. I changed out of my wrinkled shirt and skirt and slipped into a comfy pair of sweats and an old college T-shirt.

Deciding not to wait for Betts to return from work, I got the ice cream and a glass of wine and sat at the table with my tablet, looking up job opportunities in the Las Vegas area. I'd already been through most of them, but there were several I had not applied to because I had set my sights on bigger roles. Maybe it was time to lower my standards.

I saw an entry-level opportunity at a social media marketing agency, and as I searched the website, I realized that the owner of it was the wife of the man who owned the club where I had met Reed. Amelia Clarke. I wondered if she and her husband had been able to rent the suite where it all began for them. I hoped so. It would be nice to think that somewhere in the world, happily ever after really existed.

I submitted my application to her agency knowing that I was overqualified for that role. But Amelia Clarke, who I had remembered as a social media influencer before she was married, could be a good mentor for me. Maybe someday, I'd open my own agency.

When Betts arrived home, she gave me a hug and told me to tell her all about the interview. It was only then that I realized I hadn't told her what happened the night she had gone out with Paul, and instead of staying home like she thought I had, I'd gone and hooked up with a man who turned out to be the billionaire owner of a fantasy sports business.

Pouring myself another glass of wine, I settled in to tell her the whole story. When I finished, her mouth was agape in surprise, but her eyes were narrowed in what looked like hurt.

"Why didn't you tell me this before?"

I shrugged. "You were flying high on being with Paul, and I guess I was still sort of surprised that I did it at all. I guess I worried you wouldn't approve."

She waggled her spoon at me. "Well, it's not the safest thing in the world to go pick up a perfect stranger in a club and sleep with him, but at the same time, it sounds really sexy."

I gave her a wan smile. "I'm sorry I didn't tell you. It's not that I didn't want you to know. It's just I wasn't sure how I felt about it."

"So, what was it like walking into his office today?"

"Oh, my God. All I could think about were the things he'd done with his tongue. How can you have a serious job interview when you're imagining the guy who could be your boss doing things with his tongue?"

She laughed. "I wonder what he was thinking about you?"

"That's even worse. At first, I didn't think he remembered me. But then I realized he did, except it was clear that he didn't have fond memories. He acted angry."

"Angry? Why? Most men like to sleep with women."

I sipped my wine. "I don't know?"

"Maybe he didn't like that you snuck away the next morning." She picked up the bottle of wine to pour us both more.

"Isn't that how hookups are supposed to end? I thought men liked it when women knew when to leave."

"Maybe he didn't want it to be over yet. Maybe it was more than a hookup for him."

I snorted. "Yeah, right. We'd only just met. How could it be more?"

"I don't know. But you could've said goodbye."

I sagged back on the couch, nearly spilling my wine as it sloshed in my glass. "I suppose. It doesn't matter, anyway. I'm not getting the job."

"Well, I'm sorry about that." She cocked her head to the side. "You know, if he isn't your boss, maybe he could be something else. I mean, you said you had a really good time. And it sounds like maybe he did also until you ghosted him."

"You're running on love endorphins or something. I hope Paul pops the question soon. It's starting to get annoying."

She did a little shimmy. "I don't think it'll be long now." She sighed and sat back with me on the couch. "I'm sorry Chase was such an asshole."

"Don't say his name."

She laughed. "I don't know why you're still even thinking about him. Not after the night you had with Mr. Billionaire." She sat up straight, as if she'd been struck by an idea. "Let's go out tonight. Let's go to the Golden Oasis."

I was shaking my head and grabbing the carton of ice cream before the words had finished coming out of her mouth. "Nope."

"Oh, come on. It'll be fun. And who knows, maybe you'll have the opportunity to make things right with your billionaire."

I sighed as I dug for chunks of fudge in the ice cream. "There's no replicating what happened a month ago. It's one of those perfect storms, only in a good way. That's how I want to remember it. One night, I was daring and met a man who wanted to be daring too, and for one night, it was the ultimate in sexual bliss."

"I don't know. Sounds like there was a real connection between you two. We can go, and if he's there, you could apologize. If he's as nice as you said he was, he'd probably forgive you, and then you could go and he could do all those things to you with his tongue." She waggled her brows. "You're really going to have to go into more detail about what it is he did."

My cheeks heated even as I stuck a spoonful of ice cream into my mouth. It wasn't that I didn't want a chance to see him again, because I couldn't deny that I wanted to. I wanted another night like we'd had a month ago.

But as I told myself when I drove out of Chicago heading to Las Vegas a month ago, the past was the past. What was done was done. I would always remember my night with Reed, but that's all it would be from now on, a memory.

3

Reed

Fuck. Fuck. Fuck.

She was the one who ghosted me last month, but I was the one being an asshole now.

She held her head up high when she told me she didn't think she was a fit for the job, but in her eyes, I saw disappointment. I doubt it was disappointment in me, since she was the one who had taken off the morning after our spectacular night together.

She had come in here hoping to get a job, and I had doused those dreams with a single look. With petty hurt feelings. She had gone through the interview like a true professional, and I was a dick.

Of course, I wouldn't have been able to hire her, but I could have referred her somewhere else.

The reason I couldn't hire her wasn't just because she'd ditched me the morning after our hookup. It wasn't even because seeing her reminded me of the fact that I got my boxers in a bunch.

No, the reason I couldn't hire her was because I still wanted her.

I hadn't even realized how much until I saw her standing there in her professional attire. It didn't matter how staid her skirt was or how prim and proper and professional she appeared. The moment I saw her, every cell in my body remembered what it was like to touch her, to be inside her. And it wanted to be there again. Badly.

But what was done was done. I regretted being a jerk, but in the end, it was for the best. So, I pushed it out of my mind, leaving the conference room and heading back to my office.

"Your next candidate is here. He's early, but since you appear to have finished quickly with Ms. Watts, maybe you'd like to see them."

I stopped and stared at Catherine. "I have more interviews? How many do I have?" This was proof that I wasn't as involved mentally in my business as I should be since I had no clue what was on my calendar. Then again, I didn't have to know, as Catherine made sure I was where I needed to be when I needed to be there.

Any other admin would probably roll their eyes at my ignorance of my own schedule, but Catherine gave me a sympathetic smile. She probably thought I couldn't get through the day without her, and I'm not sure that she was entirely wrong.

"There are four more. But then that's it. Hopefully, you'll find one you like out of this bunch."

I nearly asked her if she could conduct the interviews since she was probably more knowledgeable about what I needed. But I had to suck it up and be a boss. I needed to stop whining and start taking control. "Let me get a cup of coffee, and then I'll be back to the conference room."

She nodded. "I will let him know."

I grabbed my coffee and headed back for the interviews. Catherine led in the next candidate. This one was a young man, whose hair was slicked back, and he made me think he'd be more fitting working for a bookie than a respectable online gambling establishment. There was something about him that just felt a little bit off, so when he left, I put him in a "no" pile. Right on top of Analyn's.

The next three were women, and all of them looked like they had just rolled out of their Instagram profile. I wondered if they had somehow been able to change the lighting in the room into one of those filters that made them look smooth and flawless.

Not that I had anything against their being heavily coiffed and attractive. If we'd been in a club, I might have . . . Well, no, I wouldn't have. For one thing, they looked too young, and for another, too fake. However, they did know everything they needed to know about social media, but nothing about fantasy sports and online gambling. I knew all too well that social media marketing could turn disastrous on a dime.

Not just ruining a reputation by saying something stupid, but breaking the law as well. Gambling was one of those vices made legal only because it could bring in money to the state (prostitution was another). As such, gambling was highly regulated, and stepping out of line could cost me millions of dollars and my reputation.

I couldn't afford for a social media manager to accidentally post something that could ruin my business. For that reason, I needed someone who didn't just understand marketing, but laws regulating marketing, the internet, and gambling. I wondered if Analyn knew any of that. Wait, no I didn't. I couldn't hire her.

When I finished interviewing the candidates, I told Catherine I needed to take a break and we'd meet after lunch to discuss them. I had done the interviews, but Catherine had done all the research on them. I'm sure she had visited all their social media accounts and websites, had already contacted their former employers, and when she greeted them for their interviews, she probably chatted with them to get an impression of them. I would rely on that to help me pick which of the three Barbies I should hire.

When I got back from lunch, Catherine had already had the candidates' files reorganized and set on the conference table as she waited for me to return.

I loosened my tie, unbuttoning the top button of my shirt, and sat down in the chair with a heavy sigh. "Alright, let's get this over with. Why don't we start with you telling me which one of these five you think I should hire?" I'd make this easy on both of us and hire the one she liked.

She pushed the file over. "Analyn Watts. I don't know why her interview was so short, but I think she'd be good."

I held back an annoyed growl as I pushed the file back to Catherine. "Not her. Who else?"

Catherine's eyes narrowed slightly, but being the consummate professional, she looked through the remaining folders. "Well, the young man seemed to know a lot about gambling, but he made me think of a loan shark or a used car salesman. I don't know, there was something smarmy about him."

"Agreed. So of the next three, which do you think would be best?"

She looked through each of the folders and then sat back, giving me a look that said I wasn't going to like what she had to say. "I still think Analyn Watts is the best."

I pointed to the three folders sitting in front of her. "One of those three should be able to do. They all know social media. Why don't you like any of them?"

"These three seem to know a lot about social media, yes, but it's all about them and being an influencer. They know how to make themselves look good on social media, and maybe push a few products, but Analyn has a degree in marketing. She didn't walk in here thinking she was going to be the supermodel for your social media account. Now granted, many of the people who are your consumers can be swayed by tits and ass, but surely, you want somebody who knows something about marketing too."

I suspected other bosses wouldn't be pleased to hear their admins using words like tits and ass, but over the years Catherine's and my relationship had evolved so that she could be frank with me, to a certain extent.

"And besides, you don't need women like that prancing around here, distracting everyone else from their jobs. There's no chance that Analyn will distract anyone."

I frowned because, in fact, I knew Analyn would distract at least one person. Me.

"Analyn is professional without trying to be provocative or sexy," Catherine finished.

And yet, to me, she was. "I don't want to hire her."

Catherine narrowed her eyes even more than she had before. I stared at her, hoping that through telepathy, she would know not to ask me why.

Because I knew it would only be so long before she did ask, I said, "Let me think about this." I rose from my chair. "I'll let you know later."

I went to my office, shutting the door, taking a seat in my chair, and scraping my hands over my face. Just my luck that the one woman who would be perfect for the job is the one woman I can't hire. I took the folders of the three women, mixed them up, did eeny, meeny, miny, moe, and drew one, deciding to hire whichever one I randomly picked from the pile.

I looked up her number and picked up the phone to call. But I couldn't get my fingers to poke the buttons.

Fuck. Catherine was right. Analyn was the most qualified professional for the job. But how could I hire a woman who with one look, I was back in a bar thinking about how she'd awkwardly sauntered up next to me and completely charmed me?

When I'd woken the next morning to find her gone, and felt the crushing disappointment, I tried to deal with it by telling myself that her company, and the sex, hadn't been as good as I thought. It was an illusion because booze had clouded my memory into thinking it was better than it was.

But who was I kidding? Analyn had a body that never ended. Curve after sexy curve. Her skin was soft. Her tits were round and full, and I'd have spent the night only focused on sucking them except her pussy tasted like an exotic fruit. When she came that first time, I drank her juice like it was the elixir of life. And then it just got better.

She'd pushed me to the bed, knocking me back on it and then doing a Vegas striptease. I couldn't explain why, but I loved it. I don't think it was that she was pushy or demanding or knew what she wanted. I'd been with plenty of women who took control during sex. It might have been the innocence of it. Not that she was sexually innocent. I was sure she'd had sex before. But she hadn't done this before. She hadn't hooked up with a man. She hadn't allowed her sexually playful side out before. She was nervous yet daring, and I ate it up, wanting to give her a night she'd never forget.

When she'd freed my cock, it was all I could do to keep from tugging her over me and sinking into that hot, sweet pussy of hers. I let her get her fill of me through all her senses—sight, touch, taste. I wanted to experience the wonder and joy she was exuding as she explored my body. Sex had always been a physical release more than anything. Like a scratch to an itch.

But with Analyn, it had been something entirely different. When I finally sank into her body, it was beyond anything I could remember. More than sensual delight. More than delicious torture. I didn't want it to end. Not that night. Hell, maybe not ever.

But it did end. I woke up and she was gone. Like a phantom. All I had was the memory, which haunted me as she continued to star in my nocturnal fantasies when I jerked off in the shower. And because of that, I couldn't hire her. I couldn't look at her and think about bending her over my desk . . .

Fuck . . . the image was there. Her sweet, round ass exposed me as she bent over my desk. My cock pounding away, bringing us both to the pinnacle of pleasure.

I shifted as my dick reacted to the scene. I'd never jerked off at work, but I might have to if I couldn't get rid of the image of fucking Analyn on my desk.

I rolled my shoulders, wondering how my life had gone from ultimate boredom to this conundrum.

But then I had to consider that perhaps Analyn's walking into my company was the answer to my boredom. Working with her, and wanting to touch her, would definitely be a challenge. A challenge that might make life more interesting.

4

Analyn

I was able to convince Betts that we should stay in. I mean, why go out when we had all the ice cream and wine that we needed?

I was dressed comfortably, and to be honest, I didn't want to risk running into Reed. Whatever connection or chemistry or whatever it was we had a month ago wasn't there today. In some ways, it might've been worse if it was, because the situation was totally changed.

"I still say that if he's not going to be your boss, it might be worth looking him up again. It sounds like you had a really smokin' night. But even more than that, it sounded like you two hit it off. You enjoyed each other's company. That's something you could build on."

I wouldn't deny that deep inside, I liked that idea. Although I didn't feel I needed a man to make my life complete, it would be nice to have a partner. Someone to support and who would support me. Someone to have fun with. And yes, someone to have really great sex with.

There were aspects of the evening I spent with Reed last month that felt like things could have developed into something beyond a hookup. If I'd been living in Las Vegas at the time, I might've actually stayed the next morning, although I woke up feeling a little embarrassed and uncomfortable.

BUT I'D STILL BEEN LIVING in Chicago, so there didn't seem to be much purpose in my staying. I imagined if I had stayed, the morning would've been awkward. Things were always different the day after.

Maybe Betts was right and his attitude today was about how I'd left. Or maybe he was just annoyed that a woman he'd slept with on a whim had walked in wanting a job.

"Right now, I need to get a job. That's my only focus. Besides, Reed, as it turns out, is totally out of my league. He's a billionaire, and he's probably twenty years older than me. Surely, he's looking for somebody a little more mature and sophisticated."

Betts reached over, giving me a push. "Don't sell yourself short, girl. Maybe there's an age difference, but it's not like you're just out of high school or college or something. You're a grown ass woman. A professional grown ass woman. You're smart, you're beautiful, you're kind. He'd be lucky to have you."

I smiled, tilting over and resting my head on her shoulder. "You're a good friend to have around."

"And don't you forget it."

She reached over to grab the carton of ice cream and the bottle of wine. They were both empty. "Do we need more?"

Since we weren't going anywhere, I thought, why not? "I'm game if you are."

She rose from the couch, grabbing the empty bottle and ice cream container and heading to the kitchen.

While she was there, my phone rang. It seemed a little late to be getting a call regarding a job application, but maybe it was somebody who wanted me to come in for an interview the next day.

I grabbed my phone from where it sat on the coffee table. I checked the caller ID but didn't recognize the number. Normally, I'd ignore calls like this, but again, it could be a potential employer.

I poked the answer button. "Hello?"

"Analyn . . . Ms. Watts."

Immediately, I tensed. "Mr. Hampton."

Betts's head appeared from around the corner, her eyes wide. She mouthed, "Is that him?"

I nodded.

Her eyes glinted as she hurried back into the living room and sat on the couch to watch whatever was about to unfold.

"I was hoping that we could meet to discuss the position," Reed said.

I pulled the phone away from my ear and looked at it like that would tell me what the heck was going on. He'd been really disagreeable during my interview, so why was he calling me to talk about the position? "It seemed clear today that I wasn't going to be the right fit."

"The interview ended abruptly, so I would like to have the chance to meet with you again." He rattled off an address. "I'd appreciate it if you would meet with me."

Betts was nodding and making all sorts of gestures telling me I needed to agree to meet him.

"Please," he finished.

I'd be a liar if I wasn't intrigued, even if I was uncertain. "All right. I'll need a half-hour or so." I definitely wasn't dressed for a job interview.

"I'll meet you there in an hour."

The call ended, and I wondered about the address that he'd given me. It wasn't his office building. He wasn't inviting me to his home, was he?

I set the phone down and looked at Betts.

"Well?" Excitement shone on her face.

"I guess I'm going to meet him at this address." I rose from the couch and headed to my bedroom.

Betts trotted along behind me. "Is it about the job, or does he want a date?"

"It's about the job." I flung open my closet. "I don't know what to wear." I wasn't going to put on the outfit I wore this afternoon, partly because it was wrinkled and partly because I didn't want to look too eager for the job. I started rummaging through my closet.

"If he wants to hire you, are you going to take the job? Would you be able to work with the guy without thinking of mind-blowing orgasms?"

The words were teasing, and at the same time, it was a reminder of why this might not be a good idea.

I stopped as a new idea came to me. "You don't think he's doing this just so he can sleep with me again, do you?" I looked at her over my shoulder.

She shrugged. "With men, it's hard to know." She shook her head. "I think it goes without saying that men would like to have sex, but maybe because the interview went badly, he wants to do it again, either to give you a chance or maybe because he knows he was a jerk."

"I suppose you're right. But I want to get the job on my own merits, not because I slept with him."

Betts sat down on the edge of my bed. "Absolutely. Integrity is everything. If he does make some sort of rude proposition, just leave. But if he's on the up and up, if he's the kind of guy you thought he was a month ago, maybe he's just trying to do the right thing, in which case this is the perfect job for you. I know you're thinking that maybe this move wasn't a good idea and you should go back to Chicago, but I want you to stay. So if this job turns out, then you should take it and we can be best friends here together."

I slipped out of my sweats and T-shirt and settled on a dress. It was casual and yet nice enough to meet with a potential employer. More than that, it was comfortable, which I was going to need when meeting with my potential boss who I just happened to have slept with the month before.

I stood in front of Betts with my arms out. "What do you think?"

She held her hands up, making a square with her thumbs and forefingers as if she were a photographer. "Casual yet confident. Besides, red is a great color on you."

I remembered that I had worn another red dress the night I met

Reed, and because of that I second-guessed whether I should wear this one. The one I had on now veered closer to burgundy than red and was more casual and subdued. But still, I didn't want him to think I was expecting to replay the night we had a month before.

"Maybe I should wear the black one instead."

She shook her head. "Nonsense. You like this dress, you feel good in this dress. This is the dress you should wear."

Not liking how much I was overthinking seeing a man I didn't plan to sleep with again or ever work for, I gave her a nod and headed to the bathroom where I combed out my hair. I didn't want to put it up like I had today, but at the same time, leaving it down might be too casual. So I pulled it back into a loose ponytail. I refreshed my makeup just to give me some color.

"Still casual and confident?" I asked Betts.

She nodded. "You're gonna knock him dead."

Putting on my coat and grabbing my purse, I headed out to my car. I poked the address into my phone for directions, and the Golden Oasis popped up on the screen. I hesitated as I realized that was the same club I had met him at a month ago. Why was he having me meet him there? Was he expecting something completely different from a job interview?

I nearly got out of the car, deciding not to go, but ultimately, I started the car and made my way to the club. I needed to put an end to this thing, whatever it was, with Reed. It needed to go back into the past where it had been until I walked into the interview this morning. The best way to do that would be to meet him again and let him know that while I thoroughly enjoyed last month, we couldn't see each other again, personally or professionally.

I parked my car and made my way toward the front of the club, slowing down as I drew closer to the door. This seemed like a bad idea for so many reasons. With a breath to shore up my courage, I opened the door.

Memories of that night a month ago filled me. Memories of how I decided to be daring and go out on the town on my own. To pick up a man, if only just for drinks and conversation. Of how much fun I had talking with Reed, then dancing, and then of course touching him and having him touch me. My entire body tingled, which wasn't good when my intention was to cut things off with him.

I scanned the club, seeing him standing in the back and waving. Goodness, he was handsome. His smile was sheepish, and it softened my hard attitude toward him. That was dangerous, but I couldn't back out now.

I made my way over, a tug-of-war playing out of my head about the wisdom of meeting him here.

"Thank you for meeting me. I was worried you wouldn't." He held out a chair for me to sit.

"I'll admit I'm questioning this."

"And yet you came? Why is that?"

I studied him, wondering what he was getting at. A month before when we spoke, everything that he said was clear. But today, in the interview and then now, his words seemed to have more meaning behind them.

Finally, I said, "You said you wanted to talk about the position."

He nodded as he sat down, and I was trying to decide whether I saw disappointment in his expression.

Stop trying to read things into his words and his mannerisms, I told myself. Whether he offered a job or not, I couldn't take it. It wasn't just that I had slept with him or even how he had acted toward me during the interview earlier in the day that required me to turn down any offer made. It was a bad idea to work for a man I was still desperately attracted to.

5

Reed

I didn't know what the hell I was doing. When I had called Analyn earlier, I'd dialed the number and started talking to her before I was even consciously aware of it. But once I'd done it, I couldn't back out.

What an idiot I'd been to choose the Golden Oasis as our meeting place. For the life of me, I couldn't figure out why I'd chosen it except for I didn't want to meet her at the office, and I couldn't very well invite her to my home.

Besides, if she was new in Las Vegas, the one place I knew she was aware of was the Golden Oasis. But the memories that flooded my mind as I entered the club for the first time since I had seen her a month ago were not ones a man should have about a woman he was planning to hire to work for him.

Memories like how sweet and adorable she was to have singled me out to sit with at the bar. How open and fun she'd been, making me feel things I hadn't felt in a long time. For a single night, she brought light into a world that had dimmed. Perhaps that was why I had been angry to wake up the next morning to find her gone. When she left, she took the light with her as well.

When she entered the club tonight, I watched her make her way to me, and although it was inappropriate, I couldn't stop from admiring the sway of her hips or the way her dress accentuated her curves. It made me yearn to touch her again.

But if things were going to work out, I had to douse those feelings. I needed to treat her as an employee. I needed to push away that night we'd had a month ago and figure out how to look at her and not be reminded of how well we moved together.

It was stupid to ask her why she had decided to come. I had told her it was to talk about the job, so clearly, that was why she was here. Deep down, I must've hoped that she was here for another reason. That was stupid.

"I apologize for my behavior earlier today. I was rude and inappropriate, and I'm sorry."

Her eyes rounded, as if she was surprised by my apology.

I laughed uncomfortably. "I guess you hadn't been expecting an apology."

"No, I wasn't."

I hated how my behavior had taken something out of her. She wasn't the same open, friendly, and vivacious woman I had met a month ago. It proved how much of a dick I'd been earlier that she could only look at me with skepticism and suspicion.

A server arrived, and I looked over at Analyn, wanting to ask whether she wanted a cranberry and vodka drink. But I knew that bringing back memories from a month ago would be inappropriate when I was here to offer her a job.

"Would you like something to drink?" I asked instead.

She glanced up at the server. "Can I just have a soda? Maybe with a little lemon in it?"

"Sure." The server looked at me. I probably should order something nonalcoholic too, but I needed to go with the drink I normally had when I was feeling less than perfect. "Bourbon and water." Sure,

I'd had it a month ago, but it wasn't a unique drink to trigger a memory.

Our server left to get our drinks, and I forced myself to focus on the task at hand. "I invited you here because I wanted to let you know that I want to hire you as the new head of social media marketing."

I'd anticipated surprise in her expression again, but instead, her eyes narrowed.

"You didn't even interview me."

"I don't need to."

Her eyes narrowed even further, and I got the feeling that I was fucking up, even though I wasn't quite sure how or why.

"How can you hire me without interviewing me?"

She leaned forward, glancing from side to side as if she didn't want anybody to overhear. Then her gaze zeroed in on my face. "You can't hire me based on what you know of me from a month ago."

Is that what she thought? "I'm hiring you because your resume shows that you are the ideal one for the job. And even though I didn't get a chance to interview you, I interviewed several other people today, and it was clear that you had the professionalism and the knowledge that I need for this position. I'm not the only one who thinks so. My admin does as well."

She sat back, her features softening somewhat, making me hope I had given her the right answer.

"You essentially had an advantage over all the other candidates because I know how creative and inventive you can be."

Immediately, she stiffened, and her cheeks reddened in rage. Her jaw tightened, and her dark eyes narrowed like lasers, trying to disintegrate me on the spot.

Only then did I realize how my words could be construed. Fuck. Everything I was saying was giving her the impression that I wanted to hire her because I wanted to continue to fuck her. And while I couldn't deny that getting her into bed was an appealing proposition, I knew that if I hired her, it would be an impossibility.

How was it that things between us had been so easy a month ago, and now we were like two different people? I suppose it was the circumstances. Tonight, we weren't two strangers wanting company at a club. I was a CEO and she was a job applicant.

I started to open my mouth to see what I could do to defuse the situation and get us back on the topic, but she shot up from her chair, nearly tilting it back.

Fuck. She was leaving.

6

Analyn

I stared at Reed, wondering how I'd misjudged him a month ago. He was a misogynistic pig.

Then again, I had picked him up in a bar and had sex with him. What else was he supposed to think about me? Well, if he thought that by hiring me he was going to have a piece of ass to play with all day, he was sorely mistaken.

With indignation filling my tone, I let him know the facts. "My qualifications for this job are strong. I have the education and experience. If you think you're hiring me to be a little side piece, you've got another thing coming."

There was no sense in staying because there was nothing he could say. Even if he apologized, I couldn't work for him. Not if he saw me as the woman he fucked a month ago.

I started toward the door, but his hand reached out, wrapping around my wrist. Heat shot through my arm, and the image of him holding my wrists over my head as he thrust into me flashed in my brain. Stupid hormones. Stupid memories.

I gave my head a shake to clear the image out and tugged my arm free.

"You've got the wrong idea. I want to hire you, but not to sleep with you."

Yeah, right. "I find that hard to believe."

He motioned to the chair. "Please sit. Let me explain."

I glared down at him.

"Remember that night a month ago? How I bet you that a man would hit on you or that you were a better dancer . . .?"

I stared at him in shock. What was he getting at? If he didn't want to sleep with me again, why was he bringing up what happened a month ago? "I don't see how that's going to make your case that you're not trying to hire a mistress."

He nodded toward the chair. "Please. Sit, and I'll explain."

Leave, leave, leave, ran like a mantra in my mind. And yet, I pulled out the chair and sat, crossing my arms as if somehow proving my resistance to him. "Okay, I'm listening. What do the various bets we made have anything to do with the job?"

Then it occurred to me that his business was a gambling establishment. Maybe that's where the betting came in. Still, it was weird for him to bring up our night together at a job interview that he was telling me had nothing to do with our night together.

"My life has become boring as hell."

I rolled my eyes and scoffed. "Oh, yeah, Mr. Billionaire can't afford any fun in his life." I leaned forward. "How many other women have picked you up in this place since I last saw you? How many before that? Seriously, you are the epitome of First-World whining."

He mimicked me, leaning forward, his eyes staring directly into mine. "None."

"What?"

"I haven't been with a woman since you, and before you, well, let's just say it'd been a while. And the last person hadn't been someone who picked me up while I was sitting by myself, minding my own business, in a bar."

I flinched at the reminder that the whole reason we ended up together a month ago was because I'd started it. But I'd ended it as well.

"So, what does your being bored with life have to do with me?"

He sat back. "You'll bring some excitement to the office."

What the hell? "What is that supposed to mean? For somebody who's trying to tell me that you didn't bring me here because you want to sleep with me, everything out of your mouth suggests the opposite."

He shook his head. "I didn't realize I was so bad with words. Even if we hadn't slept together that night, I enjoyed your company. I like your personality, and I think it would bring a lot to the office."

I narrowed my eyes, studying him, trying to decide whether he was telling me the truth. "So that means you're saying you have no interest in sleeping with me. You just think I have a good personality—"

"And as you pointed out, you have the education and experience."

"Yes, I have that. So this is just about my qualifications. You don't have any interest in me personally?" I was a little bit shocked to find I was holding my breath as I waited for his answer.

The right response had to be no, he wasn't interested, because we couldn't work together if there was a chance we'd sleep together. But I didn't want to hear no. I wanted him to be interested in me. God, I was a mess.

He sat and watched me for a moment. "Do you want total honesty?"

I nodded.

"The attraction is still there."

My stupid hormones did a little dance at that. Thank goodness I had my good sense with me. "If that's the case, then there's always the potential that we'll end up in an inappropriate office entanglement."

He frowned. "There would be no inappropriate office entanglement if you didn't want it. Now, if you found you were still attracted to me, that of course would be a challenge, which is why I have a new wager for you. If you take the job, I bet that I'll be able to resist sleeping with you."

I hated how confident he sounded. Shouldn't it be a little bit hard for him to resist me?

"If I make it a year and I haven't seduced you, I'll host a victory party at my house, and you'll have to do all the dishes and cleanup afterward."

I studied him, thinking that was the dumbest bet of all. "And if I win?"

"If I lose the bet, I'll double your salary."

As much as I would've liked to have kept my face impassive, my eyes and my mouth shot open in shock. Already, the starting salary was better than I'd ever earned before. I wouldn't be rich by any means, but I'd be able to finish paying off my debts, including my student loan, and even buy a house within the next year or two.

But doubled?

That was ridiculous, and at the same time, I felt like I'd be a fool if I didn't take it. If he won the bet, then I would be safe from being a cliché employee sleeping with the boss. But if he failed, I'd be making more money than I ever thought possible.

"This doubled salary, for how long would it go? One month?"

He shook his head. "As long as you have the job. And as long as you do a good job." He leaned forward, his expression turning cheeky. "That's a pretty big incentive for you to try and make me lose."

It took me a moment to realize what he was saying. And he was right. For double the salary, I could wear tight skirts and flaunt my breasts in front of him to make him lose. If I were that sort of woman.

He sat back. "But I'm not worried that you will purposely tempt me into losing because having the job on your own merit is too important to you."

That's right, Buster. I nodded. "It's the most important thing."

He arched a brow. "So, do we have a bet?"

Once again, common sense was urging me to decline and walk out. There were other jobs out there I could apply to. But goodness, none that paid as well or were as important as this one. And while this little wager was stupid, I believed he wanted to ensure that I felt confident that he was offering me the job because I was the best candidate, not because he wanted to sleep with me again. Or maybe I was just talking myself into it.

Either way, I couldn't help myself. I extended my hand across the table. His large one wrapped around mine, and it was all I could do to push out the memory of the way his hands had felt on my breasts, the way his fingers had slipped so deep inside me. I gave a quick shake and quickly released his hand.

He smiled, and for a moment I wondered if it was a smirk, like he'd known where my thoughts had gone. "You start on Monday."

7

Reed

I skidded my mountain bike to a stop, the desert dust flying out. Pierce brought his bike to a stop next to me.

I reached down, grabbing my water bottle. "You're getting old and slow, man." I smirked at him as I took a long gulp of water. It was still early morning, so it wasn't hot, but the desert was dry, and it was easy to get dehydrated without even knowing it.

"You do know you cheat, right? You took that cutoff back there."

I shrugged. "The refs didn't call it, so it can't be a foul." It was a joke we had from back in our hockey days. Any misdeed the ref didn't call didn't exist.

He rolled his eyes, but his lips twitched upward. Like me, Pierce missed our days of professional hockey. Unlike me, he seemed to have made the transition better than I had. He was coaching a team that might possibly make it to the Stanley Cup this year if their star player, Bo Tyler, stayed healthy and out of prison.

"I saw that Bo snuck back onto the golf course, but this time he wasn't hitting neon colored golf balls. Unless he was using a stripper's tits as a tee."

Pierce shook his head and looked down. "Fucking idiot. He acts like a horny teenager all the time."

"So, why don't you put the kibosh on it? It can't be good for the team."

"Me and the rest of the team are starting to hate him, but the owner and management fucking love him. They love the publicity. Apparently, ticket sales are up. People want to come see that asshole play. He's a fucking genius on the ice, and as long as he continues to play like that, he can do whatever he wants." He gave me a pointed stare. "When we played, it was so much easier. I'm beginning to think you're right and our glory days are behind us."

I shrugged as I took another long gulp of water. The truth was, with Analyn coming to work for me on Monday, it felt like things were looking up.

When I finished my drink, I realized Pierce wasn't talking. I turned to look at him, and his eyes were narrowed, scrutinizing me.

"What?"

"What the fuck has gotten into you? You've been like Oscar the Grouch for a decade, and now all of a sudden, you almost seem happy. What's going on?"

"I ran into a former flame of sorts." I didn't want to call Analyn a hookup because it felt like there'd been more to it, even though there hadn't been. "I just hired her to work for me."

Pierce was taking a large gulp out of his bottle, but it didn't prevent me from seeing the way his eyebrow quirked up. Once he swallowed his water, he said, "You hired a woman you slept with?"

I smiled, a wave of happiness filling my chest. "Yeah, I did."

"Jesus, Reed. What's with this woman? Seriously, dude, I don't think I've seen you smile like that since last time you played hockey."

I hadn't told Pierce anything about Analyn. It wasn't that it was a secret. I just wasn't the kind of man to kiss and tell. Besides, after she left, there really wasn't anything to tell.

"She picked me up at the Golden Oasis."

"No shit. She picked you up?"

The memory filled me with another wave of happiness. "We got to talking, we got the dancing—"

"And you got to fucking?"

I flinched because it sounded sordid even though that was exactly what happened. "Yeah, we did. But it was more than that. She wasn't one of those women who was all teased up and pushed up." Usually at the club, women's tits and hair were both lifted for optimal appeal. "She was real, you know? Sexy, yes, but more than that."

Pierce narrowed his eyes at me. "Do you think it's a good idea to hire a woman you fucked? Especially since it looks like there's still something going on there?"

"There's nothing there really. The next day, she took off. Story of my life. The woman is there one minute, and then she's gone. Until the other day when she walked into my office wanting a job."

"Let me ask you again, do you think it's a good idea to hire her? I mean, you still want to fuck her, don't you?"

I fucked her nearly every day in my fantasies. It would have to be enough. "I suppose I do, but I won't. It will make life interesting. And as you pointed out, my life has been pretty dull."

Pierce gaped at me. "Most people with dull lives get involved in an extreme sport or travel to Peru. They don't purposely put temptation in their way at work."

"I like the challenge of it. Besides, I made a bet with her. If we can go a year without me sleeping with her, I'll have a big blowout party. You're invited. She's going to be there to clean up afterward."

"And if you lose?"

"I double her salary."

This time, his expression went from shocked and concerned all the way to *have you lost your mind?* "What's to keep her from shaking her ass around you so that you lose that bet?"

"Integrity."

Pierce looked at me now like I was being naïve. Who knew the guy had so many expressions?

"No, really. She wasn't going to take the job because she wants to earn it on her own merit, not as payback or for favors. I respect that. I have no doubt that she wants that more than she wants more money." It was a bit of an ego-buster, but I still admired her for it.

Pierce shook his head. "You know this arrangement skirts all sorts of ethical lines, don't you? I don't know what the policies are at your company, but generally, it's not a good thing for a boss to be lusting after one of his employees. You've set yourself up for potential sexual harassment problems. And worse, what if this goofy smile I'm seeing on your face is reciprocated by her? What happens if you wind up getting together and falling in love?"

I shook my head. As nice as it would be to find a woman to love, I knew my history. "Look, we both know that I have zero luck with women. Would I like to fuck her again? Yes. But I also like her as a person. She's refreshing. She's herself without any guile or pretense. And she's smart. I'd be an idiot not to hire her. I don't think temptation is going to be a problem."

I didn't need Pierce's dubious expression to tell me I was probably lying to myself. But my intentions were good.

"Sounds like you've thought it all through." It was clear that he thought I was playing a dangerous game.

Maybe I was, but that was the allure. I'd felt so fucking dead inside for so long, and this little challenge had lit me up.

"Oh, ye of little faith."

He rolled his eyes. "I want to get in on the wager. I haven't met her, but seeing you like this, I have no doubt that you'll fail."

"Sorry. I'm not taking that bet." Clearly, I didn't think I would succeed either. But I'd try. I'd count on Analyn to put the kibosh on anything that could lead to my losing.

"How about I make you a bet that I can beat you to the bottom?" He gripped his handlebars and took off, pedaling full speed toward the Red Rock Canyon parking lot where we left our cars.

That was one bet I would take. I started after him, determined that I would win. I'd win this bet and the one with Analyn.

As I pulled up next to Pierce, ready to take the lead, I realized that

I was willing to lose one of the bets. As I pulled ahead of Pierce and entered the parking area ahead of him, it was clear which bet I was hoping to lose.

8

Analyn

Like anyone would be, I was both excited and nervous to start my first day of work. But my feelings were heightened by the idea that I would be working with Reed.

Despite the bet, there were so many ways things could go wrong. Although there had been a great deal of friction between us the last two times we'd met, the chemistry was there too. At least for me. I hoped that once I settled into the job, I'd be too busy to think about him. Plus, he was the CEO while I was the head of social media in the marketing department.

Except for maybe an occasional meeting, which the director of marketing would probably be more likely to attend, I didn't anticipate that I would see him on a daily basis. So everything would be okay. Fingers crossed.

When I arrived, I was greeted by a smartly dressed woman who introduced herself as Catherine Smalls, Reed's executive assistant. She was direct and efficient as she gave me a tour and let me know the expectations of the job. If I didn't know that Reed was the CEO, I might've guessed that she was. She had an air of authority about her.

It was clear to me that she was the gatekeeper. In my mind, that was a good thing. It added an extra layer of protection between me and Reed. Not that I was going to go seek Reed out, but if I did, she'd likely be in the way.

We finally ended up in the area of the building where the marketing team worked. She introduced me to the team, who were all friendly and welcoming. It added to my feeling that this was a good job decision.

I settled into my office and met with members of my immediate team to find out what they were working on now and to begin brainstorming ideas for the next campaigns. When that was done, I familiarized myself with my office and resources.

I was surprised I had an office, although it wasn't necessarily private as the upper half of the walls were windows. I could see out into the main marketing department section. It also had windowed walls to designate the area.

My office, while in the marketing section, ran along a corridor to the other parts of the building. Across that corridor was a large meeting room, also with windowed walls. As I looked over, I stopped when I saw Reed standing at the head of the room, talking to a group of a half-dozen people or so.

When I first met Reed, he was wearing a T-shirt and jeans that made my mouth water. When I first saw him in the interview, he was wearing a suit, complete with coat and tie, and to be honest, he wore that well too. Now, in the meeting, his jacket was off and his tie was loose.

He'd unbuttoned the sleeves of his shirt and rolled them up. And goodness, if he didn't look delicious like that as well. I had an image of grabbing his tie and leading him somewhere secluded and then one by one unbuttoning the buttons of his shirt, exposing the hard planes of his chest and the hard pack of muscles on his abdomen.

It brought back the memory of the night we'd been together and I'd first seen him naked, and how I'd wanted to touch every inch of him, so I did. He let me explore his body, looking almost amused as I drew my fingers over his pecs, scraping my nails over his nipples, making him hiss, and then dragging my hands slowly down over his rock-hard abs and lower.

When I'd freed his dick, a thrill ran through me, although admittedly, there was trepidation as well. In his case, large hands did signify a long, thick cock. It was magnificent as it stood up straight, a pearl of precum sitting on the tip. I used my finger to rub it around the head and along the edge, loving how he sucked in a breath and then let out a long groan.

He did his best to let me explore his dick, but finally, he sheathed himself, pushed me back, and drove home. I arched and gasped as he filled me. I clung to him as the sensations swept me up. I'd enjoyed sex with my ex, but there was something different about it with Reed. There was more energy in the air. It whipped around me, tingled my skin.

It was also different because he wasn't driving toward the finish line as fast as he could. I'd get to the edge and then the tables would turn. All of a sudden, I'd be on top, riding him, feeling more feminine and sexually free than I'd ever felt in my life. It was like a dance, moving, swaying, writhing until finally, neither could hold back. I came hard, feeling it through my entire body.

And the best part was that when it was over, it wasn't really over. Once we had an orgasm, there were a few minutes to catch our breaths, but then he'd start all over again. I had more orgasms that night than I'd had in the last year combined.

"Ms. Watts?" Catherine's terse voice broke through my memory.

I flinched and turned to her, embarrassed at having been caught ogling my boss. It was clear by the way she looked at me that I had been lost in my memory, and she'd had to say my name a couple of times to get me out of it.

"Yes. I'm sorry, I was just thinking."

Her expression was impassive, and yet I saw disapproval in her eyes. Not a good way to start my new job.

I motioned to the chair by my desk. "Would you like to sit?"

She entered my office, standing in front of my desk holding an envelope.

I took a seat behind the desk, using the few seconds to get myself sorted and putting on my professional mask.

She lifted the envelope. "What's in the envelope?"

I glanced at the envelope, confused. "I don't know." Why would she think I knew what the envelope contained?

Catherine set the envelope in front of me on the desk. She studied me in a way that made me want to squirm, but I did my best not to.

"Mr. Hampton canceled an important conference call on Thursday night without any notice."

I thought back to Thursday night. That was the day of my interview, and that evening, Reed had called asking him to meet him. He'd offered me this job.

"And then the next day, he told me that you were hired. That was after he was adamant that he couldn't hire you. I'm wondering if there's some sort of correlation between those facts."

Ah. I could see why she was suspicious. My belly fluttered with nerves. She struck me as the type of woman who could read minds. She'd be able to ferret out my history with Reed if I didn't do better to hide it.

I ignored the part about his being adamant that he couldn't hire me. I knew why. It was for the same reason I didn't think I should take the job. Or close to it. But I wasn't about to tell this admin my history with Reed, including having met with him on Thursday evening. If he didn't tell her about it, it seemed like he didn't want her to know.

I shrugged. "I don't know what it means."

Catherine continued to study me, and then her gaze moved to the envelope. I got the feeling she wanted me to open it in front of her. She wanted to know what was inside. The fact that she didn't know told me she didn't put it together for him. I had to assume he didn't want her to know.

I picked the envelope up and stuck it into the top drawer of my desk. "I'll be sure to check it over later. Right now, I want to review the data on all social media campaigns over the last ninety days."

Catherine frowned, but just as quickly, her expression changed, going back to the professional façade she wore. "I hope you're settling in."

I nodded. "I am. I'm really excited about the work I'm going to be able to do here with the marketing team."

I fully expected her to turn and leave, but she continued to stare at me from the front of my desk.

Finally, she said, "Mr. Hampton is a very good boss. And I know I don't have to tell you that he is a very rich and handsome man."

I worked to keep my face impassive and wondered if maybe she'd give me lessons on how to pull it off.

"You wouldn't be the first woman to set her sights on him. But any interest you have in him personally will be in vain. We are all professionals, and so there is no fraternization here—"

I shook my head. "I'm not setting my sights on Mr. Hampton." Well, maybe in my dreams, but not in reality.

She didn't look convinced. "I like to let all the new hires know the situation. He's off limits."

I got a weird vibe from her comment. Like he was off limits because he was taken.

Had she set her sights on him?

Maybe I should read the HR manual to find out if there really was a policy of nonfraternization. Then again, what would it matter if she wanted him? It didn't make any difference to me.

Liar.

"I don't blame you for being attracted to him. But you need to know that nothing will come of it." She turned and left my office, shutting the door behind her.

"Have you told him that?" I said when I knew she was out of earshot.

I hated that I had gotten caught staring at him. I wondered if she'd tell him about it, and what would he think? Would he like the idea that I was watching him? Would he worry that I was going to try and win the bet by seducing him so I could get my pay doubled?

I pulled the top drawer of my desk open, taking out the envelope.

I studied it, wondering what the heck it was. Was it related to work? It seemed like if it was, Catherine would know what was in it.

I turned it over to open it but worried that she might come in again, so I shoved it into my purse and headed to the restroom. Once I was in the bathroom stall, I opened the envelope and pulled out a sheet of paper with the official company letterhead on it. On it was a handwritten message:

You are cordially invited to a victory party, one year from today, to celebrate my winning the bet.

My lips twitched upward. Below his signature, he'd written his home address, as if adding an extra little dig at me.

My first thought was, *we'll see about that.* But then I shook my head realizing what I was thinking. My goal was to be seen as a professional. If he lost the bet by our having sex again, I'd risk my reputation.

Certainly, Catherine would judge me as a gold digger or someone trying to get perks by sleeping with the boss.

No, I needed to support him and his goal of winning the bet.

I put the paper back in the envelope, allowing myself to feel the disappointment that he would have to win the bet for me to maintain the respect I wanted in the workplace.

But then I thought of his large hands on my body. What a shame that we wouldn't be together like that again.

I put the envelope in my purse and exited the bathroom, going back to work. It was time to focus on the job, not my boss. I didn't know what I was getting myself into, but I knew I wanted this to work out. So, as I sat at my desk to get started on analyzing the social media data, I marked my calendar one year from now to attend Reed's party as the cleanup crew.

9

Reed

I was intently looking at my computer, going through sports results from the night before. I had people in the company who tracked all this and input the data needed to run the fantasy sports leagues. but I liked to keep up for myself, being a sports fan, and I needed something to occupy my time to keep from going to check on Analyn.

I was glad that I had a Monday morning meeting with other executives, just to have a chance to see her over in the marketing department. If I hadn't had a meeting, I might've scheduled one, which might make Catherine suspicious.

I respected Analyn's desire to have success on her own merit and to be treated as a professional, and I didn't want to do anything to mess that up for her. I was smart enough to know that I didn't have to sleep with her for there to be a hint of scandal. I had to continue to act normally and not give her any extra attention that I wouldn't give to anyone else.

But I wouldn't lie. When I looked over to the marketing department and saw her meeting with everyone on the team, looking confident, and everyone on the team welcoming her and treating her as the professional she wanted to be, I wanted to join in. At one point during my meeting, I glanced over and thought I saw her watching me. But Catherine was there delivering the envelope that I had asked her to take to Analyn. So maybe she was just looking over because of that.

In hindsight, it might have been better if I'd delivered it myself. I felt pretty sure Catherine wouldn't open it, but I knew she'd be curious about it. Nearly every communication in the business was drafted and delivered by her. But if I had brought the envelope to Analyn, that might've raised even more suspicion.

The knock on my door interrupted my thoughts. "Come in."

Catherine entered, walking straight up to my desk. "I delivered the envelope to Ms. Watts for you."

I nodded. "Thank you."

She stood quietly for a moment. "She didn't open it while I was there, so I have no message back."

"That's fine." Inside, I chastised myself for not considering whether Analyn would open it in front of Catherine or Catherine would wait for a response. Fuck. I needed to think these things through better.

I THOUGHT HAVING Analyn work for me would be an interesting challenge. It was a challenge alright, but not interesting. More like tormenting. God, how I wanted to visit her in her office.

I'd had more meetings in the large conference room just to have a chance to see her. She looked so fucking confident as she met with the team or worked at her desk. On occasion, I'd catch her and her team talking, and they'd all laugh, and my heart would squeeze. I wanted to be a part of their group so fucking badly. As the boss, I could walk in there and demand to be a part of it, but heads would turn. Suspicions would rise.

On Friday, I was in my office, watching a clip of Bo Tyler's latest antics when Catherine entered. "A Gino Palmieri of Paradise Limited is here. He doesn't have an appointment, but he insists on seeing you."

I frowned. I knew of Paradise Limited because they were a major player in online bookmaking. I couldn't imagine what anyone from there would want with me. But at least it would occupy my time. "Go ahead and clear anything on my schedule for the next hour and show him in."

She nodded and left my office. A few moments later, a forty-something-year-old man with dark, slicked back hair and beady eyes entered my office. He looked like somebody who just walked off a Mafia movie set. He reminded me of the young man I'd interviewed last week. I wondered if somehow, the two were related.

He reached his hand across my desk, giving me a firm, almost too firm handshake. "I knew you'd see me. Everyone says you're a shrewd businessman."

I released my hand and resisted wiping his smarm off on my jacket. I motioned to the chair in front of my desk. "How can I help you, Mr. Palmieri?"

"Well, I know that you are well aware of Paradise Limited. We are the industry leader in online bookmaking."

I gave a short nod but didn't respond.

"We like to keep an eye on everyone in the business, and when we see a star, we like to connect. You're going places, Reed, and I'm here to make an offer. We can go in together and become filthy rich."

The way he just said all that, including using my first name, was an attempt at flattery and personal connection, but I found it disrespectful. I did my best not to roll my eyes. I was already filthy rich. I considered telling him that but determined I'd have a better chance at getting rid of him if I acted grateful for his attempt at a compliment.

"I'm flattered that you think my company is worthy, but we're doing just fine. We have no reason to change things up here."

Gino maintained his smile, but his eyes darkened slightly. I got the feeling few people ever said no to him. "An extra percentage on each transaction would be a good reason to switch. Plus, we have many other perks we could offer to the partnership."

I had no idea what other perks he could be talking about, but I couldn't help but think that they skirted the line of legality. I now wished that I hadn't had Catherine clear my schedule. I wanted an excuse to get out of this meeting. Then again, he didn't know that I told her I cleared my schedule.

"I'm sorry I can't give you more time, but I'm late to another meeting." I stood, hoping he'd get the hint.

Gino remained sitting. "I haven't finished going over the perks."

I buttoned my coat. "As I said, I'm not interested in making any changes at the moment."

Gino stood and visibly worked to give me an affable smile. "I'll tell you what. I'll hand-deliver a proposal tomorrow. It's going to be so good you won't be able to say no to it."

I shook his hand, again trying not to cringe. I let out a sigh of relief when he left.

The door had no sooner shut behind him than Catherine strolled in. "What did he want?"

"He wants to have a partnership with us. I'm not sure it's on the up and up. I don't suppose you have a handwipe or hand sanitizer." I really wanted to get Gino's handshake off me. Hell, maybe I'd go to the gym so I could shower him off me.

Catherine nodded to my desk. "There's hand sanitizer in your top drawer."

I sat down, opening the drawer and finding a small travel-size bottle of the clear disinfectant. I squeezed a large glob of it onto my hand and rubbed it in.

"I'd be happy to do a little digging on Paradise Limited," Catherine said.

I shook my head. "It's not important. The business is doing great, and there's no reason to change anything."

She let out a sigh. "Sometimes, change is good. Like realizing maybe you've overlooked something that's right under your nose."

I looked up from where I was putting the hand sanitizer back into the top drawer, trying to decipher what she meant. But before I could ask, I saw Analyn walk past my open door. I needed to let her pass by without acknowledging her. I couldn't do anything that would have anyone, especially Catherine, question my relationship with Analyn. But the urge to go talk to her welled up like a tsunami.

As casually as I could, I stood. I checked my watch and realized it was lunchtime. It was the perfect excuse. "As I said, I'm not interested in a partnership. And in particular, not one with Paradise Limited. I'm heading out for lunch."

I didn't wait for her to respond. I made a beeline out of my office, turning in the direction that Analyn had gone. Warning bells clanged in my head that this was probably a mistake. Going out of my way to see her could quite possibly result in my losing the bet.

Of course, I wanted to lose the bet more than I wanted my next breath. The only reason I wasn't going to try and seduce Analyn was her desire to be taken seriously at work. I didn't want to fuck that up for her.

But surely, we could find a happy medium. We could be colleagues, maybe even friends. Something in the back of my skull told me I was kidding myself, but I pretended not to hear it.

10

Analyn

By the end of the week, I was feeling really good, not just about my job but also at having Reed as my boss. Although I saw him around on occasion, for the most part, we didn't talk to each other. We barely looked at each other. He was doing exactly what I wanted. He was acting like my boss and like we hadn't slept together a month ago.

Even so, sometimes, like a stupid lovesick teenager, it bothered me that I wasn't catching him looking my way when I was looking at him. As it turned out, I was the one struggling not to let our history interfere.

So when I heard him call my name as I was heading down the hall toward the elevator to go out and grab lunch, I stopped short, wondering why he wanted to talk to me. I reminded myself that he was my boss, not the man I'd picked up at a bar a month ago. Chances were he wanted to tell me something boss-like, such as checking in on my first week or maybe offering praise on how I was settling.

I plastered on a smile and turned as he approached.

He pointed to his watch. "It's nearly time for lunch. Now that you've been here for a week, I thought we could meet, and you can let me know how things have gone."

Ah . . . okay, so boss-like and yet, I hadn't seen him take anyone else out to lunch. I studied his face, and he appeared sincere. Like he really wanted to check in on me as his new employee, not as the woman he slept with last month.

I was hungry, and a girl's gotta eat. I decided I need to take him at his word. "I wouldn't mind some lunch."

He smiled, and for a moment, I was dazzled until I reminded myself, again, that he was my boss.

We walked together to the elevator, and he said, "We've got a really good Chinese restaurant on the ground floor of the building."

"I like Chinese." I stepped into the elevator next to him. I looked over at him until the memory of when he'd bet me that he wouldn't be able to wait until we reached the hotel room to kiss me, and to prove it, the minute the elevator doors had shut at the hotel, he had pressed me against the wall and his lips were hot and thorough on mine before the door even closed.

I cleared my throat and looked forward. He didn't speak, and in fact, he took a step sideways, putting distance between us. Had he had the same thought and he was trying to behave? Maybe I had inadvertently given off sexy vibes, and he was worried I was going to try and make him lose his bet. This was why avoiding each other at work was for the best. Whenever he was around, my mind went all sorts of places it shouldn't go.

When we reached the ground floor, we exited the elevator and made our way across the lobby to the Chinese restaurant.

A lovely Asian woman met us at the hostess station. "Mr. Hampton. Right this way."

I remembered back at the bar when I'd been so impressed that Reed had known the owners and the bartender. And now here we were at a restaurant that clearly knew him as well.

We followed her through the main dining area and to the back.

Curious. "Are we going to eat in the kitchen?"

The hostess looked over her shoulder at me like I was a country bumpkin. "We have several private eating areas where businessmen can have meetings or privacy for any reason."

Huh? What did that mean? What else were businessmen using these dining rooms for? Had Reed used it for something else? I imagined him with another woman, who interestingly enough was Catherine. No wonder I didn't like her.

The way my body tingled, it hoped it was my turn for the non-business private dining experience.

"We celebrated my buddy Pierce's birthday here once," Reed said.

Oh, right. Life wasn't just business or sex.

She led us into a room with a single table. How odd to have a private dining room.

"I hope you don't mind if I order for us," he said as he pulled out my chair.

I shook my head. "That's fine. I haven't met a Chinese dish that I didn't like." I sat down.

"All of the usual, but for two," he said to our hostess.

She nodded. "I will let your server know."

"What's your usual?"

Reed sat next to me at the round table. "Dumplings, shrimp, toast, and Mongolian chicken wings."

I grinned at him, noting these were all finger-foods. "You don't know how to use a fork?"

He laughed. "It turns out that all my favorite Chinese foods can be eaten with my hands." He held up his hands and wiggled his fingers. I had to stifle a groan as once again, the memory of his hands on my body returned. My body remembered too, and it got noticeably hot. I wondered if my skin was turning flush.

I looked away. Seeing a glass of water on the table, I reached over and took a large gulp, hoping to cool my hormones down.

"Of course, if there's something else that you would prefer—"

"No, those all sound very good."

He studied me for a moment and then he took a sip of water. "So, how was your first week? Are you enjoying the job?"

"I am. I really am." I knew I sounded giddy, but I wanted him to know that I appreciated that he had gone against his judgment and offered me the job. And that he was following through on his promise, or bet, to protect my reputation by not bringing up our past or doing anything to have the other staff question why I was there. "You have a really good marketing team, and your social media people are very good at taking a concept or idea and turning it into a compelling visual."

He nodded. "Good to hear. Do you have any new ideas? Especially to attract new users?"

I had several new ideas, but the one I was most excited about was the one that the rest of the team wasn't so sure of. Maybe if Reed liked it, I could go back to the team and let them know. "I have this idea about a social media video campaign of having a fantasy league made up of magical creatures."

He frowned, tilting his head to the side. "What do you mean by that?"

"I mean like having teams that have dragons and Minotaurs and unicorns and Bigfoot—"

"Bigfoot is magical?"

"Not just magical, but mythical too."

"So, like a yeti?"

I nodded. "It would be a minigame that featured all the best elements of what you do with all the other sports, but instead of using people, it would be these mythical creatures."

"What sport would they do?"

"It could be anything. They could run. You could have them play football. Or hockey," I added quickly, remembering he had once been a professional hockey player. "Or it could be a game we make up. I know you have fantasy sports leagues, but fantasy can also include the magical realms. Fantasy fiction is big right now, so it's a play on that. If it's too strange to use current sports, we could use historical sports like fantasy jousting or sword fighting."

He sat quietly thinking, but I couldn't decipher if he was trying to find the words to tell me my idea was terrible or if he was considering the idea.

Finally, he nodded and said, "That is an unusual and unexpected idea, but I sort of like it. I knew you were creative. I haven't stopped thinking about how you—" He stopped short and his cheeks reddened, telling me that he was about to bring up something from a month ago.

At first, I wondered what I'd done that he thought was so creative? When I rode him backward? When I licked the underside of his balls as I stroked his dick, making him come in a huge mess on his perfect abs and chest? I didn't think those were creative. Mostly, I did it out of curiosity and exploring sexual pleasure, something I'd never felt free to do until that night. Until Reed.

But then I remembered we were only boss and employee now. "It's best not to go there. Think of all the money you're going to lose if you have to pay double for losing the bet."

His head tilted to the side. "You make it sound like losing the bet could be a possibility."

Of course, it was. I couldn't tell him that, but I wasn't sure how to respond. Thankfully, at that point, a server entered carrying our food.

Once he'd put the plates on the table and left, Reed cleared his throat. "Like I said, I think the idea is interesting. I know that when it comes to marketing, it's important to stand out, and that sounds like something that would make us stand out."

I decided that he'd put his stamp of approval, and I was eager to get back and let the team know. In the meantime, I served myself a couple of dumplings and chicken wings.

I took a bite of a dumpling and the flavor burst on my tongue, making me moan. "This is so good. I've never had a dumpling so good."

"How about shrimp toast?" He picked up one of the shrimp toasts, dunking it into sauce and holding it out to me. Automatically, I opened my mouth and took a bite. I closed my eyes as more delicious flavor filled my mouth.

When I opened my eyes, he was still leaning in close, and I realized how intimate his feeding me was. In that second, the energy in the room changed. The atmosphere was charged with electricity.

He used his thumb to wipe my lower lip. "You have a little sauce there." His voice was rough as he brought his thumb to his mouth, sucking off the sauce.

My blood pounded as erotic energy coursed through me with heat and intensity. Our gazes held as the world dropped away, and there was only here and now, me and him, and a magnet pulling me to him.

When his lips touched mine, there was nothing else to do but to kiss him back. Fireworks exploded. Need pumped fire through my body straight down to my pussy.

He was too far away. I needed his hands on me. I needed my body against his.

His arm wrapped around me, and I willingly let him pull me to him, straddling him in his chair, rubbing my body over his hard length. But it still wasn't enough.

Our lips fused as his hands slid up my thighs and under my skirt. I sent a silent thank you out to the universe that I still hadn't replaced my nylons, and so the only thing blocking his access to my center were my panties. His finger slipped under the panel, rubbing my clit and then sliding down to tease my entrance.

It still wasn't enough. My fingers unbuckled his belt and the button and zipper of his pants. I freed him and rose up as he pulled my panties aside. I impaled myself on him. Relief and pleasure and perfection hit all at once.

11

Reed

I should stop, but now that her body was wrapped around my cock, I was powerless to stop. Her pussy was wet and hot, sweet perfection.

"Fuck," I groaned. I wrapped my hand around the back of her neck and pulled her to me, consuming her with my mouth. Fire rushed through my veins. Light filled my chest. Life . . . life like I hadn't felt since I played hockey radiated through me. This . . . fucking her, in a restaurant, no less, might be wrong, but it felt right. Perfect.

Her body rocked, sending a feral growl from deep in my chest. "Yes . . . fuck, Analyn . . ." I gripped her hips, helping her rise and fall over my dick. God, how I wished we were naked so I could bury my face in her tits, suck her nipples.

Her fingers gripped my shoulders, her breath coming in pants as her pussy grew tighter with each slide.

"Yes . . . fuck, yes . . . I'm gonna come." I was teetering on the edge, but I did my best to hold off. I focused on her. Moving with her.

Knowing she was close too as our bodies rocked and rode until I could hardly breathe.

We peaked together, flew together, our bodies in perfect sync as pleasure consumed us both. It was like our bodies were made for each other. As we came down from the high, I wished more than anything that we were at my house. In my king-sized bed. I could picture her there, her lush, soft body warm and wanton in my sheets.

Unfortunately, we were in the middle of a restaurant. Yes, it was a private dining room, but our server could enter at any moment. As much as I wanted to draw this out, I knew I couldn't. Still, I savored the sweet sensations for as long as I could. That was until Analyn's head lifted and her gaze captured mine and in her eyes I saw regret.

"Oh, God." She scrambled off me, stumbling to her seat. She pressed the palms of her hands on the table like she was falling apart.

It fucking hurt to see her response because this wasn't wrong. Except it was. At least in her mind. Sleeping with the boss would ruin her reputation and make those around her question whether she'd earned her job. So I did my damnedest to push away my own feelings and waited for her.

Her breaths were low and shallow, but finally, she took in a long breath, letting it out. Her head turned to me, and in her expression, I saw anger. "You couldn't even go a week."

She blamed me. I supposed I started it by kissing her. Or maybe it started by feeding her. Or inviting her to lunch. Hell, it might have started when I hired her.

"Well, at least you got a raise." Even as I said it, I knew it was weak and stupid. I was already wondering how I was going to justify doubling her salary when asked about it by HR or Catherine.

The anger was still in her eyes, but so were tears, and I hated even more how dismissive of her situation my words were.

"Right. A raise for services rendered."

Her tears got me, but her words pissed me off. This thing between us, despite how it started, wasn't sordid. But again, I pushed my feelings away because I didn't want her to feel the way she clearly felt. I needed to figure out a way to fix this, but how?

The obvious answer was to end the bet, but the bet seemed like the best way to put roadblocks between us, what just happened notwithstanding.

"Okay, so how about we go double or nothing?"

She looked at me like I was a complete douchebag, and maybe I was.

"You've lost your mind."

I took a breath. "Hear me out. This time, the bet won't involve a raise, or promotion, or anything related to your job. I promise I won't touch you, and at the end of the bet, I'll pay triple your salary to the charity of your choice."

I was feeling desperate to keep her from walking away while at the same time, agreeing with her that I'd lost my mind. I had to face it —what happened just now was inevitable from the moment I brought her to have lunch at my private dining area.

Our having sex was bound to happen.

Hell, it was probably bound to happen the moment I asked her to work for me. A smart man would let her go. He'd let her quit her job, as I was sure she wanted to do. A part of me thought I should let her. After all, the problem we were having was that I was her boss. If she didn't work for me, we could be together.

But that wasn't what she wanted. Sure, she'd climbed into my lap, released my dick, and ridden me to paradise, but what she really wanted was the job as my head of social media marketing. She'd earned it. She'd done well in school and worked hard, her job history showing deliberate strategic moves up the corporate ladder. The position with my company was perfect for her, and her for it, and I'd be a selfish bastard to get in between her and her goals, especially since her career was the most important thing in her life right now.

And why shouldn't it be? She was still young. At twenty-five, she had time to think about things like family. I was the old fogey who'd already achieved his success in two careers. My life was in a different place from hers, and if I were any sort of man, especially one who found himself drawn to her in a way beyond lust, I would support her. I was in a position to make her dreams come true, not by giving her the world or making her a trophy wife, but by supporting her career.

It was also clear that she didn't trust me. A part of me wanted to point out that she was the one who climbed into my lap, but that would be petty. I searched my brain, looking for something I could say that would change the look in her eyes from regret to a smile.

She continued to stare at me like I'd grown a third eye or horns on my head. That was probably how she saw me. Like the devil who'd seduced her.

Finally, she shook her head and picked up her purse. "I can't do this." She stood, and after giving me a look of despair, she turned and left the room.

I had an urge to go after her, but what for? In the end, I'd probably only make it worse. And besides, it wasn't like I wasn't used to women walking out on me.

I turned my attention back to my lunch, eating only because I knew it would be best for Analyn if we didn't arrive back at the office together. I was the dirty little secret that she didn't want anyone to know about. Who gave a fuck if that hurt my feelings?

I finished my meal and then took my time returning to the office. I was barely out of the elevator when Catherine met me, her mouth in a grim line and her jaw tight as she forced a smile. It was a sure sign that she was upset with me but was trying to hold it in.

"You're late for a video conference call."

Who cares? "I'm here now." I made a U-turn, heading toward the larger meeting room where we held videoconferences.

"Where were you? I was calling." She walked with me.

"Having lunch." Hadn't I told her that when I left? I was pretty sure I had, so why was she asking?

"Was it a business meeting? Or . . . a date?"

It's none of your fucking business. "Do you have what I need for the meeting?"

She was quiet for a moment but then finally said, "It's already on the table."

"Thank you." As I strode past the marketing department, I glanced into the area, relieved to see Analyn at her desk. It didn't look like she was packing up, so maybe she was going to stay.

I hoped now that she did stay, although my reasons for it were in contrast to what she wanted. I wanted to be around her, get to know her, and support her goals. To that end, I needed to do everything I could to keep my hands to myself. My feelings to myself. Ugh! Cupid was a fucking sadist.

12

Analyn

I totally and completely lost my mind. I'd had sex in a restaurant! How did that happen?

I blamed Reed, even though I knew that was unfair. He didn't undo his pants and pull out his dick. I did that. Hell, I was the one who climbed into his lap and sank over him and rode him like my life depended on it.

But he's the one who fed me, and then kissed me, so it was his fault, right? I wanted to put all the blame on him, but I knew that I was culpable as well. I could have pushed him away. I could've said no. But I didn't. Like before, I got swept up in his charm and status. The guy had his own dining area in a restaurant. I didn't even know that sort of thing existed.

But good God, what if someone had walked in on us? I was really enjoying my job, and the last thing I wanted was to be considered the office slut. Fear of that had me nearly packing up my belongings and quitting the job. It seemed clear now that I couldn't resist Reed, and apparently, he couldn't resist me either.

That thought sent a little thrill of happiness through me, but I tamped it down, knowing that our attraction didn't mean anything and all it would lead to was humiliation.

I glanced over toward the meeting room where Reed was sitting as someone on a video screen spoke. Reed was the epitome of a sexy boss. He was sharp, shrewd, and confident. He was the last person I should be falling for.

I gave my head a shake. Not falling for him. *Surely, it's just lust, right?*

Okay, so maybe more than once, I'd wondered what it would be like to be with him beyond the physical. I imagined living in a big house and waking up in the morning next to him. Maybe we'd shower together and then get ready for work. We'd carpool to the office, where we'd part while I created amazing social media marketing campaigns that turned his company into the number-one fantasy sports betting business in the world.

My fantasy had us having lunch in his office, and by lunch, I meant sex. But now I could amend that to having lunch in his private dining room, eating amazing food and having spectacular sex.

I recognized that my job and my desire for respect were the big issues between us. If I did leave this position, those barriers would be gone. I'd be free to pursue whatever it was between us. To make those dreams a reality.

I let out a groan at my silly thoughts. There were so many reasons it was a stupid fantasy. For one, he was my boss. Then there was the fact that he was so much older than me and a billionaire. He wasn't married, but that didn't mean I wasn't just viewed as a little something to bring excitement into his life. Didn't he say that his life was boring? But I wasn't a woman he would get serious with. At his age, it seemed possible that he preferred to be a bachelor.

So no, I'd keep my job. I wasn't a woman who'd let her career be derailed by a man, which meant I needed to be more careful. God, if anyone caught wind of my having had sex with Reed, before and after he hired me, I'd be accused of being a gold digger or wanting extra perks.

I'd known all this when I went to lunch with him, but my brain had short-circuited. My body had taken over. The memory of it warmed my blood. I couldn't stop from thinking about the way he touched me.

Stop, Analyn! You have got to get yourself under control.

I tore my gaze away from Reed and worked to focus on developing a storyboard for our mystical animals campaign. Not that it worked.

My phone rang, and I was relieved to have something interrupt my thoughts of Reed. I checked the caller ID and saw it was Betts.

I answered. "Hey. What's up?"

"I just want to check and make sure you're going to be home tonight in time to help me pick out an outfit for my date. I think tonight's the night that Paul is going to pop the question."

I smiled, happy that my friend was finding happiness. "I'll be there."

For a moment, I wondered what would happen if Paul did ask her to marry him. That meant my living situation would be changing, which was all the more reason I needed to make this job work. I needed to get my hormones under control.

"You're going to be my maid of honor, right? I'm going to need you right there by my side."

"Of course. I'm going to help you put together the grandest wedding that ever was."

"Oh, my God, Analyn. I think I'm getting married."

I laughed. "I'm happy for you."

"Of course, this doesn't change anything between us. You know that, right? We're the epitome of BFFs."

"Best friends forever."

When I hung up the phone, I tried to imagine what it would be like to know the man you loved was about to ask you to marry him. That he wanted to spend the rest of his life with you. I glanced over in Reed's direction, where he continued to run a meeting.

Don't be a dope and imagine such a life with him. It would be some time, if ever, before I knew what Betts felt like now. But that was okay. I had my job, a job that I was really enjoying.

I pulled myself together, refocusing on creating a storyboard for the mystical creatures social media campaign. When I finally came up for air, several hours had passed, surprising me. But that's how it was when I had a job I loved. I got lost in the creativity of social media campaigns.

It was nearing five o'clock, so I gathered my things to go. I looked over toward the meeting room and was surprised to find that Reed was still there. He was by himself, his attention on a laptop.

He looked up, and I cursed myself for getting caught staring at him. He gave me a slight smile and then turned back to his work.

I started to leave but then worried he might head me off as I was leaving. I wasn't ready to talk to him. I was too worried that my staff, or anyone in the company, Catherine in particular, would see me talking to him and be able to tell what we had done during lunch.

Then again, I had to get home to help Betts. Knowing I'd have to risk it, I pulled my bag together again. I closed down my computer and walked out of my office. I said goodbye to a few of my staff who were still there and made a beeline to the elevator. I sent up a silent prayer that I would be able to leave without having to talk to Reed.

I stepped into the elevator, and as I leaned over to press the button for the ground floor, Reed rushed toward the elevator, stepping in before the door could close.

13

Reed

My meeting ended over an hour ago, but I stayed in the conference room, working, hoping that I would have a chance to talk to Analyn. I figured I'd catch her when she was leaving for the night and walk her out.

Risky, maybe. But I needed to find out what she was thinking.

I was brooding over my epic fuckup and needed to make amends. Yes, she had been an active participant during sex this afternoon, but I was the one who'd said I wouldn't touch her. Hell, I'd made a bet that I wouldn't. Had I not put us in a highly charged situation, it wouldn't have happened, so in the end, it was my fault.

The thing that bothered me the most was a fear that she had the wrong idea about me. Yes, I yearned for her, but that wasn't why I hired her. She needed to know that I didn't expect her to sleep with me in order to keep her job or to get perks. I hated that somehow, what we had done could impact her job. Even if nobody found out about our sexual past, which I was going to make sure nobody did, I knew it impacted her mentally.

What I thought would be an interesting challenge had turned out to be more difficult than I had anticipated. Resisting her was nearly impossible, but I wanted to keep her around even if I couldn't touch her. Seeing her, talking to her, made me feel things I hadn't felt in a long time, and I wasn't just talking about my dick. She was the epitome of a breath of fresh air. Around her, I felt something instead of empty and numb. In order to keep her around, I had to get my shit together.

Movement in the marketing department caught my eye. Analyn stood and gathered her belongings. She exited her office, saying a few things to her , and then she headed for the elevator.

I was out of the meeting room in a flash, although trying not to look too eager. I nonchalantly hurried to the elevator to catch her before the doors closed. I stepped in just as the car doors slid shut.

She looked up at me with a combination of nerves and wariness.

I hated that. I hated that I was the source of it. "I'm sorry."

She held up her hand and shook her head. "I don't think it's a good idea for us to be alone together."

I ran my hand through my hair. "I know that I made a miscalculation by inviting you to lunch. The truth is, Analyn, I'm stuck on you."

Her breath hitched, and I hoped my revelation didn't do more harm than good.

Just to make sure I wasn't fucking up worse, I hurried on. "I hate that I've made you feel uncomfortable or that you might think that I hired you for any other reason than that you were the best candidate for the job. From now on, I promise I'm going to be hands off." I held my hands up and then shoved them in my pockets to highlight my sincerity. "You're going to be able to focus on your work without my interference." I sent up a silent prayer for the strength to allow me to follow through with that. "I will work to avoid you, and of course, you can do the same. I don't want you to quit. Or if you are going to quit, I don't want to be the reason for it."

She didn't say anything as the elevator arrived at the lobby. When the doors opened, I followed her out, through the lobby and out of the building.

Finally, unable to deal with the uncertainty and needing to know what she was thinking, I gently took her arm, turning her to look at me. "I hope you'll stay. "

She was silent for a moment, and I damn near got on my knees to beg her to stay. What was going on that she had such an effect on me?

She scanned the area, and I cursed myself for not paying more attention to who might see this conversation.

Finally, she let out a sigh. "I like my job, Reed. I want to stay. But I really need to think about things." She turned away, heading toward the parking garage, and as much as I wanted to run after her, now was the moment I needed to prove to her that I could follow through on my promise. I needed to leave her alone. I needed to avoid her.

Reluctantly, I turned away, heading back into the building and up to my office's floor.

As I entered my office, Catherine followed me in. "Is there a problem with Ms. Watts?"

"Not at all." I sat down in my chair thinking I'd bury myself in work, but I didn't think I'd be able to stop my mind from ruminating on Analyn.

"It just seems that you're paying a great deal of attention to her. I checked in with the rest of the marketing department, and they all seem to like her. They say she's competent and creative. But if there is something going on, you can let me know."

"I was just making sure she's settling in properly." I found myself irked at Catherine's interference. I wanted to ask her why she was watching Analyn so closely, but maybe she watched all the staff so closely. Hadn't I relied on her to take care of things so I didn't have to?

"I don't remember you paying this much attention to our previous hires. What's going on?"

What the hell? She was acting like my mother. Or wife. She was overstepping. At least that was what it felt like.

Perhaps this was normal, and I was the one who was different. It didn't matter the reason. What mattered was that I didn't like her interference or her feeling that she was entitled to know the inner workings of my mind.

I looked up at her, and my expression must've been fierce because she flinched. "I appreciate all that you do for me, Catherine, but you don't run my life. What I do or don't do, who I pay attention to or ignore, is really none of your business unless I say it is. Again, I appreciate that you're looking out for me, but I don't need you to delve into every little thing that I do in the office. Now, if you'll excuse me, I have work I want to finish."

Catherine straightened, lifting her chin, almost in defiance. "Of course. I'll leave you to it." She turned, leaving my office. The door nearly slammed as she closed it behind her.

Fuck. I couldn't afford to have Catherine be upset with me. Everything I had just said to her was true. She wasn't entitled to know every little thing about what I did at work. But I had given her enough power and control that of course she would be observant about what was going on at the office. I had to hope that she didn't read anything into the attention I had given Analyn.

It was apparent even more now than it had been before that I needed to avoid Analyn, if only to protect her from Catherine. Catherine struck me as just the sort of person who might question Analyn's intentions. Since I hadn't wanted to hire her at first, Catherine could be suspicious of my attention toward Analyn, thinking it was Analyn's doing.

I remembered how annoyed Catherine was about the call I missed when I'd met with Analyn to offer her the job. She'd been suspicious, but I felt I'd done a good job covering up where I'd been and why I'd changed my mind about Analyn. But maybe I hadn't. If I wasn't careful, Analyn's fears could come true. Catherine wouldn't play nice if she felt Analyn was trying to get special attention from the boss.

As long as I followed through on my promise and kept my distance from Analyn, Catherine shouldn't suspect anything between us. God, I hoped that was true. Even more, I hoped I could keep my promise.

14

Analyn

I was five minutes late getting home, but Betts was so preoccupied trying on dresses that she didn't notice. I swept in, looking at the dresses strewn on the bed that she'd already tried on, which was nearly every one in her closet. Then I took in her current ensemble.

"I just don't know what to wear. Should I put on something sexier? I don't want to look like a skank when Paul proposes to me, but I want to look great, you know?"

In my mind, Betts always looked good in everything she wore. "What makes you feel beautiful, confident?"

She stopped in the middle of discarding the next dress she'd been about to try. "I don't know." She looked at me with an expression of panic and excitement.

"Maybe you should go with something bold." I remembered the red dress I'd worn to the bar the night I decided to be bold and go clubbing on my own. As much as my current situation messed up my life, I couldn't deny how great that night was. All because I'd been bold.

Betts looked at the dresses she'd thrown on the bed. "What do you think would be bold?"

All her dresses were nice, and several were sexy, but I wasn't sure that any were bold. "I think you should go with the emerald or royal blue one. Both make your red hair stand out."

Betts put on the emerald-green dress, and I was right. She looked confident and smoking hot. If Paul wasn't planning on asking her to marry him already, surely, he would when he saw her in this dress.

I helped accessorize the outfit and do her hair. By the time Paul arrived, she was ready. She looked so happy, and I was happy for her.

Once she and Paul left for their date, I went to my room and changed into pajamas, which was actually a pair of shorts and a tank top.

I grabbed some dinner, and while I knew I should think about what I needed to do in my job, I didn't want to. I liked the distraction that helping Betts had given me, and I didn't want to spend the rest of the night in a tug-of-war over my feelings about Reed. Instead, I decided to distract myself with ice cream and wine and bingeable TV.

I considered watching a romcom but decided that might make me think of Reed, so instead I watched back to back episodes of *Deadly Women*, surprised at how often true love could turn to murder.

I was well into the middle of the fourth episode when Betts and Paul charged into the condo. Betts was absolutely beaming with happiness, and both of them looked like they had been celebrating, if the glassy eyes and giddiness were any indication.

"I'm engaged." Betts thrust her hand forward, showing me the lovely ring Paul had given her.

I gave her a hug and then hugged Paul too. Congratulations."

Betts whirled around, looping her arms around Paul. "I don't want this night to ever end."

He smiled. "It won't. Marriage is forever, right?"

Betts got a sappy look on her face. "Isn't he romantic?"

I smiled and tried not to roll my eyes. Of course, had Reed said something like that to me, I'd probably have a sappy smile too. God, I was a mess.

"I want to keep the party going. We should have another toast." Betts headed to the kitchen but then a few moments later came out pouting. "We don't have anything to toast with." Then she lit up. "I'm going to run down to the corner store and grab a bottle."

Our area was safe, but it still seemed like she shouldn't go alone. When Paul didn't chime in, I said, "I'll go with you."

Betts shook her head. "You're in your pajamas. You stay here and keep Paul company. I'll be back, ten minutes max."

She was out the door before Paul or I could stop her. I looked at Paul, shrugging at Betts's behavior. But I stopped mid-shrug when I caught him looking at my body like he wanted to lick it from head to toe.

"So, these are your pajamas?"

Immediately, I went on alert, but I calmed down by reminding myself that he'd had a little bit to drink. Maybe it was messing up his thinking.

"How about I go make something to eat? I think you and Betts could use something to sop up all the celebratory champagne."

I went to the kitchen looking for something bread-like to soak up all the alcohol. I was putting some crackers on a plate when hands settled on my hips and lips nuzzled my neck.

Shocked, I jerked away, gaping at Paul.

He gave me another appreciative body scan. "I always thought you were hot. Maybe we could hook up."

My jaw couldn't drop any further. I moved away from him. "You just got engaged to my best friend." What the hell was he thinking?

He shrugged and started walking toward me, or stalking was more like it. I felt like prey.

"Hooking up is no big deal. It's just a little fun. Something we can keep between ourselves. I'm sure you'll like it. I'm pretty good at it. I'm sure Betts has told you."

Gag! I shook my head, working to put the table between the two of us. "I'm sure I wouldn't like it because I would never do that to Betts. How could you?"

Paul's eyes narrowed, his lips curling into a sneer. "You should be happy someone like me is even paying you attention."

What happened to he always thought I was hot? I didn't ask him, of course. Instead, I decided I needed to get away. Like right now.

I hurried out of the kitchen and to the coat closet, where I pulled out my overcoat, shoving my arms through the sleeves as I grabbed my purse and headed out the door. I was just exiting the building when Betts came in.

She stopped short and frowned. "Where are you going? We have celebrating to do."

Oh, God, how did I tell her that her fiancé hit on me? I knew I needed to tell her, but I couldn't find the words. At least not at this moment.

"I had a work emergency." I hated lying to her. I hated that I couldn't blurt out how Paul hit on me. I started to congratulate her again but then realized I couldn't do that either. I couldn't wish her well in marrying a cheating douchebag. Had he already cheated on her with others? I couldn't imagine he hadn't.

Her head cocked to the side. "Are you okay?"

Tell her. "Yeah, sure. Just a potential social media scandal. I'm sorry." I hurried off, wishing I could tell her that my apology was for not revealing her cheating fiancé, not that I had to leave.

Once I got in my car, I gripped the steering wheel, not knowing what to do. Clearly, I had to go somewhere, but where? And crap, I was in my pajamas. Thank God I had already been wearing my slippers, but God, they were slippers. I couldn't go anywhere like this.

I supposed I could go to a hotel. I started the car because it was getting cold, and I didn't want Betts to look out the window and wonder why I was still sitting here in the parking lot.

As I pulled out, I remembered that there was one other person in town whom I knew. One person whose home address I had.

I reached into my purse and pulled out the envelope Catherine had given me on my first day. This was a mistake too, but in the middle of a cold night, escaping my best friend's letch of a fiancé, and realizing that I was going to have to ruin her happiness, where else could I go?

15

Reed

Insomnia sucked. And what made it worse was the inability to find something to do late at night when I couldn't sleep. I considered watching porn, thinking it could kill three birds with one stone. First, it would pass some time. Second, the physical nature of it might tire me out. And third, maybe by watching another naked woman get off, I'd stop fantasizing about Analyn. I couldn't fuck things up at work anymore, and the best way to do that would be to end this gnawing attraction I had for her. But I couldn't do that when she so frequently starred in my fantasies. Replacing the fantasy seemed like the best option.

The only problem was that all my porn video options left me flat, figuratively and literally. My dick was a flaccid sad sack.

Finally, I decided maybe I'd read. I put on my robe and made my way out of my bedroom, up the long hall, and through my expansive house to the library. All the way, I was cursing the size of my home.

I didn't need all this room, and having it only highlighted how alone and empty I was. I'd bought it not long after I retired from hockey, thinking I'd start a family and fill it up with children. All these years later, the house was empty except for me. I didn't even have a fucking dog or cat. Maybe I should get one. I'd be the old crazy cat guy.

I was scanning my old paperback thrillers when a knock echoed through the house. I checked my watch. Nearly midnight. Who the hell was here?

It had to be Pierce, but it was unusual for him to show up so late, especially without calling first. So maybe it was Bo, but that would be odd too. Bo and I were acquaintances but not friends. Why would he come to my place unless he needed help and knew that Pierce would kick his ass for whatever trouble he'd gotten himself into?

I left the library, heading out to the foyer, whoever was at the door knocking again.

"I'm coming."

I looked through the peephole and my heart stopped. Analyn. I looked again to make sure I wasn't hallucinating. She stood on my porch with her hands clutching the lapels of an overcoat as she shivered.

I yanked open the door. "Analyn? Are you okay?"

She let out a long sigh. "I'm sorry to just show up like this, but . . ." She seemed at a loss for how to finish the sentence. She shivered again, and it was only then I realized her legs were bare and instead of shoes, she had slippers on.

What the fuck?

I held the door open wider. "Come in. What happened?"

Was she running from someone? Maybe she had an ex-boyfriend who hunted her down. It wasn't out of the realm of possibility. It wasn't that long ago that another resident in Las Vegas, Max Clarke's sister Vivie, was a victim of a stalker.

Had Analyn's ex decided he wanted her back? Maybe he realized what an idiot he'd been to let her go, so he'd shown up, and when she told him she'd moved on, he'd tried to force her.

Realizing I was letting my mind get the best of me, I shut the door behind her. "Can I take your coat?"

She clutched her lapels closer and gave me a sheepish smile that was adorable. I desperately wanted to wrap her up in my arms and comfort her.

"I'd rather keep it on. And I'm sorry again to just show up like this, but I couldn't stay in my apartment for another moment. I couldn't think of anywhere else to go."

"I'm glad you came here. How about we go to the living room, and we can sit and talk? Do you want some tea or something to warm up?"

"No, thank you." She looked down to her fidgeting fingers. "I shouldn't have come, but—"

"It's fine, Analyn. Come on. I'll show you to the living room." I led her from the foyer through the double doors into the elaborate space called the living room. I had the requisite furniture, but again, I had anticipated having a wife who might want to decorate, so it was fairly sparse except for the couch, the side tables, and a couple of throw rugs. It did have a fireplace, and I thought maybe I should light a fire to help her warm up.

As I made my way across the room, I heard her yelp, and as I turned, she fell to the floor.

Good Christ, was something wrong with her?

As I rushed to her, I saw a throw rug bunched around her feet and realized she must've tripped.

She dropped her head, letting out a laugh, and I was relieved that she was okay.

As I reached her to help her up, I noted that there wasn't much to whatever she wore under the coat as there was a great deal of bare leg. My dick immediately took notice. Traitor.

I helped her up and led her to a chair.

She sat down, shaking her head, still laughing, though not necessarily with humor. "I have the worst luck in the world."

I sat on the couch across from her, linking my fingers together to prevent me from getting up and going over to take her into my arms. "Oh? How's that?"

"When I came to Las Vegas, I moved in with my best friend. She's the one who encouraged me to move out here."

I smiled even though there was a part of her statement that stung. She hadn't moved out here for me.

I shook the thought away, calling myself an idiot. Of course, she didn't move here for me. If she had, we'd be together.

"Anyway, her boyfriend finally proposed to her tonight, and she is on cloud nine. She ran out to get more champagne to celebrate, and while she was gone, he propositioned me."

My fingers tensed. "Propositioned?"

She nodded, her eyes wide in surprise. "You know, like he wanted me to have sex with him right then and there. While his fiancée was out getting champagne."

Her shocked expression morphed into anger. "I told him no, and he turned into a total asshole, acting like I should be so lucky to have a guy like him want to screw me."

I'll kill him.

She let out a breath and sagged back into the chair. "I was a coward. I didn't know what to do. So, I just grabbed my coat and purse and ran out. I know I have to tell her. I just couldn't get my brain to work right. And then I ended up here."

"Did he touch you?" My mind kept going back to the part where she said he'd propositioned her. What the fuck did that mean?

She stared at me and blinked. "What?"

My jaw tightened as the image of another man putting his hands on Analyn made my blood boil. "Did he touch you?"

She cocked her head to the side, and I realized that perhaps this wasn't the reaction I was supposed to have. But right or wrong, I was connected to Analyn, and another man touching her wasn't something I could deal with.

"He put his hands on my hips and tried to nuzzle my neck." She shuddered like a bug or snake had touched her. "But I got away from him, and then he turned mean, so I left."

I remembered how at one point, I thought that Analyn and I could be friends since we couldn't be lovers. Or more. This was my opportunity to show her that we could still be in each other's orbit without the sex.

Instead of acting like a jealous, possessive jerk, though, I needed to respond differently. "Under the circumstances, you can stay here, if you'd like. It appears you're already in your pajamas, and I have extra toothbrush and toothpaste." It didn't escape me that I didn't mention I had a guest room. In fact, I had several. I suppose deep down inside, I hoped she would stay in my room.

It took her a moment, but finally, she nodded. "I can't go home, and I don't really want to go to a hotel."

Deciding I needed to be gallant, I said, "If you'd rather go to a hotel, I'll take you and pay for it. Whatever you feel most comfortable with." I knew her staying the night at my house, if found out, would make people talk about the things she was trying to avoid.

She closed her eyes, scrubbing her hands over her face, looking so tired. Again, I had to resist the urge to get up and put her in my lap to make all her worries go away.

"I think I'd like to stay here, if that's okay." She stood up and unbuttoned her coat.

I did my damnedest to look uninterested as she slipped the coat off, revealing she was wearing a tank top and shorts and nothing else but the slippers. My blood ran like liquid fire, but I rolled my shoulders, reining in my libido.

"Do you happen to have something else I could wear over this?" she asked.

I nodded and rose. "I'm sure we can find something in my closet." I led her out of the living room and down the long hallway to my bedroom.

I walked over to my closet, opening the double doors and stepping in. I knew the closet was bigger than most studio apartments, but again, in my defense, I'd expected to share it with a woman. And while I wasn't a clothes horse, I did have my share of expensive suits, shoes, and casual wear.

"Oh, my God." The words came out of her mouth with humor.

I glanced over as she scanned the closet, amusement lighting her eyes. I knew it was at my expense, and yet it was so lovely to see that for a moment, I just watched her.

She let out a laugh as she caught sight of the shelves of shoes. "I bet you have more shoes than I do."

She pointed a finger up and began to count my pairs of shoes. When she got to the lower shelves, she bent over, giving me a stellar view of her sublimely round ass. I stifled a groan as I imagined holding onto her hips and sliding into her from behind.

It occurred to me that this was a really bad idea. I could lose the bet. Then again, as she turned around and I saw her face lit up in delight, I was willing to bet everything I had to be with her.

16

Analyn

By now, I wouldn't have expected that seeing Reed's opulence would faze me. I knew the guy owned a billion-dollar company. I knew he had his own private dining area in a restaurant. And yet, I was still mesmerized by the size of his house and his closet. Why did one guy need all this room?

The closet was practically the size of Betts's condo. I noted that while Reed had very nice clothes, and more shoes than I did, there was still room in the closet. Perhaps for a woman? There were no signs of a woman at the moment. That shouldn't have given me as much joy as it did.

Teasing him, I started counting his shoes. There were fancy black ones and brown ones, and even a couple that were a slate gray. He also had more sneakers than were necessary.

As I finished counting his shoes, I stood up laughing, only to find Reed watching me with an intense expression. My laughter dropped away, and I worried that perhaps he didn't like being teased.

He cleared his throat and took off his robe, revealing that he was wearing a T-shirt and lounge pants underneath. I thought perhaps I saw evidence of arousal, but he handed me the robe, saying something about wearing it, and then he walked out of the closet.

I'd been thinking of borrowing something more along the line of sweatpants, but I suppose the robe would do. Especially when I slipped it on and its warmth and the scent of him wrapped around me. Yearning to get wrapped up in him filled me. If only he weren't my boss.

Not wanting to get caught standing in his closet fantasizing about him, I exited and caught a glimpse of him as he headed back to the hallway. I followed him, taking another look around his bedroom. Of course, my gaze stopped on the large, sumptuous bed.

What would it be like to spend the night in it with him? I could picture him naked, and I nearly groaned at the desire the image filled me with. I wondered how many other women had enjoyed the experience of staying the night with Reed. That thought effectively doused my libido.

"Everything alright?" Reed popped his head back into the bedroom.

I started toward him. "Yes, of course. Thank you for the robe. Is there a room for me to stay in?"

He nodded and led me down the hall and into a guest room. It was large and luxurious like his own bedroom. The bed might not have been quite as big, but it was still a good size.

"This room has its own ensuite as well." He led me to a door, opening it to a bathroom that was nearly the size of my bedroom. In the middle was a large soaking tub and a tiled shower with a rain spout.

"Make yourself comfortable," he said, as he moved back into the middle of the bedroom.

I followed him and sat down on the edge of the bed. Reed's world was so different from mine, but as a person, Reed didn't feel out of reach. He had an authenticity and a down to earth quality that belied the opulence that he lived in.

"I'll leave you to get some rest. If there's anything you need, just let me know."

I nodded, and then realizing the imposition I'd put him in, I called after him. "Reed?"

He stopped at the door and turned to look at me.

"Thank you. I know I'm asking a lot, especially considering how I behaved this afternoon."

He smiled and shook his head. "Not at all, Analyn. What happened today was my fault, and you had every right to be upset. I'm just glad that you can still see me as a friend and that you trust me."

Guilt filled me that he was taking the blame for this afternoon. "You know what they say? It takes two to tango. It was my fault too. You have been exceedingly good to me, and I want you to know that I appreciate it."

"Have a good night, Analyn."

He exited and shut the door. I flopped back on the bed, letting out a breath. I actually felt remarkably calm and content considering what was going on in my life.

My best friend's fiancé had hit on me, and I hadn't been brave enough to tell her. And I knew I would have to. I hated that I was going to have to ruin her dream. Ruin her happiness.

A part of me wondered if she would believe me. We were so close that I couldn't imagine she wouldn't, but when it came to affairs of the heart, sometimes, that took precedence over everything else, including friendships.

I rose from the bed, taking off the robe and inhaling the scent of Reed one more time before I laid it on the bed. Then I pulled back the covers and sheets and climbed in. I turned off the light on the side table and snuggled in to get some sleep.

Unfortunately, while my body was tired, my brain couldn't stop flitting from one thought to the next. Most of it had to do with figuring out how I would tell Betts about Paul.

But other times, my thoughts were of Reed. Of imagining him alone in that large bed of his. There was the desire to join him, but then also the need to be taken seriously at work. I didn't want to risk my work reputation by being found out to have slept with the boss.

Just coming here was a risk. Staying the night was riskiest of all. But it was a risk that I was glad I took.

Reed was a good and decent man. I could see that he respected me, and it was good to my ego that he was attracted to me.

I tossed and turned, and finally, at three in the morning, I gave up. I got out of bed and slipped on the robe. As quietly as I could, I opened the door to my bedroom and made my way back up the hall. It seemed to take forever, but I finally reached the foyer, and after a little bit more searching, I found the kitchen. It didn't feel right to rummage through his home looking for a bottle of wine, but I had hoped that a glass might help me go to sleep.

I didn't bother to turn the lights on. I didn't need to with how the light from the moon illuminated the kitchen well enough to see what I was doing.

I found an open bottle of white wine in the fridge and took it out, placing it on the counter. Then I began the process of opening the cabinets, of which there were many, looking for a wine glass. I finally gave up and just grabbed a juice glass and poured the wine into it.

I'd just taken a long gulp when I heard, "Are you okay?" Startled, I turned to the entrance to the kitchen. The lights might have been out, but it was bright enough for me to see that Reed was in his lounge pants, and only his pants. His chest was bare, and as he approached me, I was transfixed by the hard planes etched to form his pecs and strong abs. The memory of touching and kissing them a month ago flooded back to me.

"I'm sorry I didn't ask first."

"It's not a problem, Analyn. I'm just checking to see if you're all right." He stopped a few feet away, opening the cupboard and pulling out two wine glasses. He brought them over and set them on the counter next to me. Then taking the wine bottle, he poured us each a glass.

He handed me one and picked up the other. "To insomnia."

I smiled, embarrassed at being caught but at the same time happy to have his company again. "I'm not so sure we should be cheering to insomnia."

He shrugged. "At least we don't have to suffer it alone."

I laughed. "I suppose there's that." I clinked my glass with his and took a sip. It really was very good wine.

"Is insomnia a common issue for you?" He leaned against the counter, and I did my best not to stare at his chest.

"Only when I have the weight of ruining my best friend's life bearing down on me."

He nodded. "But I imagine her life would be more ruined if she marries someone who was willing to cheat on her with her best friend. What are the odds he hasn't cheated on her already?"

"I wondered the same thing." I hoped Betts would see things like that. "What has you up so late?"

He looked from me down into his wine glass. "I suppose, like you, I've got things on my mind."

The vagueness of his answer got me curious. Was my being here keeping him up? Or maybe that was just wishful thinking on my part. Maybe there were issues at work.

He finished his wine, setting the glass on the counter. I worried that he was getting ready to go back to bed, and I didn't want him to leave.

"The team is on board with the mystical creatures fantasy league," I blurted out.

His lips twitched upward. "I look forward to seeing it. It looks like this bottle is kaput. We should have some more."

I nodded, pleased that he wasn't leaving. He leaned closer to me, reaching above me, and it was only then I realized he had a wine rack built into his cupboards. Of course, that knowledge slipped away the closer he came to me in his effort to get a bottle of wine. I closed my eyes, inhaling his scent, awareness of his body heat sending sumptuous sensations through my body. Unable to help myself, I pressed my hand on his chest, feeling the beat of his heart.

He flinched. "I'm sorry, I don't mean to crowd you."

I looked up into his eyes and saw the craving, the hunger that I had for him reflected in his eyes. It was like lunchtime all over again, and this time, my brain was sounding alarms, reminding me of how important it was that I retain my reputation at work. But with Reed so close, his body heat radiating around me, his scent filling the air and making me dizzy with desire, and seeing the need burning in his eyes, I was helpless.

I couldn't figure out what words to say, so I simply went with instinct. I leaned in, pressing my lips against his chest. He growled, the rumble of it shaking me to my core.

"Analyn." His voice was strained, like it was all he could do to restrain himself. It was another thing that boosted my ego.

I looked up at him. "I'm sorry."

He let out another frustrated growl as he set his hand on my hip. "You don't have to be sorry. I like it when you touch me. It's no secret that I want to touch you."

I nodded. "I like it when you touch me too."

His eyes flashed with wild passion. He set the bottle of wine on the counter, and then his hands and lips were on me.

No, no, no, my brain screamed, but there was no turning back. I wanted this. I wanted him. Reed had a way of touching me that went beyond pleasure.

"Analyn," he murmured against my neck. "Fuck, I want you."

I responded with a groan. Finding his dick, I wrapped my hand around it and squeezed. In an instant, I was moved across the room. The robe and my clothes were off by the time he lifted me onto the kitchen table.

He dropped to his knees. "My mouth has been watering to taste you again."

I didn't have time to respond before his mouth was on my pussy, devouring me.

"Reed!" I cried out as pleasure rocketed through me, pushing me up and up. I gripped the edge of the table, sure I'd scatter into a million pieces when he made me come.

"Come, Analyn. Let me drink you up." His tongue lapped through my folds and then slid inside me, flicking along my sensitive walls. His thumb rubbed over my clit. The dual sensations shot me to the heavens.

He made noises like he was enjoying a sumptuous meal as he licked and sucked, and I came long and hard until I fell back like a wet noodle on the table.

He lifted my legs, which had to be a feat since they were dead weight. He rested them on his shoulders and then he plunged inside me. I arched and moaned again as wondrous sensations shimmered through me again.

"Jesus fuck, you feel good." He rocked back and drove in again.

That was the problem. This was so good. Too good. I was risking it all for an orgasm from this man. It was crazy. No orgasm, no man was worth risking my job for . . . right?

"Do you feel me inside you? Do you feel what you do to me?"

"Yes." He felt magnificent. And with each thrust the friction only got better.

"Tell me. Tell me you feel it."

For a moment, I wondered if he was talking about something else. That he was feeling more. Oh, how I wanted that. Except no, I couldn't want that.

He withdrew. "Tell me."

"I feel you. God, don't stop."

He rewarded me by thrusting in hard, making me see stars.

17

Reed

We shouldn't be doing this. She'd made the first move, but I felt certain that when we were done, there would be regret. I wasn't sure I could handle that.

Oh, who was I kidding? I wouldn't like it if she regretted this, but I would handle it because the alternative would be to stop now. Stop kissing her. Stop touching her. And I couldn't stop even if I wanted to. Well, that wasn't exactly true. If she told me to stop, I would in a heartbeat. But she wasn't telling me to stop. She was telling me the opposite.

"I feel you. God, don't stop."

I thrust in hard, wanting her to feel how we were together. I understood her concerns, but Jesus, wasn't this . . . whatever this was between us . . . worth exploring? I knew it was for me.

I watched her tits as they swayed each time I plunged in. God, I wanted to touch and suck them. I removed her legs from my shoulders, wrapping them around my hips. Then I leaned over, and holding her tits, I sucked a hard pink nipple into my mouth.

"Oh!" She gasped, her pussy contracting around my dick and making me groan.

I refocused, sucking on the other nipple as I pinched the first one. All the while, I drove into her in a steady rhythm. A rhythm that was getting harder to keep as need coiled tight in my balls.

"Come, Analyn. I want to feel you come all over my cock."

"Oh, God!" Her body arched and her hips rocked, her head tilted back. She was close. Reaching for pleasure. She was so goddamned beautiful.

And then she was there. Her breath caught, and her pussy clamped around my dick like it wouldn't ever let go. I wished it wouldn't. I wished she wouldn't let go.

"Yes! Fuck . . . yes." My orgasm slammed into me like a freight train. I gripped her hips and fucked her fast and hard until I couldn't see straight.

When I went over the peak, disappointment filled me. I didn't want to be done. Not yet. Not when I knew she'd pull away from me again.

I collapsed over her, my breath harsh against her neck as my heartbeat continued to thunder in my chest. Could she feel it?

I nuzzled my lips just below her ear. "Please don't regret this." It was pathetic how fragile my ego was at this moment. Being with Analyn was unlike anything I'd ever experienced before. Seeing regret in her eyes would gut me.

She sighed, pressing her hand against my chest, pushing me back to give her space.

I moved, but only slightly. Only enough to look down into her beautiful face. But she kept her head tilted down. Did she do that so I wouldn't have to see the regret?

"It's not regret." She lifted her gaze, and I looked into her lovely dark eyes. Maybe it wasn't regret, but it still wasn't good.

The coward in me refused to ask her what it was she was feeling. Instead, I said, "The attraction is strong. We can't seem to keep our hands off each other." I wanted to let her know how much I desired her but also have her know that it wasn't one-sided. Was I the only one feeling this? It couldn't be. Tonight, and earlier in the week at the restaurant, she'd been an active participant. Hell, she'd made the first move tonight, unless the way I brushed up against her to get the wine counted as a move on my part. It might have. I could have let her know what I needed, and she'd have stepped away. But I took the opportunity to get close to her. Fuck. Maybe it was my fault again.

She gave me a wan smile. "I know." Her smile faltered. "We're going to have to try harder to resist."

Irritation flared deep in my gut, but I worked to keep it under control. Getting upset wasn't the answer. "I don't know about you, but I felt like I was trying pretty hard tonight."

She shifted, and I stepped away, allowing her to slip off the table. She picked up my robe and put it on. "It's my fault for coming over tonight. You had a plan to avoid each other, and if I had stuck to it, this wouldn't have happened."

I ground my teeth together again, holding back an angry retort because that statement sounded like regret. This woman was killing my ego. I had to remind myself why she was acting like this. She didn't want to be the woman sleeping with her boss.

But more than that, I had to find a way for her to accept what was between us. The chemistry was off the charts. And despite the way she acted after we had sex, I believed there was mutual respect.

"You know, we have another option here," I said as another idea came to me.

She looked up at me with hope in her eyes. "What's that?"

"We give in to it."

Her head was shaking before I finished my statement. I held my hand up to stop her from speaking. "Hear me out on this. I think it's clear that this thing between us is stronger than we are able to resist. So we give into it in secret. At work, I'm just your boss and you're one of my employees. We stick with the avoid each other plan. But away from work, away from anyone who could possibly see us, we allow ourselves to indulge in this."

"It's dangerous."

I reminded myself that she was the one with all the risk here. She was the one whose reputation could be ruined if an affair between us was discovered.

"We can be careful. Discrete." I knew she wanted me, otherwise she wouldn't have touched me or kissed me, and yet I still couldn't help myself from asking, "Unless this thing has already burned out for you. Maybe you're not feeling the attraction anymore."

Inwardly, I kicked myself, hating how pathetic I sounded.

She didn't roll her eyes, but she was probably thinking it. "I think you know that's not true."

Taking a chance, I stepped toward her, my hands rubbing up and down her arms. "Before you came back to town, that night we spent last month stayed with me. You have brought something into my life that I'm not ready to let go of yet. But something this intense generally burns itself out. All I'm asking is that we take advantage of it. Go with it. Let it run its course."

"I know what you're saying, Reed. And I feel it too. I really do."

I had a moment of happiness fill my chest. She admitted to what was going on.

"But I don't think I can do that."

"You don't have to decide right this minute. Think it over." I hated how desperate I sounded. Why was I fighting so hard knowing I was asking her to risk so much? Maybe I needed to cut and run. I'd made my pitch, and she didn't want to do it.

Unfortunately, I wasn't ready to hear no just yet.

She gave a single nod. "Okay. I'll think about it."

I grabbed my lounge pants, slipping them on. "I'll walk you back to your room."

Her lips twitched upward slightly. "Good, because this house is so big, I'm not sure I could find it."

I laughed, knowing she was eager to move away from the topic of our affair.

"Why do you have such a big house, anyway? Were you married once and your family was here?"

I stopped short at her question, realizing we hadn't talked in great detail about our history. I knew she had jerk of a former boyfriend, and I thought that I had told her I'd been unlucky in love, but maybe I hadn't.

"I've never been married. I wouldn't mind being married and having a family, but that hasn't been in the cards for me."

"You talk like that option is unavailable to you anymore."

"I've given up trying too hard. You can't force someone to love you." I looked down at her, and for a moment I thought I saw her in this house with me, children running up and down the hallways. I gave my head a quick shake. I couldn't even get her to give me a chance. The Reed love 'em-and-leave 'em curse continued. "Have a good night, Analyn."

"You too, Reed."

I waited until she entered the room and shut the door, then I made my way to my own bedroom. *Let her go, let her go*, ran through my mind like a mantra. But it was so clear to me that ignoring this chemistry between us wasn't going to make it go away. We needed to give into it and let it run its course.

Analyn didn't want to do that, and I had to respect her reasons for it. I wished I could come up with another solution. One in which we could indulge this crazy attraction. Interesting that I didn't wish for the desire to simply vanish. I wanted to be with her. And it wasn't just the sex. Analyn was an intriguing woman, smart and creative. More than that, she was real. There were so few people in my life who felt truly authentic to me. Pierce was one. Analyn was the other.

Knowing I wouldn't have any relief from this difficult situation, I went to bed. Maybe she'd change her mind once she had a good night's sleep. *Yeah, right.*

18

Analyn

I woke up the next morning having slept surprisingly well, even though I woke up confused about where I was. Then it all came back to me in a rush.

Running out of the house after Betts's fiancé tried to hit on me. Thinking that Reed's house was the best place for me to go. And it was until I couldn't sleep, and I got up to get wine and ended up jumping him in the kitchen. After all that, it was a wonder that I slept so well.

Perhaps it was exhaustion from the day coupled with the sex and the silky-soft sheets on the most comfortable bed I'd ever slept in.

Now it was the awkward day after. I was pretty sure I wouldn't be able to sneak out of the house without Reed knowing this time. Besides, I got the feeling he was upset that I had done it the last time.

Then I remembered I'd come over in my pajamas and slippers. It was one thing to show up in the middle of the night dressed like that. It was a whole other thing to do the walk of shame out to my car and drive home like that.

I got out of bed and went immediately to the ensuite bathroom.

My dark hair was a mess. I'd run out of the condo so fast, I hadn't brought anything I needed like a comb or toothbrush.

I opened the drawer and found an unopened toothbrush and toothpaste. Deciding it was there for guests, I used them. I ran my fingers through my hair, pulling it back after I found a rubber band in my purse. I had no choice but to put on my pajamas and the robe again.

When I was about as presentable as I was going to be under the circumstances, I made my way out of the guestroom and found my way to the kitchen. I heard movement. I peeked in to see Reed at the stove cooking up something that smelled delicious. The scent of coffee also caught my attention.

Most importantly, Reed was dressed. He wore jeans and a Henley shirt that stretched tight along his shoulders. His hair was damp, suggesting he just got out of the shower. He looked yummy. *No touching*, I reminded myself.

I stepped into the kitchen and his head turned to me. "Good morning. Did you sleep alright?"

I nodded. "I'll have to find out where you got your bed. I think that's the most comfortable sleep I've enjoyed in a long time." I doubted I'd be able to afford such a nice bed, even on the good salary he paid me.

"I'm glad you were comfortable." His piercing eyes stared at me, and I understood that his words were laced with something more. Like he wasn't just concerned about my physical comfort, but emotional as well. That was the nice thing about Reed. Despite the fact that we kept breaking our vows to keep her hands to ourselves, I believed he truly did want me to be comfortable around him.

He turned back to the stove, rotating the knob and moving the pan to a different burner. He grabbed a couple of plates and began to serve us.

"Have a seat. I hope you like eggs and pancakes."

"I love eggs and pancakes, but you didn't have to go through all this trouble." I sat at the table, relieved that the awkwardness of last night was gone and yet sad that this couldn't be more.

"What trouble? It's Saturday. Saturday isn't right if pancakes aren't included in breakfast." He grinned as he set the plate in front of me. "Can I get you some coffee?"

"I would love a cup of coffee." It was so strange to be waited on like this. My ex never made me breakfast. Or coffee. Even when I was sick.

Reed went back to the counter, picking up a coffee mug and pouring me a cup from the carafe. "I like it pretty dark. Would you like milk or sugar or something?"

"I wouldn't mind a little milk."

When he returned to the table, he set the coffee mug and the carton of milk. "I suppose I should put it in some other container."

I waved his comment away and picked up the milk. "That would be too much fuss and would make me feel like I wasn't posh enough for your home."

He let out a laugh. "I don't know how to be posh." He returned to the counter, picking up his plate and then sitting across from me at the table.

"I don't know, I think you're posh in some ways. This house is pretty fancy. You have your own dining room at two establishments, and people know you wherever you go. You're Mr. VIP."

"Knowing people isn't posh. Just because you have money doesn't mean you're fancy. I didn't grow up rich. And I don't think there's anything that posh people do that I feel compelled to do myself. I live exactly the way I want to."

"So, you like having this big house. I bet you could roller-skate up the hallway."

He poured syrup on his pancakes. "I like that bet. It could be fun to find out."

"You were able to get all this from online gambling? Do you feel bad that you have built your home on the backs of people who've lost their money?"

He looked at me, his brow arched as if he was trying to decide if I was serious or teasing him. I suppose it was a little of both.

"If you have a problem with people gambling, you might need to reconsider your job since you create the materials that lure them in."

Oh. Yeah. "Well, it's not like you're forcing them or stealing from them."

"People enjoy games and like putting wagers on them. It's a form of entertainment. Yes, some people have a problem, but I suppose many businesses have people with problems using the products or services. Beer, wine, cookies."

"Cookies?"

"Sure. A lot of people out there eat too many cookies. The point is, at some point, individuals are responsible for themselves."

I nodded.

"Life doesn't always go as you plan. You have to take what life serves you and do the best you can with it."

Was that what his proposal was about last night? Taking this lust and making the best of it until it burned out?

"Is that what you did?" I cut my pancakes and took a bite. They were really good. I wondered if he made them from scratch. I also wondered where he'd learned to cook. Had his mother taught him? Another woman?

"I suppose I did. I would've liked to have played hockey a little bit longer, but the universe had other plans. That's when I decided to start my business. I've been very fortunate."

It was an interesting comment. He was talking about taking responsibility for his life, but then he suggested that luck had something to do with his success. "Do you think it's luck or hard work?"

"There's definitely hard work. But a lot of the time, when you make a choice to do something, you don't know if the hard work is going to pay off. There's a little faith and luck thrown in the mix when you make a big change in your life."

I took a sip of the coffee and then reached over to pour a little bit more milk into it. He was right. It was dark.

"What about you? Do you feel that making the move here was a good one?"

His mannerisms were nonchalant, but I swear I could hear concern that I might regret moving to Las Vegas and taking the job.

"No. I needed something different, and coming to Las Vegas has provided that. Of course, life is filled with challenges. I slept with my boss."

He let out a snort.

"I've also discovered that my best friend's boyfriend is a cheating douchebag. But if I hadn't moved here, I wouldn't know that about him. Since I'm going to tell her about him, and hopefully, she'll believe me and not marry him, my moving here will have saved her from a bad marriage."

He took a sip of his coffee, setting it down, his eyes piercing as they looked at me. "And sleeping with your boss? Have you thought about my proposal from last night?"

This conversation had been going so well, so easily, but with that question, it changed.

"It's not a good idea, Reed." It was a terrible idea. It wasn't that I didn't want to do it. It was that the risk to me was too great. He had very little at risk. He'd be considered a cliché. Maybe he'd have concerns about a sexual harassment lawsuit, but considering I jumped him, twice, it wasn't something he'd be worried about.

"I respect your position, Analyn. I really do. And I don't want to do anything that would result in anyone at the office thinking you didn't earn your job."

"Thank you."

"But I think it's clear that despite our best efforts, we are unable to keep our hands off each other. And quite frankly, I don't want to ignore this. I want to spend time with you. Two times, the desire was out of control, and we succumbed. So maybe a better option would be for us to stop trying to resist it and instead control it."

I understood what he was saying. Theoretically, it made sense. But it still put me at risk. We could act like total strangers at work, but maybe somebody would see me here at his house, and they'd tell somebody, who'd tell somebody else.

According to the six degrees of separation theory, it would only be a matter of time before it got back to work. And then where would I be?

I didn't want to work at a place in which my staff and my

colleagues questioned how I got the job. And judging by the way Catherine hovered around Reed, and of course her earlier warning to stay away from him, she would make my job difficult. I didn't need people looking down at me and creating a hostile workplace.

Especially just for sex.

If there was a possibility that there could be something more, then I might have considered it. I loved my job, but I wanted a home and a family someday too.

If I found a man I could love deeply, I might make compromises with my job. But it was clear that Reed was not that man for me.

Yes, we had great sex. Yes, we got along well. But we lived in two different worlds. For him, I was just an interesting escape from a life that had become boring for him. But how long would it be before the novelty wore off? No, an affair with the boss was too big of a risk.

"I'm sorry, Reed. I just can't decide right now. Especially since I need to deal with Betts and her cheating fiancé." It would be too much to manage both situations. I needed to focus on my best friend and save her from a disastrous marriage.

He was quiet for a moment, but then he nodded. "I understand. Is there anything I can help you with regarding your friend?"

Couldn't imagine how. "No, thank you. You've been more than generous to me. You must think I'm ungrateful to show up on your doorstep in the middle of the night and then be unwilling to participate in your proposal."

He shook his head. "Not at all. One really has nothing to do with the other. I hope that anytime you feel like you need something, you will come to me. No strings. No expectations."

Looking at him, I knew he was sincere. He was a sweet and kind man.

He picked up his coffee mug, bringing it up to his lips but not taking a drink yet. "Of course, if you touch or kiss me, all bets are off. My ability to resist you only goes so far."

My cheeks warmed, and I couldn't stop the smile on my face. "I will work harder at not tempting you."

"That is an impossibility. I'm tempted just by looking at you. But if we maintain our distance, I will do my best to resist."

"I will too." It seemed like an easy thing to agree to, but since we'd agreed to it before and failed miserably, I questioned my ability to hold fast to the vow this time.

REED WAS nice enough to lend me a pair of sweatpants and a sweatshirt to return home in. "They're going to be too big for you, but they're warmer than what you arrived in. I'm sorry I don't have any shoes that will fit you, so you're stuck with your slippers."

His clothes were large on me, at least in the length. I was sure I still looked like I was taking the walk of shame, but at least my legs were covered.

When I arrived home, the condo was quiet. I went to my room, took a quick shower, and changed into jeans, but I put on Reed's sweatshirt again. It was silly, but I liked having his scent on me.

I spent the rest of the morning cleaning up my bedroom and sorting my laundry, but I didn't start a load because the in-unit washer was a little bit loud and I didn't want to wake Betts. I prayed that Paul wasn't in her room with her. The last thing I needed was for him to get up first and corner me again. I didn't want to have to deal with him again. It was bad enough that I needed to tell Betts what he had done the night before.

It was just after noon when Betts made her appearance. I was in the kitchen making lunch when she staggered in. Her hair was a mess, and she was bleary-eyed, likely from a hangover, but she still had a smile on her face. To be smiling during a hangover could mean only one thing—she was happy about her engagement. And I had to be the one to burst her bubble.

"Hey, thanks for taking off last night and leaving me and Paul here to celebrate our engagement. I won't go into details about how we did that, or where we did that." She glanced at the dining table, and I reconsidered eating my lunch there. Funny how I hadn't considered that after having breakfast this morning on the table on which Reed had taken me to Pleasureville.

"Sure," I said, scanning my brain to figure out how I could tell her what Paul had done.

She made her way to the coffee machine, putting in a pod, and after filling a cup with water and pouring it into the coffee maker, she pressed the brew button. She leaned forward, resting her forearms on the counter, her head down.

"Are you sure you're okay?" Maybe I should wait until she felt better to tell her about Paul.

"Oh, yeah. It's just being upright is hard at the moment. It'll be fine."

I found a glass and filled it with water and then got her two pain relievers. "Maybe you should have this before you have your coffee."

She popped the pills in her mouth and washed them down with the water. "It's so great having you here, Analyn. That's the only bummer thing about getting married. We won't be able to be room-mates anymore." Her face then morphed into concern. "But I'll help you find a new roommate or a new place or whatever. I'm the worst, asking you to move in and then leaving you like this."

"Don't worry about me. I'll be fine. Besides, unless you're leaving Las Vegas, we'll still be able to see each other, right?" I should be telling her not to marry Paul, but the words weren't coming.

"Right. We're going to stay in town. We're actually talking about buying a house."

Marriage and a house were huge commitments. I couldn't let my best friend get trapped by them with a man who was willing to cheat on her with her best friend. What were the odds he'd already cheated on her with somebody else?

I tried to act nonchalant as I poured myself a glass of seltzer water to have with my sandwich. "I know you and Paul are in a good place now, but you've had some rough spots in the past. You're sure about getting married, right?"

"Of course. I wouldn't have said yes otherwise."

Inwardly, I kicked myself because I knew that was true. It wasn't like she was going to tell me she had concerns but said yes anyway. Maybe I needed to treat this situation like a Band-Aid and just blurt out what happened.

"Listen, Betts, when you were gone last night—"

"I appreciate your concern," Betts spoke over me. "But Paul and I are in a really good place. Both of us have grown, and we know better who we are and what we want."

Crap, she was making this hard.

I opened my mouth to try again to tell her what he'd done, but she turned to get her coffee and began prattling on and on and on about Paul and how he proposed, and how romantic it was, and all the promises he made to her. I swore I could see joy and happiness emanating like an aura around her. I knew I had to tell her the truth, but my courage and strength to do so in this moment failed me.

I gave her a hug but didn't tell her I was happy for her. She'd assume that was what the hug meant. In my mind, the hug was an apology that I was going to have to ruin her happiness. Not right now, but later today.

We spent our day doing our own things. I finally got my laundry done and bills paid. I started to look for a new place to live but then remembered that I wouldn't need to once Betts learned about Paul.

As dinner time approached, I knew I couldn't put off the truth any longer. I went to Betts's room expecting to find her resting, recovering from her hangover. But after I knocked and she told me to come in, I opened the door to find her preening in a full-length mirror.

She turned to me. "What do you think? Does this dress show confidence too? I don't want Paul to forget why he proposed to me."

Oh, God. "About Paul. Last night, when you went out—"

She walked over to her dresser and grabbed a pair of earrings. "I overslept during my nap, so I'm running late. You think I look alright?"

"You look beautiful. Confident. But—"

She grabbed her purse and then pushed past me out the door. "He's going to be here any minute."

I followed her out to the living room, determined to tell her that

Paul was a dirty, rotten cheater. "Betts, I'm trying to talk to you about something that happened last night."

She turned to me. "Okay."

A knock on the door had her turning away from me. She looked back with an apologetic expression on her face. "I'm sorry, Analyn. Can this wait?"

She didn't wait for my answer as she went to the door and opened it.

Paul stepped in, looking at me and then to Betts. "We're still good for tonight?"

I got the feeling he was trying to find out whether I had told on him or not. Betts smiled, radiating with happiness. "Of course."

He looked at me, probably wondering why I hadn't told her what happened. He'd better not think it was because I changed my mind about his proposal. Weird how I was propositioned twice in one night.

Betts put on her coat and then she turned to me. "We'll talk tomorrow. I promise."

I nodded, my gaze still on Paul, letting him know his time was running short. Maybe he'd realize it and he'd do the right thing and tell Betts the truth.

His smirk over his shoulder as he walked out the door told me that his douchery was still in full swing.

19

Reed

Gino and his company spared no expense on this presentation he brought me regarding a partnership. But it was all gloss and shine. It was clear they'd decided that I was motivated by money and money only because there was no substance to what they outlined. I wanted to toss the material back at him about two seconds into the presentation, but I let him give his spiel. I'd decided that I'd be polite, but my answer would be no.

To be honest, I wasn't paying that much attention as Gino rambled on. My mind was on Analyn and wondering whether she was considering my proposition. It was all I could do not to call her over the weekend to find out. Now it was Monday morning, and there still hadn't been any word.

Gino finished his presentation and sat across from me. He didn't look expectant like he was eagerly awaiting my answer. No, he looked smug. Like he was certain I was going to say yes. And based on all the things that he explained, I could see where someone who was only interested in money would say yes.

But I had plenty of money, and I wasn't impressed. I knew that by raising objections, he'd end up sticking around to respond to each and every one of them.

So instead, I gathered up the information, putting it in a pile on the corner of my desk. "I will bring this to my team, and we will thoroughly go through it and get back with you."

Gino arched an eyebrow at me. "You're the CEO of this company. You look weak if you have to get permission from your team."

Instead of looking offended, I stared at him in surprise, maybe even projecting that I thought he was an idiot. "Any leader who doesn't utilize the men and women he's hired for their very specific talents to advise him is an idiot."

Gino's eyes narrowed for a moment, but then just as quickly, his smile was back in place. "You must have faith in your team."

"I do. That's the whole reason I hired them. And that's why we're number one." I really wanted to put this guy down a peg or two, and reminding him of my placement in the marketplace was one way to do it.

Thank goodness he seemed to catch on as he stood and buttoned his coat. "Well, in that case, I know I'll be hearing from you as soon as you and your team meet. This is a solid plan. I know you and your team will see that."

I doubt it. But I reached across my desk and shook his hand. "I'll let you know."

When he left, I opened the top drawer of my desk, pulling out the bottle of hand sanitizer and using practically the whole thing to wipe Gino's essence off me.

Once I felt cleansed, I pulled up recent financial reports and was scanning them when my phone rang. Checking the caller ID, I saw it was Pierce.

"Hey, Pierce. What's up?"

"I've noticed that your private VIP spot at the rink has been empty the last few games. Have you actually solved your women problems, or are you just at home drowning in your tears?"

"Har-har. Neither."

"Listen, if you're not going to use the space, you should donate it to charity."

"That's not a bad idea." I felt bad for not paying attention to the fact that I hadn't been to a game in a while or that I could have helped a local charity by donating the spot.

"So, are you going to be at the game tonight or not?"

I was scanning my brain on who I could donate the use of my booth to when I decided I would invite Analyn to attend the game with me instead. "I'll be there."

"Good. Your absence was beginning to worry me."

"All is good, my friend." At least I hoped it would be.

When I ended the call, I intended to go to the marketing department to talk to Analyn, but then I remembered that if I looked like I was giving her any special attention, she'd be worried other people would be suspicious.

So instead, I buzzed out to Catherine. "Can you have Analyn Watts come to my office, please?"

"Oh? Is there anything you need for me to get ready for you to meet with her? Her work review isn't due yet."

"No, it's all right. I just need to check in with her on an idea she pitched to me." That sounded official, didn't it?

"Would you like to see her now? Or did you have a time?"

"Have her come up now. Unless she's in the middle of a meeting or something." I winced. Should I be more commanding? Was Gino right that I was weak when it came to exerting my authority?

"Of course."

I felt like a foolish teenage boy as I waited for Analyn's knock to come on my door. It seemed to take forever. Then finally it came.

"Come in."

The door popped open, and Analyn stepped in, her expression a mixture of wariness and concern.

I stood. "Ms. Watts, come in." I hoped I sounded official.

I must have because the wariness morphed straight to concern. She entered my office, shutting the door behind her.

"Is everything okay with my work, Mr. Hampton?"

"It's okay, Analyn." I hoped that by switching to her first name, she'd relax. "If you're worried about how being called to my office will look, it's not unusual considering you're a new hire, and you have an employee review coming up soon."

She lifted her head, standing taller as if she were trying to be professional. "Is that why I'm here?"

"No."

The wariness returned to her eyes. "I see."

If she was concerned about that, I was pretty sure she wasn't going to like my asking her to attend a hockey game. But I couldn't very well send her back to her office now.

"I asked you here to invite you to attend a hockey game tonight. My VIP box has been sitting empty, and I thought maybe you would like to attend with me."

She shook her head. "I don't think that's a good idea. In fact, it defeats the purpose, doesn't it?"

"I know it seems like it does, but I've invited staff to attend hockey games with me before. I brought Clive with me just a few months ago," I said of the head of the entire marketing department. "I even once brought Catherine." She had expressed interest in the game, so I brought her along.

"As a date?" Analyn asked.

"What? No." What the hell? Did I give off relationship vibes with Catherine? God, I hoped not.

Analyn studied me in a way that made me uncomfortable.

"What?"

She shrugged. "It's nothing. It's just that sometimes, Catherine is overly protective of you. Sometimes, I wonder if there's something there."

I stood and came around my desk, sitting on the edge. "No. There's nothing between Catherine and me. There never was. I've never had an interest in her that way." I began to wonder if maybe Analyn's question was coming from jealousy.

"Coming to a hockey game with me has become a reward of sorts.

I'm sure if you ask Catherine or Clive or even several other people on staff, they'll tell you that I've brought groups to watch hockey."

"Groups?"

Boy, was she nitpicky. "Yes, usually groups. But Clive, I brought by himself, and Catherine too. The point is that no one will think anything of it. Maybe after some time together at the game, you'll have an answer for me about my proposition."

She walked over to the window, crossing her arms around her. Was she protecting herself? Was she protecting herself from me?

"I got the feeling that things were tense at home. This could distract you. Take your mind off things." God, I was desperate if I was using her challenges at home to get a date.

She let out a sigh. "I don't know anything about hockey, but I suppose a distraction would be nice. All Betts talks about is the wedding, and the guilt is killing me."

That had to mean she hadn't told her friend about what her fiancé had done. It couldn't be an easy position to be in.

"But I still don't think it's right for us to be seen together in public. People might talk."

"First of all, I have a private box. Second, people talk all the time, seeing things that aren't there. We can't control what other people do, Analyn. But like I said, your coming to the game with me isn't unusual."

She didn't respond.

I decided to go another route. "You know when we first met, we hit it off long before we ended up having sex. Since you've moved to Las Vegas, we haven't been able to keep our hands to ourselves, but we haven't spent time together like we had that first night. You know, just talking. This would give us a chance to do that."

She looked at me over her shoulder. "And consider your offer?"

"Yes. And consider my offer."

By now, I was resolved that she was going to decline. And maybe she was right. I was playing with fire here. Recent events proved that I was at risk of getting burned.

She gave a curt nod. "Okay. It'll be interesting to see a hockey game."

I nearly shot off my desk and jumped for joy. Instead, I cleared my throat and stood. "I could pick you up, but if you're concerned about how that will look, I'll arrange for a driver to come get you."

She nodded. "Thank you."

When she left, I sat at my desk, leaning back, lacing my fingers behind my head, and sporting a grin. She said yes when I'd been so sure she'd say no. All of a sudden, things were looking up.

20

Analyn

This was a bad idea. I knew it when Reed asked me to attend the hockey game with him. I knew it when I had agreed to go. But I suppose the discomfort of being with Reed was less than that of being at home with Betts, who was frequently there with Paul.

He was there much more than he used to be, and I began to wonder if that was because he wanted to intimidate me into keeping my mouth shut. I think he was clear that he wasn't going to have another chance with me because on the few occasions when Betts was indisposed, he didn't come near me.

My not telling Betts the truth about what happened had nothing to do with Paul and his continuously lurking about. It had to do with the way Betts walked on air at being engaged. There were wedding magazines everywhere. She was watching wedding related YouTube videos, and of course, binge watching *Say Yes to the Dress*.

And each time I made an attempt to tell her, her exuberance prevented me from following through. I was going to tell her. Really, I was. I just hadn't found the courage yet. And going to a hockey game was another excuse to put it off.

Even so, I found the game intriguing. It moved so fast, I usually had no idea where the puck was. It was a little disconcerting how exciting it was when one player rammed into another, a move that Reed explained was called checking. And I suppose I enjoyed once again seeing how the one percent lived by watching it from a private VIP box filled with decadent snacks and wine, along with its great view of the ice.

"So, you used to play this game?" I asked as I sat in a chair next to Reed overlooking the ice.

"I did."

I glanced over at Reed, noting the amusement in his voice and eyes. But I also saw that he was glad that I was enjoying myself.

"Did you used to get hit like that?"

He laughed. "Yes, and I did my fair share of checking as well."

I frowned as I looked at him.

"What?

"You still have all your teeth. I thought I saw somewhere that hockey players were always losing their teeth. The way they get hit, I can see why."

He grinned, showing off a straight set of pearly whites. "I lost two teeth. And I left them lost until I retired. Losing a tooth is a rite of passage."

I laughed. "Really? It must be painful."

He nodded. "Sure, but getting hit with a stick, being slammed into the boards, hitting the ice . . . hockey is a painful sport."

It was a crazy sport. "Why do people do it? Why not have more protections? Football is always updating their equipment."

He sat back, looking at me skeptically. "Football is for pussies." Then he grinned again. "Hockey has a long tradition of being fast and violent, where your bruises and lost teeth are like medals of honor. It's part of what makes the sport fun."

I heard a buzzer go off.

"That's the end of the first period," Reed explained. "Now we have an eighteen-minute intermission."

"How come you quit playing?"

His jovial demeanor faltered. He let out a long sigh as he sat back in his chair. "Some injuries are harder to overcome than others. In my case, it was my knee."

It had to be horrible to have your dream stolen by an injury. "I'm sorry."

He shrugged. "It's one of the risks. And it's not like I didn't have a full career. Most hockey players are out in their early thirties. I'd made it a little bit longer than that."

"Is that when you started your business?"

He nodded, reaching over for the bottle of wine he'd set on the table between us and pouring me another glass. I'd had two already, so it didn't seem wise to have another. But I was enjoying myself, and so far, the chemistry between us hadn't combusted. Oh, sure, it crackled and snapped sometimes, but it hadn't consumed us.

"Yes. I sort of started on a whim. I wasn't ever a gambling person, but I always enjoyed little wagers or bets."

I nodded. "You've made a few bets with me."

"And I think I've lost them all."

I cocked my head to the side to study him. "You don't seem too bothered by that."

He looked at me intently, making my insides fire. "When it comes to you, even when I lose, it seems like I'm winning." He clicked his glass with mine.

The door to the private room opened, and a man who had to be in his late thirties or maybe early forties with dark hair and bright blue eyes entered.

Reed stood up and went over to the man. "Pierce. What the hell are you doing here? Shouldn't you be down getting your team ready for the third quarter? Bo is looking a little sluggish out there tonight. Is he hung over?"

"I wouldn't doubt it. But even hung over, that kid plays better than anyone I've ever seen."

"Pierce, I'd like you to meet Analyn Watts. Analyn, this is Pierce Jackson. He's the coach of the home team."

Pierce glanced at Reed and then at me, extending his hand and smiling. "It's nice to meet you, Analyn." He patted Reed on the shoulder. "This is quite a difference, Reed. When we were playing hockey, your taste in women was always the cougar. What is it called when you're dating a woman who could practically be your daughter?"

Reed growled at him.

Pierce grinned at both of us. "I believe it's called a cliché."

"Just for that, I might have to put money against you."

Pierce laughed. "You can bet against me, old friend. But I wouldn't bet against Bo." He gave me another smile. "It was good to see you. I hope you're enjoying the game and being with this guy. He might be old, but he's a good man. I'll head out and leave you two to your date."

Date? This couldn't be a date. If it got back to work, I'd be viewed as the office slut. Gold digger. Catherine would probably gouge my eyes out with her long, sharp nails.

"We'll connect after the game for my critique," Reed said.

"Or tomorrow. Whatever."

As Pierce left, I realized that the two of them weren't just friends, they were close friends. Like brothers.

I arched a brow. "Cougars?"

Reed's cheeks blushed, and it was adorable. "I'm in need of another drink to explain that one." He went over to a bar area and poured himself something stronger than wine.

After he poured his drink, he came over and sat back in the chair next to me. While he'd been getting his drink, I made a plate of the fancy little quiches that were available.

"A lot of the women who enjoy coming to watch hockey are older. There's a time in a man's life when he isn't always very discriminating about women."

"They're happy to have sex with any woman?" I arched a brow.

He shrugged. "Pretty much. My life was mostly filled up with hockey, so I didn't have time to meet women and date. I wasn't looking for a relationship—"

"You were sowing your oats."

He took a sip of his drink and nodded. "I suppose that was it. I wanted more than anything to play hockey, but I was a young man, and I figured taking care of other urges was easily done through the women who just happened to show up and wanted to hang out with players. So I took advantage of that."

I narrowed my eyes at him. "That sounds like you've been with a lot of women?"

Again, his cheeks turned pink. "Not as many as you're thinking, I'm sure. Don't let Pierce know, but I often went home alone."

I looked at him skeptically but didn't challenge him. "Who's the Bo person?"

Another buzzer went off, and all of a sudden, the skaters were flying across the ice, hitting the puck and each other.

"Bo is number 98. And he's probably the greatest player I've ever seen."

"I thought you said somebody named Greg was the greatest?"

He made an *ugh* sound. "Wayne Gretzky is the greatest hockey player ever. But Bo could probably beat him if he got his shit together. The kid is fearless, but there's always a sense of him like he's running from something. Like the devil is at his back. I don't know how to explain it. But he's as reckless off the ice as he is on it. And while on the ice, it makes him a great player, but in life, it makes him dangerous."

I looked over the rink, finding number 98 and watching him as he sped across the ice, ramming into somebody and taking control of the puck, then zooming away.

"Doesn't the coach try to keep the players in line?"

Reed let out a laugh. "Pierce is the only one who tries to keep Bo in line. As it turns out, his crazy stunts make the news, but not in a negative way. He's like everyone's eight-year-old, rambunctious child. They find him charming. So when he does things like drunkenly play golf in the middle of the night with glow-in-the-dark golf balls, it's good publicity. The stands are full tonight because of Bo. And because of that, the ownership and manager give him a little bit more leeway than Pierce would like."

There was something sad about that. A young man was living his life recklessly, and the people who should be looking out for him were only paying attention to the dollar signs he could bring in. I suppose hockey was a business and Bo was a grown man. But still, how many times had I read stories about athletes or other celebrities who burned out too soon or who got in trouble because no one was there to rein in their darker parts?

"Do you know him? Maybe you could mentor him," I suggested.

Reed cocked his head and looked at me quizzically. "I know him, although not well enough to mentor him. But you're right, he might be in need of a mentor. Knowing Bo, he wouldn't agree. You can't help somebody who doesn't want to be helped, right?"

It made me think of Betts and whether or not she would believe me when I told her what Paul had done. The fact that I hadn't told her right away could work against me. Would her enthusiasm for the marriage, her love for Paul, keep her from recognizing that he wasn't the man she should be with in the same way that Bo's reckless behavior could ruin his career?

It didn't seem like twenty minutes when the buzzer went off again, announcing the next intermission.

"Can I get you another drink?" Reed asked.

"Sure." Again, I wondered at the wisdom of drinking too much. But we were in a public place with windows all around us. I figured I was safe from throwing myself into Reed's arms like I had at the restaurant. Or in his kitchen.

Reed went to the bar for another glass of wine. I took the opportunity to check out more of the selection of food left on the buffet at the back of the room. There were only two of us, but it was enough food to feed the hockey team.

At the end of the buffet, there were several little cakes and cookies. I picked up a new plate and grabbed a few of the delicious chocolate ones.

The door opened again, and this time a man in full hockey gear entered the room. He looked at me and then over at Reed.

He returned his attention to me and grinned. "Hello."

Reed came out from behind the bar with a scowl on his face. "Bo, what are you doing here?"

So this was Bo. The player who was making mincemeat of the other team on the ice. The one Reed said frequently got into trouble off the ice. I imagined some of his exploits had to include other women, as he was handsome with his blonde hair, hazel eyes, and boyish grin.

Bo winked at me. "Excuse me for a minute." Then he turned his attention to Reed. "Pierce said you were up here, and I decided I needed to come and get that money I won off you. You said I couldn't get a hat trick against the Ducks and I did. So pay up." He held out his hand, wiggling his fingers.

"What's a hat trick?" I asked.

Bo turned and walked over to me. He looked at my plate of cookies. "A hat trick is when you score three goals in one game. Can I have one of those?"

I held up my plate. "Sure."

"Bo, you can get your own cookie from the buffet." Reed's voice was tense.

Bo picked up a cookie and grinned at me as he took a bite.

"Is scoring three goals in a game hard?"

"Not for me," Bo said with a mouthful of cookie. "If you want, I'll do it tonight for you. I'm Bo Tyler." He held out his hand.

I put my hand in his. "I'm Analyn Watts."

"Are you here with the old man?" He nodded toward Reed.

I was, but I couldn't have him think it was a date. "I work for Mr. Hampton."

Bo looked over his shoulder where Reed was still scowling at him. "Are you sure?"

I nodded. "I'm sure. I only just started, and Mr. Hampton was nice enough to bring me to a game."

"Are you enjoying it?"

I nodded. "It's fast, and I have a hard time watching the puck, but so far, I'm enjoying it. I don't know much about the game, but Mr. Hampton pointed you out, and I can tell that you're good at it."

"Next goal I score will be for you, Analyn. And if you want, you can come with me to the next game."

"Bo!" Reed's voice made me jump. "Shouldn't you be in the locker room getting coaching points from Pierce?"

"Like I said, I came for my money." He looked at me again. "I can't help it that I'm distracted by your new employee."

21

Reed

I didn't like the way Bo was looking at Analyn. Or talking to her. I especially didn't like that Analyn had explained to him that I was her boss. I knew it was the truth. And of course, she would say that because of her concern about the world finding out our true relationship.

True relationship? I didn't know what the hell that was, but I knew I didn't want it to be that I was simply her boss.

The fastest way to get rid of Bo would be to pay him his money. I reached into my pocket, pulling out my wallet and nearly all the money I had in it. It was way more than I owed him, but I didn't care. I slapped it into Bo's hand and then shoved him out the door. "Go back to playing the game and not picking up fans."

With him out of the room, I turned to Analyn, whose brows were raised in surprise.

"If you're worried about your reputation, he's the last person you want to be seen with."

"Is that why you pushed him out of the room like that? Because you're worried about my reputation?"

There was amusement in her eyes, but I was too worked up to join in on her game. "You're the one who tells me that you're concerned about your reputation. Or is that just around me?"

Her head tilted to the side, the amusement still glinting in her eyes. "If I didn't know better, I'd think you were jealous."

I took a step toward her. "What is it that you think you know better about?"

The twinkle in her eyes dissipated slightly.

"I was pretty sure we were both in agreement that there's something between us. Just because you're trying to deny it, or are trying to ignore it, doesn't mean it's not there."

She let out a sigh. "You know I couldn't say anything different to him, right?"

I nodded, not liking the clawing feeling in my gut. The one that wanted to claim her once and for all.

"All of a sudden, the atmosphere changed between us. Maybe I should go."

Her words were like a punch to the gut. It told me that my behavior was making her uncomfortable.

"There's no reason to leave." I went to the table where I'd set her wine and picked it up, bringing it to her. "I think Bo stole one of your cookies so you might want to get another one."

She eyed me warily.

I got my drink and went to sit down on the sofa. "Once you've got your cookie, come sit here, and I'm going to quiz you to see if you've been paying attention."

She looked at me for a moment longer and then with a smile, got another cookie and came to sit next to me. "I'm pretty sure I'm an expert now. Speaking of gambling and being an expert, isn't it against the rules for you and Bo to be making wagers?"

I shrugged. "It was just a little bet. The kid is cocky, and I decided to encourage him to put his money where his mouth was."

"It sounds like he won."

"He did. Speaking of wagers, I've got one for you. For each question I ask, you can use this private box each time you get one right."

Her eyes narrowed. "And if I get it wrong?"

I was taking a big risk, but damn it, I was having a hard time not touching her. "If you get it wrong, you have to kiss me." I expected her to pull away and remind me of all the reasons we couldn't be together.

"You seem to think that I haven't been paying attention, but I have. As long as you play fair, I am certain I'll be able to answer all your questions."

I stared into the depths of her dark eyes, willing her to give in to me. To this thing between us. "Well then, you shouldn't have any problem with taking on this bet."

She held up her wine glass. "You're on."

I clinked my glass with hers. "What is it called when a hockey player pulls the stick back almost to parallel to the ice, and then swings forward to hit the puck?"

She smiled victoriously. "A slapshot."

"And what is the other type of shot a player can take?"

"A wrist shot."

So she was paying attention. "What is it called when one player slams into another player?"

"Checking."

"What is it called when a player scores three times in one game?" I wondered if my line of questioning was too easy.

"Hat trick." She sipped her wine, her eyes glinting in triumph at me.

"Which type of shot is harder for a goalie to stop? The slapshot or the wrist shot?"

She looked as if she was going to answer but then stopped, her eyes turning away and her brow furrowing. "Did you tell me that one?"

I nodded. "I did."

"Okay, give me a minute? Can you give me a hint?"

My eyes had already settled on her lips, intending to have her pay up on the bet. "I told you about it when I was explaining the T-push maneuver the goalie was doing."

She bit her lower lip, and I really wanted to cross the distance between us and nibble on her lip myself.

Her gaze looked up at me. "I have to guess. The slapshot looks harder and faster."

"Is that your answer?"

Indecision hung on her face, but she nodded.

Triumph filled my chest. "Wrong."

"Really?"

I moved closer to her and was pleased that she didn't move away. "You're right in that the slapshot is harder and faster, but it takes longer to pull off. The goalie can see the stick coming back and therefore anticipate the shot. The wrist shot is quick and harder for the goalie to anticipate."

I pushed a tendril of her hair behind her ear, letting my fingers caress down her neck. I loved the way her eyes closed and her breath hitched at my touch. If she was going to tell me to stop or bring up her concerns, that was the time to do it. If I were a better man, I wouldn't ask her to pay the bet. But I wasn't a better man, and unless she told me to stop right now, I was going to collect my winnings.

"I still got more right than wrong," she whispered.

"True. You have access to this room for three games. Maybe you could bring your friend Betts. The aggression of the game will help her get over her two-timing fiancé."

Analyn's eyes rounded and then she smiled. "That's a great idea."

"Now, how about paying on your wager?"

"You like playing with fire, don't you, Reed?"

I inched closer, hoping my nearness tempted her as much as it tempted me. "I think I've already told you that you are irresistible to me."

"Well, I wouldn't want to be known as somebody who didn't pay their bets. If I didn't, would you send somebody to come break my kneecaps?"

I shook my head. "If you don't want to pay up on the bet, you don't have to." As I inched closer, her eyes clouded and her cheeks flushed, telling me she wanted this. She wanted to kiss me. "But you did make the bet. You don't want to be known as somebody who backs out on their bets, do you?"

Her gaze had drifted down to my lips. "No."

For a moment, I wasn't sure if her answer was no, she didn't want me to kiss her or no, she didn't want to be known as someone who reneged on their word.

"I'll pay my bet." In the next instant, her lips were on mine, and I did my damnedest to keep the kiss within acceptable limits. But it didn't take long for desire to rush through me, for need to coil tight and beg for release.

I groaned, tilting my head, my tongue sliding through the seam of her lips, rejoicing when they parted and she let me in.

Just a kiss, just a kiss, I repeated in my head to stop myself from pushing her back on the couch and taking everything I wanted. But a moment later, she was on her back and I was over her, my hands sliding underneath her shirt to touch that creamy, soft skin of hers.

"You're like a drug, and I'm so fucking addicted," I murmured against her lips as I settled my hips between her legs and ground against her.

If she didn't tell me to stop or push me away now, I was going to strip my clothes off and hope to hell that she would let me fuck her right here. I'd never had sex in my private box. The thought of it was thrilling beyond belief. My two favorite things in the world, hockey and Analyn, were right here together. In this moment, my life was perfect.

22

Analyn

It was happening again. And it was all my fault. I knew the correct answer to the question. Wrist shot. I remembered when he had explained it to me. But with him sitting so close, looking so handsome, and seeing his jealousy at Bo's attention, all I wanted to do was throw myself at him. So I got the answer wrong.

I should've known that Reed and I were unable to stick to only a kiss. Since the first time I met him, a kiss always led to sex. And like all the other times, I was helpless to say no. I didn't want to say no. The way he looked at me and touched me, a woman could live her whole life and never feel the way Reed made me feel. I was helpless to resist it. Hell, I craved it.

"Analyn." His voice was strained, pained even.

I cupped him, squeezed.

He groaned, and all restraint left us both. He pushed my shirt and bra up, his lips wrapping around my nipple. Electric erotic sensation burst through me. In moments, our pants and underwear were off enough for him to slide inside me. God, it was like the most decadent chocolate when he entered me. My pussy throbbed and pulsed with need around him. My blood was coursing thick and hot through my body.

"You feel so fucking good." He lightly bit my nipple and tugged.

"Oh!" My hips arched up as need ramped up. "Reed." Desperation filled me. My orgasm sat on the edge, teetering as he moved in and out, in and out. I needed to come so badly, and at the same time, I never wanted it to end. I knew what awaited me after the big O. I didn't want it. Not yet. All I wanted was to feel this man in me, around me. He made me feel things I never felt before. Things I always wanted to feel, and I cursed the gods for the obstacles in our way.

"Fuck. I'm coming." He levered up on his hands, giving into his need. His thrusts became harder, faster, and it sent me soaring. Pleasure filled me, stealing my breath.

We continued to move together, drawing out the pleasure until finally, he collapsed over me.

As the high dissipated, regret took up the space it emptied. I did it again. I'd given in to desire when I shouldn't have. Not only that, but we were in a public place. More public than the restaurant had been. Could fans at the other side of the rink see us? The door hadn't been locked. Anybody could've walked in.

"Don't, Analyn," Reed said, his fingers gently rubbing my cheek as his blue eyes looked down on me.

As risky as having sex in this location was, I knew that the real problem for me was the well of emotion in my chest. I wanted to give in to this thing between us, just as Reed had said.

But all the same problems existed—the risk of ruining my professional reputation. Our worlds were different. But the biggest problem was that I was falling for him, and that couldn't happen. Sure, Reed was attracted to me, but he felt that this was a chemistry that would eventually burn out. He wasn't in love with me. He wouldn't fall in love with me. So, allowing myself to fall deeper and deeper into him meant the biggest risk I was taking was with my heart.

I pressed my hands on his chest, gently pushing because it was hard to think with him looking at me so sweetly, continuing to feel the pulse of him inside me.

"We can't keep doing this. If we do, we're going to get caught, and things will explode for the both of us."

His expression showed reluctance, but he pushed away, helping me sit up. "Didn't we already determine how little control we had over this?"

I pulled my clothing back together. "What if the camera had caught us just now? We'd be on every news site and social media platform in a second. I can see the headline already. Billionaire Bangs Employee on a Bet at the Hockey Rink."

He adjusted his clothing. "That's a clunky headline."

Exasperated, I shot up from the couch. "You're not taking me seriously. We can't keep doing this."

The buzzer went off again, indicating the end of the game. On the ice, Bo, his teammates, and the home crowd let out a cheer.

"I need to go home."

"I'd like to see Pierce, and then I can arrange for you to go home."

I shook my head. "No, I want to go home now. I think it's better that we leave here separately so nobody sees us leaving together. So your friends don't see us together."

"My friend already saw us together."

"They think I'm here as your employee. We need to keep it at that."

He put his hands on his hips and turned his head, looking out toward the rink. I knew he wasn't taking in the celebration on the ice. He was frustrated, and at the same time, I could see he was trying to respect my wishes.

Finally, he turned back to me. "You're right, we can't continue on like this. Considering this is where we always end up, we need a different plan."

"The answer is for us to stay apart. I'm going to go now." I felt a bit histrionic as I hurried to the door and exited. I also felt a little bit like a bitch. It was wrong to always give in and then get mad. It was a wonder he didn't have whiplash.

I made it to the lower level. The crowd was thick and full, making it difficult to find a quick exit. I wound my way through the crowd trying to find an exit, ending up near the locker rooms.

"You're not supposed to be down here," a security person said to me.

"I'm sorry. This is my first time at a hockey game, and I guess I got lost."

"I'll show her out."

I looked over the security guard's shoulder and saw Bo sauntering toward me. He was dressed in jeans and a T-shirt with a coat over it. His hair was wet, suggesting he'd just come out of the shower.

"Great game today, Mr. Tyler."

Bo patted the security man on the shoulder. "You didn't expect anything less, did you?"

The security guard grinned. "Not at all."

Bo looked at me. "Did you see that score I made for you?"

I hoped the warmth of my cheeks didn't give away that I had missed the score because I was having sex with Reed on the couch. I didn't like to lie, but I didn't feel like I had any choice. "It was impressive."

"Nah. All in a day's work." He tilted his head to the side. "Are you alright?" His gaze scanned the area behind me before returning to me. "Where's Reed?"

"We came separately. Like I said, he invited me as his employee." That wasn't a lie, and yet it still felt like one, considering what I'd just done with him.

"How about we grab a drink, and you can tell me what the old man said that got you so upset?"

I pressed my hands to my cheeks, wondering how he could tell I was upset. "Oh, I'm sure you want to go celebrate with your friends."

"Not at all. You're much prettier than them. And probably more interesting."

"The press is outside and waiting, Mr. Tyler," the security man said.

The press?

Bo draped his arm around my shoulder. "Come on, let's give them something to talk about."

That didn't seem like such a good idea.

"Maybe when they see me with this beautiful, smart woman, it will improve my reputation."

The security guard snorted. "Good luck with that."

"What does that mean?" I asked.

"I have a bit of a reputation for getting into trouble. But I'm confident you're going to keep me out of it tonight. Maybe tomorrow, I won't be getting a call from Pierce yelling at me for one reason or another."

I wondered if exiting with Bo could help me as well? If I left with him, nobody would think to believe that I had just had sex with my boss. They wouldn't think that my coming here with him was anything more than just a workplace event.

"A drink would be nice."

He grinned. He was a grown man, but there was something in his smile and his attitude that reminded me of a boy. It was charming, even as I imagined it was annoying to his coach.

He led me out the doors, and we hadn't gone far before there were cameras and flashes going off. They were blinding, and to protect myself, I curled into him.

"Obnoxious, aren't they? Don't worry. I'll keep you safe." His arm wrapped around me tighter as he led me toward his car.

It wasn't until Bo had driven out of the parking lot and away from prying eyes that I was able to take a breath. It was also when the feelings of guilt burned deep in my gut. It felt a little bit like cheating, but it wasn't, was it? Reed and I weren't a couple. Yes, on occasion, we let our lust take control, but he was my boss. We had no personal commitments to each other. And in fact, even though I was going to have a drink with Bo, I had no intention of letting something grow between us. It was just drinks between new friends.

My conscience reminded me that it had been just drinks with Reed when we met. But as interesting and charming as Bo was, that spark that I had felt from the moment I had sat down next to Reed wasn't there with Bo. Bo would be safe. And it would take the attention away from anyone thinking something was going on between me and my boss.

No. I had nothing to feel guilty about.

23

Reed

I wanted to go after her and stop her, but what use would it be? She was right. We always ended up in the same place. Our passions would get away from us and then she'd run off regretting it.

What was the definition of insanity? Doing the same thing over and over and expecting a different outcome.

Analyn wasn't going to risk her career or reputation for me. I had to accept that. So I let her go and instead went to the bar, pouring myself a straight shot of bourbon. I downed it and poured another one, taking my glass and sitting in the chair. I pulled out my phone to scroll through email and news while I waited until Pierce arrived.

It was a habit of ours that we would meet after a game, and I would share any insights that I saw during the game. There was nothing pressing in my email, so I went to my newsfeed and then to social media.

I was just about to close it down when a picture of Bo with his arm wrapped around Analyn, who was cozied up against him, appeared on my feed. She was wearing the same clothes as tonight, and I recognized the area of the rink.

Who is Bo Tyler's Mystery Woman? Read the caption.

What the fuck! This was right outside. Going on right now.

I scrolled a bit further, and there was another photograph of Bo helping Analyn into his car. What was she doing? Was this some kind of joke?

"Fuck!" I threw my glass across the room. It hit the wall and shattered.

I wasn't a violent man, my hockey days notwithstanding, so the burst of violent frustration surprised me. Annoyed at myself for letting my emotions get away from me, and Analyn for being the catalyst for it, I went behind the bar to get a rag to clean up my mess. I grabbed a garbage can and brought it with me, carefully picking up the glass off the floor and wiping up the bourbon and smaller pieces of glass with the towel.

"Getting dropsy in your old age?"

I didn't bother to look at Pierce. "Not exactly."

"Jesus. Did you throw your glass?"

This time, I turned to look at him. His gaze narrowed on the wall. I looked to where his attention was directed to see my drink dripping down the wall. I straightened and wiped that up as well.

"Where's Analyn?" he asked.

"Maybe you should ask Bo. "

"Oh, shit. What's going on?"

I tossed the rag in the garbage can, leaving the rest for the janitor to clean up. "Check your social media feed."

Pierce stared at me for a moment as he pulled out his phone. It took a moment, but then he winced. "The only thing wrong with this picture is the fact that I think you're into her."

I glared at him.

"So, what's going on?"

"There's something there, Pierce. Sometimes, she seems to acknowledge it, and then she runs off like a skittish cat."

Pierce walked over to the bar, pulling out two glasses. "You can't really blame her. You are her boss. It's a big risk for her unless she doesn't mind looking like a gold digger. There's even some risk for you if she decides to sue you for sexual harassment."

I ran my fingers through my hair, knowing he was right and at the same time knowing there had to be a way through this.

"It doesn't bother you that she is young enough to be your daughter?"

I growled at him. "Whose side are you on here?" Was the age difference really that bad?

Pierce picked up the glasses, walked around the bar, and handed me one. "I'm on your side, man. But I'm not sure that you've considered all the facts. Sure, there are a lot of men who marry women who are younger than them, but is that what this is about? Or is this just a little infatuation that's going to burn itself out?"

When I had pitched the idea of an affair with Analyn, I had discussed the idea that we could indulge in it until it cooled off. But I was beginning to recognize that this could be something more. The seething anger I felt at the idea that she was with Bo proved to me that my feelings for her were more than just friendly and wanting a good fuck.

"If it is more than that, I'm happy for you. But your track record with women isn't so great. I think part of the problem is the women you fall for. You shouldn't be picking a woman who works for you. And I have to question a woman who comes to a hockey game with you and leaves with Bo Tyler. You deserve a good woman who knows your worth, and I don't mean your billions of dollars. I mean that you are a good man. I know you're looking for a good woman who can appreciate you."

I downed the drink and sat down in the chair feeling like all the air had gone out of me.

"Maybe a night with Bo will make her realize just how good you are." Pierce sat next to me.

I doubted it. Bo was closer to her age. He probably had more stamina. He also wasn't her boss. He had everything going for him, and I had nothing.

"I don't know. Maybe it's like you said. I'm terrible at choosing women I find interesting. She's not willing to take the risk, so maybe that's the answer."

"What are you willing to risk?"

I glanced over at him. "What do you mean? The sexual lawsuit isn't enough?"

He shrugged. "We both know that's not likely to happen. And if it did, you're a billionaire. While you could get some bad publicity, your fucking your employee is more of a cliché. But she's risking her reputation. If she were to go somewhere else, she might have difficulty getting another job if this all came out. Or her new boss would expect her to put out. I guess the point is that you clearly like her, and the chemistry between you two was palpable, but is that really enough to risk it all? Maybe it is for you, but is it for her?"

I knew the answer to the latter part of that question was no. After all, she was out with Bo Tyler now. "Thanks for the pep talk." I rose from my chair and brought my glass back to the bar. "I'm just going to head home now."

"No notes about the game?"

All of a sudden, I felt mentally exhausted. "Can we talk about it tomorrow?"

He stood and brought his glass to the bar as well. "Sure. I'll walk out with you."

When I arrived home, I parked in the garage and entered the house through the kitchen door. I considered getting another drink, but being exhausted, I decided to go to bed.

I made my way out to the foyer and toward the hall to the bedrooms when I noticed an envelope on the floor at the front door. Picking it up, I noted that it had no writing on it. Opening it, I pulled out a piece of paper and immediately scanned to the bottom to find Gino's signature.

"Jesus fuck. Will this guy ever leave me alone?"

I scanned my eyes back to the top of the page to read what it said.

. . .

You are an intelligent and shrewd businessman, Reed, and so we know you will recognize an offer that you cannot refuse.
  I look forward to doing business with you.
  Gino

Because I was intelligent and shrewd, I recognized that this note was a threat. Oh, it wouldn't stand up as such in court, but I understood what Gino is getting at. It appeared that there was no swatting him away like an annoying gnat. I was going to have to deal with him head on. Knowing that Paradise Limited had ties to organized crime, I'd have to be careful how I did it, lest I ended up at the bottom of Lake Mead wearing cement shoes.

But at the moment, I didn't want to deal with it. I tossed the note onto the table next to the door, then headed down the hall to my bedroom.

I stripped to my boxer briefs and climbed into bed, letting out a sigh as I thought about the hot mess my life had become. Before Analyn came into my life, work was boring. Mostly, I went through the motions of my day, with occasional enjoyment by going to a hockey game or maybe mountain biking with Pierce. With Analyn in my life, there were moments that were fulfilling, exciting, promising, and then, like a balloon, it would pop, and I was left feeling like shit.

Before, my life was missing something, but with Analyn's on again, off again behavior, I was beginning to wonder if maybe the emptiness of my life before was a better way to live.

24

Analyn

Thank God it was the weekend. I didn't have to think about seeing Reed at work since I was off today. While I was having drinks with Bo last night, he showed me how we were already on social media and people were questioning who I was, insinuating that I was his girlfriend, or at the very least, a hookup for the night.

While I was glad that it would put any question about my relationship with Reed to rest, it felt uncomfortable.

Nothing happened with Bo. Nothing would. The sparks weren't there. I enjoyed his company, but I didn't feel the same sort of pull I did toward Reed. Bo was a gentleman, even if he could be a little immature. He didn't try anything with me. We'd just had a nice, friendly evening. Even so, I couldn't help feeling that I'd betrayed Reed.

But being home had its problems as well. Primarily, I still hadn't told Betts what Paul had done. And now I was sitting with her at the kitchen table as she went through the Internet looking at dresses. She was just as giddy as she had been the night of the engagement. I sat next to her, smiling and giving my input to the dresses that she pointed out, all the while trying to find an opening to tell her that her fiancé was a cheating jerk.

"I don't know, Analyn. I really love this ivory and lace old-fashioned style. Isn't that gorgeous?"

My eyes were on the dress, but my mind was trying to find the courage to close the laptop and tell her to toss Paul to the curb. "It's beautiful."

"But look at this mermaid style one. I love it. Although I don't know if I could pull that off. Are my hips too big?"

"I think you should wear whatever makes you feel—"

"I know. Confident." She grinned at me.

I smiled, even though on the inside, I was feeling sick. "I was going to say beautiful, but yes, confident too. It's your big day. You need to do whatever you need to do to feel like the precious bride you are."

"Aww, Analyn. You're so sweet." She put her arm around me and tugged me close. "You're the best friend ever."

Not exactly. It was time for me to tell her. "Betts, there's something—"

A knock at the door interrupted me.

"I'm not expecting Paul right now. How about you? Do you have a secret lover I don't know about?" Betts said.

"No." I stood and headed to the door so she couldn't see in my expression how right she was. But I doubted Reed would be at the door. Not with the way I left him last night. Not after going out with Bo. Unless, of course, he was here to tell me I was fired for leading him on.

I opened the door to find Bo on the doorstep. "Bo?"

He gave me his signature affable smile. "Hey, Analyn. I'm sorry to drop in like this. I had my publicist track down your address. I had a lot of fun last night and I got to thinking. I have a proposition for you."

He had to be kidding me. If I were another kind of woman, it might be a boost to my ego to have two men offering me propositions. But I wasn't that type of woman, so I was mostly annoyed.

"I enjoyed our drinks too, but I'm not looking for anything—"

He waved his hand. "I don't mean that type of proposition." He laughed. "I know that because of my antics, I have a crazy reputation, but I promise you, I'm not suggesting anything untoward."

I was sort of surprised he would use a word like untoward. Bo didn't come off as the sharpest tool in the shed, although there was a part of me that wondered if his aw-shucks country boy persona was a cover. There were a few times during drinks where there seemed to be more to him.

I opened the door to let him in. "Can I get you something to drink or something?"

He shook his head. "I won't stay for long. The thing is, Analyn, my behavior plays well for the press. While my coach doesn't love it, the owners and managers not only tolerate it, but they encourage it a little bit because it brings in fans."

"I noticed you had a great deal of fans last night. I would've thought they were there because you played hockey so well."

He grinned. "You noticed." Bo had this charming ability to say something cocky, and at the same time, his down-home, boyish charm made it endearing.

"The thing is that at home, it's making my mama crazy. She thinks I need a woman to help settle me down. She's actually started vetting some, and it won't be long before she sends someone from home out here to drag me to the Chapel of Love to get hitched. I don't need that right now. So, I was thinking, if I started dating a good woman, my mama might cut me some slack. I know for sure that my mama would like you."

"Thank you, I think." Where was this going?

"My proposition is . . . would you be willing to pretend to be my girlfriend? The media is already speculating, so it wouldn't be hard to pull off."

My jaw dropped. "I don't think that's a good idea." I wasn't sure what being a pretend girlfriend would entail, but I got the feeling I wouldn't like it.

"Like I said, it would all be fake. I mean, it would have to look like we're dating, so we'll go out. But it will all be platonic. Friendly. Just like drinks the other night."

"But the press would have to see us, right?"

He nodded. "There would be some of that. That's how my mama keeps up on my antics. But chances are I'm still going to misbehave, so over time, when I do something stupid, you can drop my sorry ass. But I figure over the next few weeks, I can behave better, especially hanging out with you."

I really should tell him no. Along with the fact that I didn't want to be in the media, I still felt uncomfortable with how it would look considering my relationship with Drew. Granted, he was my boss, and nothing could develop between us. Sure, we couldn't seem to not have sex when we were alone together, but that was all it was for him. Maybe if it was more for him, I could consider giving in because the truth was, I was falling for him. Because of that, pretending to be in love with somebody else felt wrong.

"I have to think about it, Bo."

He nodded. "Of course. I understand." He reached into the front pocket of the flannel shirt he wore. He pulled out a scrap of paper. "Here's my phone number. It's my personal cellphone. That's how much I trust you, Analyn. If you have any more questions or you're going to give me the blowoff, or maybe you'll agree to a few fun dinners, call me and let me know."

"I will. I'm sorry, I can't just outright agree to it."

He waved my concern away. "No, I get it. It's a crazy request." He grinned at me. "I'm kind of a crazy guy." He walked over to the door and opened it. Then he turned and looked at me with concern in his expression. "Am I stepping on Reed's toes? I could tell he didn't like the attention I was paying to you last night. I figured when you were leaving the rink alone and then agreed to come for drinks with me, it meant the feeling was unrequited on his side."

Unrequited? "No, there's nothing between Reed and me." The lie was burning a hole in my gut. Or maybe not a lie since Reed and I weren't a couple. But it still felt wrong.

"Okay, good. Listen, even if you decide not to be my pretend girlfriend, if you ever want to go out for drinks again or hang out, let me know. It was nice to talk to somebody who was from close to home."

I laughed. In my mind, Chicago, Illinois wasn't really close to his tiny hometown in Wisconsin. But maybe our both being Midwesterners made us kindred spirits with each other.

"I'll keep that in mind."

When he was gone, I returned to the kitchen, but Betts wasn't there. I went to her room. The door was open, and I saw her laying outfits on the bed. Surely, when a couple was engaged, deciding what to wear didn't need to be such an ordeal. I wondered if I could use that as a start to questioning whether she should marry Paul.

"Who was that?" she asked.

"He's just somebody I met when I went to the hockey game last night. What are you doing?" Like I didn't know.

"Paul said that he had work he needed to do tonight, but apparently, he was able to get out of it, so he and I are going to one of the casinos."

"Paul was going to work?" I wasn't sure exactly what Paul did, but it seemed suspicious that he'd be working on a weekend night. Then again, everything Paul did was suspicious to me.

"Yes."

"Betz, there's something—"

"I'm going to take a quick shower and get ready. He said he'd be here in twenty minutes, and I'm running out of time."

She didn't wait for me to answer as she headed toward the bathroom.

I scraped my hands over my face. I couldn't let this go on much longer.

25

Reed

By Monday morning, I had written Analyn off, decided to plead my case again, and now was sitting at my desk continuing the tug-of-war between moving on and begging. Who was this woman who one minute would charm me and fuck me and the next minute run off?

I'd been thinking that she felt the pull between us but was worried about her career. But seeing her with Bo had me questioning all that.

Had I misjudged her? Was her leaving with Bo the other night her way of breaking free from me, or had she been playing me the whole time? And if the latter, what was her end game? What reason would she have to torment me like this?

A knock at the door interrupted my inner conflict. "Come in."

The door opened, and Catherine walked through. Disappointment filled me, revealing that I'd hoped it was Analyn. It was pathetic how much I wanted her to come to me and tell me she was tired of fighting. That she wanted to see where this thing between us could go.

Catherine approached my desk and set a folder on top of it. "This is Analyn Watts's performance evaluation."

There was a tone to her voice that had me looking up at her. "Is there a problem?"

She shrugged one shoulder. "That's for you to decide."

I opened the folder and began reviewing the contents. In the basic areas of competency, Analyn's marks were about what I expected. She was doing the work that needed to be done and was doing it well enough. But when I reached the written comment section, my gut clenched at what her supervisor reported.

In essence, it said that Analyn dismissed her team's input and ignored their suggestions, apparently by telling them that she had my support to do whatever she wanted. It was true that I had supported one idea, but not at the exclusion of everyone else's. Clive praised her ideas and enthusiasm but indicated concern at her insistence that her way was the best way and that I'd backed her up on that.

"I'm sorry because I was the one who pushed you to hire her. And it's true she seems to know what she's doing, but she doesn't appear to be a team player. She seems to think that she can do whatever she wants and you're going to back her all the way. I don't know if it's wishful thinking on her part or if perhaps there's something going on..."

My gaze snapped up to Catherine. "What do you mean by that?"

She held her hands up defensively. "Nothing. Like I said, it might just be wishful thinking on her part, but she acts like she's special. That you think she's special. I don't think her team likes it."

I thought I was angry last night, but compared to the rage that flashed through me, it was no comparison. Analyn had been telling me we couldn't be together because it would hurt her reputation at work, and yet somehow, she was telling her team and behaving as if she had my full backing. It seemed she wanted it both ways.

She wanted to fuck me and act like she was worried about her career, but in fact, she wanted to gain my favor. And she had, hadn't she? I thought the mythical creature fantasy team was nuts, but I'd let her sway me. I wanted to think it was her enthusiastic and creative pitch that had me agreeing to it, but she'd fucked me right afterward.

"Tell Analyn I want to see her in my office."

"Of course. Right away." Catherine hurried out of my office, and I took the few minutes to work through my anger. She'd made a fool of me. I was a decent looking man. I was a nice man. How was it that I had the worst taste in women?

Analyn walked in, leaving the door open as she made her way to the center of the room.

I stood from behind my desk. "Close the door." I had things to say that no one else needed to hear.

"I don't think that's a good idea."

"I don't give a fuck what you think. Shut the damn door."

She flinched, and her eyes widened in shock, maybe even fear. For a moment, I felt bad about it, but then I remembered that she was totally screwing me ... literally and figuratively.

She acquiesced, shutting the door. She remained standing by it, probably wanting to be able to flee. Fine. If she wanted to run, let her go.

"Your performance evaluation has just come in, and I want to know why you think it's okay to use your relationship with me to dismiss and ignore your team."

"What?"

"You act like you have special consideration from me, but when you and I are alone, you're adamant that you need to be considered on your own merits?"

Her eyes narrowed, as if she was confused. "What are you talking about?"

I picked up the report off the desk and opened it, quoting from the comments. "Ms. Watts frequently dismisses the ideas of her team, insisting that Mr. Hampton has approved her concept." I looked at her and had to give her credit. She still looked confused. But I wasn't buying her innocent act. "For the life of me, I could not figure out why you'd fuck me and then run away, worried about your reputation. But now it's starting to make sense."

She looked at me with horror in her eyes. "I don't know what you're talking about."

"You fuck me because you want the special perks. You want me to support whatever it is you do, like monster fantasy fights. You just don't want anybody in the office to know, so then you act all high and mighty, knowing that I'm going to respect your wishes and do my best to hide your dirty little secret."

She flinched when I referred to our affair as dirty. "That doesn't make sense."

I moved closer to her, needing to look into the depths of her deceiving eyes. "I think it does. You know my interest in you. You used it at lunch. You pitched your idea, fucked my brains out, and then, wanting to make sure no one would question my support, you ran off telling me we couldn't be together."

She gaped at me. "You really think—"

A thought occurred to me that made me sick to my stomach. "How long have you been fucking Bo Tyler too?"

Her expression turned indignant. "I don't know where you're getting any of this—"

"He didn't just show up in my box in the middle of a game to get money from me." I wished I'd noted how unusual that was at the time. "He showed up because you were there. And the two of you left together. Tell me, did he notice that you'd already fucked me when he fucked you?"

Her hand came across my face hard. My words were vile, but I felt justified.

She stepped back, horror filling her expression. "I'm sorry . . . I just . . . what is going on? Whatever that report said about how I work with my team is wrong. You're wrong. I do listen to their ideas. I have incorporated many of them. Did they tell you that I didn't?"

"It's in your report. So, yes." Weirdly enough, I had a kernel of concern deep in my gut. Maybe before confronting Analyn, I should've gone to talk to Clive and some of Analyn's team.

But that would mean I was putting into question the performance evaluation, and I had no reason to do that. Every evaluation I received in the past was generally spot on. Even the employees who were fucking up generally acknowledged it and either determined to work harder or we ended up parting ways.

She stared at me like she didn't know me. *That goes both ways, baby.* Who was this woman who had come to consume my life?

She shook her head in disbelief. "I don't understand what is in that report. You can't possibly believe what you just accused me of."

"Why not? From the beginning, you told me you wanted everyone to know that you got this job on your merits, and I assured you that it would be the case. You told me you wanted to use a mythological fantasy game on social media, and I agreed to it. Then you fucked me right then and there."

Her eyes flashed with heat.

"After, you run off. So, I try to respect your boundaries and avoid you. But then, you show up at my house telling me that your room-mate's fiancé hit on you. Not only do you show up, but you're practically naked when you do, and the only place you could go was to my house. Never mind that we live in a city with more hotels per capita than practically anywhere else in the world. No, you show up at my house, and of course, we fuck again because you know I can't resist you. Then, like clockwork, you run off. You're using sex against me, Analyn. I can't help but wonder if maybe there's something else going on between your friend's fiancé and you? Maybe that's why you haven't told her."

Analyn's face went white, and for a minute I thought she was going to be sick. That kernel of doubt tried to take root again, but I pushed it away. As I recounted our time together, her behavior was making sense.

"I shouldn't've gone to the hockey game—"

"But you did. This whole time, I've been sincere with you, Analyn, and you've used that against me. Tell me, when did you concoct this scheme? Was it the night we met? Is that why you moved to Las Vegas? To fuck me and fuck with me?"

She lifted her chin in defiance, her hands fisted at her side, making me wonder if she was going to take a swipe at me again.

"If you don't believe me, then maybe this isn't the right job for me." She turned, opening the door, and stormed out.

I wondered if that meant she was quitting. Deep down, I hoped she was. She made a fool out of me, and now she was outed.

But Jesus fucking Christ, I wanted to be wrong.

26

Analyn

I rushed out of Reed's office, heading directly for the restroom. I'd barely made it into the stall when my breakfast came rushing up and out.

I couldn't believe what had just happened. The performance report confused me, but what really had me sick were Reed's accusations. I couldn't believe he thought such a thing. That I was playing him, using sex to get what I wanted at work. His reasoning made no sense. But I could see in his eyes that he meant every word. I had never been so disrespected and spoken to so vilely.

When I finished being sick, I rinsed my mouth out and then returned to my office, pulling my purse out from the desk drawer and finding a breath mint. I sat in my chair, and I looked out over the marketing department.

Did they really report to Reed that I could do whatever I wanted because I had his attention? I took time to look at each and every person who was in the office, thinking back over interactions I'd had with them. Not once had I perceived any irritation or resentment from any of them. The head of the marketing department, Clive, wasn't always the most forthcoming with praise, but he hadn't indicated that anything I was doing was wrong, either.

Part of me wanted to go out and demand an explanation from each of them. At the same time, I couldn't stand to hear a repeat of what Reed had told me in his office. Did they know what was going on between Reed and me? Was that why they said the things they did? Had all my efforts to retain my professional reputation been in vain?

I was about to pick up my purse and resign, but deep down, I liked this job. I didn't like the idea of continuing to work for Reed after what he said, but I was good at my job, dammit. I wasn't going to let anyone run me out.

And at this point, it was clear that any further contact between Reed and me wouldn't involve anything personal except for my anger at him for accusing me of essentially whoring myself out for job perks. If he wanted me gone, he'd have to fire me. I wondered why he hadn't. Maybe he worried I'd retaliate by suing him.

Determined to prove to them all that I deserved to be here, I went to work. If I had information I needed to convey to my team, or to Clive, I used email and made sure I stayed professional.

As noon came around, I needed a break. I didn't think I could eat because my stomach still roiled from what Reed had said to me this morning, but I needed to get out. I grabbed my purse and my coat and left the building, taking a walk, inhaling the cool winter air. Maybe this was just all a nightmare, and I would wake up. If that was the case, I'd heed it as a warning to do better at avoiding being alone with Reed and risking temptation.

But of course, it wasn't a nightmare. At least not the kind that came during sleep. This was a waking nightmare. This was my reality.

I ducked into a café, ordering a cup of tea thinking that was probably the only thing I'd be able to keep down. I sat at a table near the window and mindlessly watched the goings-on outside.

When my phone rang, my first inclination was to ignore it. But if it was work, I needed to answer it, if only to prove that I was a professional. Hell, for all I knew, it was Catherine calling me to tell me to empty out my desk because I was fired.

I pulled the phone from my purse and the caller ID said *Hat Trick*. It took me a moment, but then I realized it must be Bo.

"Hello?"

"Analyn. It's Bo."

I was going to ask him how he got my number, but I supposed it was the same way he had gotten my address. "Hi, Bo."

"Listen, I don't mean to pressure you, but I'm wondering if you've thought about my request?"

To be honest, I'd put it out of my mind. I had more pressing things to think about.

"Whether you have or not, I wanted to invite you out as a friend. Maybe if we spent some time together, it would be easier for you to decide. You could see I'm not really a lunatic. It would be a friendly outing. I promise."

I couldn't see him, but his affability and charm came over the line. "What did you have in mind?"

"Well, that's a surprise. "

I wasn't really in the mood for outings or surprises, but at the same time, a distraction would be good. I needed to get my life together. That meant focusing on my job and making a life away from my job. Away from Reed. "When?"

"How about tonight? I'll pick you up at about seven?"

What the hell. "Okay."

"Dress casual and warm."

WHEN I RETURNED TO WORK, I kept my head down and my focus on the job. Every now and then, I'd look up and catch one of my team or someone from the marketing department looking over my way. I couldn't read their expressions. Was it confusion? Concern? Guilt?

If they'd been unhappy with my work or attitude, why hadn't they said anything? Maybe it was because I was their supervisor. But Clive, who I reported to, could have said something.

Somehow, they thought that I believed I was special. Was it because I was caught making googly eyes at Reed? I thought only Catherine had caught me doing that, but she didn't have input on my performance review, did she?

They probably were just curious about how I took my performance review. This was how. By hiding in my office. God, I was pathetic.

After work, I had to go home, which was my other source of stress. I expected to show up to find Betts knee-deep in wedding plans. But when I got there, she was gone. She left a note saying that she was out with Paul. God, I wondered what sort of lies and promises he didn't plan to keep that he was feeding her? Why hadn't I told her yet what an asshole he was?

How did my life get so out of hand? I pushed it all away and instead prepared for my evening with Bo. I took a shower and then put on a pair of black jeans and a white long-sleeved T-shirt with a red V-neck sweater over it. This outfit was casual and warm, right?

Bo arrived promptly at seven, wearing jeans and a beige Henley with a plaid flannel shirt over it.

He gave me his signature grin. "You look perfect. Are you ready?"

"I think so. I might know for sure if I knew what we were doing."

He held his arm out toward his car. "Your chariot awaits."

As we drove toward the strip, he asked about my day. Knowing he had a connection to Reed, I kept it vague, saying it was stressful, but I focused on the job.

"Did you always want to do marketing?" he asked as he pulled into a casino parking lot.

"I don't know about always. By the time I went to college, I knew marketing was a skill that was in need no matter the economy."

"Good thinking."

"What about you? I guess you always wanted to be a hockey player."

He grinned as he pulled up to a valet booth. "Ever since I put on my first pair of skates."

"What will you do when your skating days are over?"

"Who knows? I'm not the smartest guy around, but I'm smart enough to invest well, so I don't have to worry too much once I have to retire."

"Smart."

We stepped out of the car. Bo put his hand on my lower back and guided me around the hotel and to an outdoor skating rink.

"Have you ever ice skated?" he asked.

"I have never skated in my life."

He looked at me, his jaw dropped and his eyes round in an exaggerated look of surprise. "How is that possible? You're from Chicago. It's cold there. They have a hockey team there. How is it you made it this far and never skated?"

I shrugged. "I don't know." I didn't want to admit I hadn't ever roller bladed or roller skated, either. I'd never skateboarded as well. If the activity involved small wheels, I'd never done it.

His grin this time was filled with mischief. "Well, I am proud to pop your ice-skating cherry, seeing as you're an ice-skating virgin."

I gave him a light flap on his arm. "Don't be naughty." I had a flash of Reed on skates teaching me. It was followed by a feeling like it should have been him doing this with me and guilt that I was here with Bo. But then earlier in the day came back to me and my guilt was replaced with anger.

A flash and a pop went off, and I looked toward the noise. Somebody had just taken our picture. I turned back to Bo.

This expression turned coy. "I need some pictures for the paps to post so my mom will see them."

"I don't remember agreeing to being your fake date."

"Date or not, if she sees me spending time with a woman, she'll leave me alone. Besides, I didn't tell them I'd be here. Sometimes, I think they've put a tracking device on my car, or hell, maybe they've implanted it in me."

I laughed. "I suppose that's what you get for being such a good hockey player and enjoying getting into trouble."

"It's my cross to bear."

Bo rented me skates, having brought his own. We sat on a bench to put them on. Walking on blades was no easy feat. I wobbled and my ankles kept dropping to the side.

When we reached the ice, Bo stepped on and turned around, holding out both hands. "The trick to ice-skating is to be tight and loose all at the same time."

All I could do was stare at him. How could you be tight and loose at the same time?

"You want to be tight so that you're in control. You don't want the skates to get away from you. At the same time, you gotta learn to go with the flow. Go ahead and step onto the ice, and I will hold you up."

"What's it going to look like to your mom when she sees me fall flat on my face?"

"She'll think it's cute. All the fans will think it's cute. They'll say, 'Look at horn dog, Bo Tyler, lost in love, sharing his passion with his new woman.'"

I rolled my eyes and then almost immediately, my skates slipped out from under me.

"Whoa." Bo wrapped his arm around my waist and propped me up. "Remember, stay tight."

For the first part of my lesson, he dragged me along the ice. Other skaters whizzed past us. A few fell around me, and like osmosis, I nearly fell with them. But pretty soon, I started to get the hang of it, and I was able to propel myself on the ice with my own effort. I wasn't very fast, and definitely not steady, but I was confident enough to enjoy myself. I liked the coolness of the cool wind on my face as I glided over the ice.

"You're doing great, Analyn. Maybe next time, we'll put a stick in your hand and we'll play hockey."

"I know I'm not ready for that. But I am having fun, Bo. Thank you."

When we finished skating, we exited the ice, and my feet were happy when I was able to sit down to put my shoes back on.

"Shall we see what's been posted on social media?" Bo asked, pulling out his phone.

I had gotten so into skating, I had forgotten that we were being watched.

"This is a nice one." He held the phone out in front of me. It was one in which Bo had his arm around me and my arms were winging out to the side.

"I look like I'm about to fall on my ass."

He laughed. "But look how concerned and helpful I am."

I rolled my eyes. "Because, yes, the world revolves around Bo Tyler."

"Well, according to the paparazzi, it does. Look at this one. It's a video."

I watched as Bo and I skated side by side. By then, I'd gotten the hang of it, sort of. I still looked unsteady, but it was cute.

"I'm going to send this one to my mom." Once he finished sharing, he put his hand on my back and rubbed. "I hope you had fun. I really do appreciate this."

I looked over at him and smiled. "I did have fun. Thank you."

He flashed his boyish grin and leaned over, giving me a kiss on the cheek. That little kernel of guilt at being with him tried to bloom in my gut again. I told it to shut up. After all, Reed was probably on the verge of firing me. He'd accused me of using him and sleeping with him to get benefits on the job. He thought that even though I had worked so hard for just the opposite.

Maybe if I spent more time with Bo, I would forget Reed. I liked Bo. He was fun and spontaneous. He clearly didn't take life too seriously.

I wondered what Reed would do when he saw the pictures of me with Bo. I knew what he would do. He'd already accused me of sleeping with Bo after having sex with him. I remembered the jealousy he'd shown at the hockey game. The petty part of me hoped that Reed saw the photos and felt jealous. It was stupid, but this sort of felt like payback.

I'd never really thought of myself as a vengeful person. But the things Reed had said and accused me of had cut me to my core. How I had begun to fall for him, I didn't know. He had been so different when I met him well over a month ago. And even up until today when he gave me my performance review, I'd have never expected him to say the things he had said to me.

It was time for me to move on. And what better way to get over my infatuation with my boss than to have a fake relationship with Bo Tyler?

Bo would distract me and help me forget the pain Reed had caused. And since there was no concern about falling for him, it would be safe. That was almost a downside. If I could fall for Bo, that meant I could get over my feelings for Reed.

27

Reed

"Fuck." I sat in my kitchen eating takeout Korean food while on my phone, I watched Bo and Analyn skate at one of the casinos' public rinks. Jealousy flared. I should have been the one to teach her to skate. I wondered if she did this on purpose to get back at me.

Why did I even care? Analyn had proven to be someone different from who I thought she was. When I first met her, she seemed authentic, sweet, and smart. But as it turned out, she was a very good actress. She had played me, and like a fool, I had let her. Even worse, I'd started to fall for her.

I really should fire her ass, but despite her games, she'd been doing good work. I had to hope that by confronting her, she'd take heed and continue to do a good job but knock off the idea that she was going to have any special treatment from me. Those days were long gone.

Jesus Fuck, did he just kiss her? I refreshed the page and sure enough, Bo Tyler had his lips on Analyn's cheek. In the next picture, she was smiling at him. The whole thing pissed me off, and the anger was made worse by the fact that she'd hurt me. I'd felt the disappointment of women changing their mind about me before, but I'd never been used like this. Played for a fool. I'd never fallen for a woman who used sex as a weapon.

Back at work the next few days, I focused on my job. Any time I was around Analyn, I ignored her. The few times I would look her way, she was either looking at me with resentment, or something else that looked like hurt, but I couldn't believe that was what it was. Why would she feel hurt? She was the one who had been using me.

For the most part, I stayed holed up in my office. I hated how seeing her not only reignited my rage, but also the yearning. Why couldn't she have been different?

Catherine entered my office with a handful of folders.

"Ms. Watts seems to be coming around, but I do think she's someone we need to keep an eye on. Someone like her could do a lot of damage to your reputation and this company if she continues to try and take advantage."

"I'll talk to Clive."

Catherine shook her head. "I've already talked to him. To be honest, I don't know why you haven't fired her."

I looked up at Catherine. "You talked to Clive?"

She nodded but shifted uncomfortably. Like she knew she was overstepping her place. "You know I try to anticipate and take care of things so that you can focus on what you do best."

It was a good answer, but it still made me suspicious about what I didn't know.

"Of course, firing her eliminates all that. Unless, of course, she has something that she can use . . ."

That niggle of uncertainty grew. "Lately, you've been skirting the line of inappropriateness, Catherine. I'm not planning to fire Analyn because despite what she's been telling her team, she's been doing good work. She's done what we hired her to do. Performance reviews are opportunities to give feedback, particularly around areas that need to change. Hopefully, Analyn is going to change her attitude. If she doesn't, then we can talk about firing her at her six-month review."

Catherine gave me a curt nod. "Of course. Would you like me to set up a meeting between you and Clive?"

I shook my head. What was the point if she'd already talked to him? "Just make sure that he watches her and helps her work on the issues highlighted in the review."

"Of course."

I buried myself in work until it was nearly seven. When I left the office, the idea of going to my large, empty house made me feel even more empty. So instead, I drove over to the Desert Oasis. Did I hope that Analyn would be there? I hoped not. Besides, she was probably out with Bo.

I sat at the bar and ordered a drink.

"It's been a little while since we've seen you," the bartender said.

"Just been busy. While you're at it, make it a double."

"Sure thing, Mr. Hampton."

Around me, people were talking and music was playing, but I wasn't paying attention to any of it.

A voluptuous blonde woman with tits that were too big to be real came and sat next to me. "You look like someone who could use a friend."

God. Analyn had done something similar, although there had been an innocence about it. Not obvious like the woman here now.

"I'm not in a friendly mood." Where was the bartender with my drink?

She pouted. "Maybe I could help?"

"I don't think so."

She huffed out a breath but took the hint and left me alone.

"You look like somebody who has lost your best friend. Not many single men turn away an obvious good time like that. Hell, not many married men would turn her down."

I glanced over to where Max Clarke took a seat on the stool the blonde woman had recently vacated. "Including you?"

"Fuck no. I've got all the lovin' I want and need from Amelia." He cocked his head to the side. "Something is up. Woman troubles?"

The bartender set my drink in front of me, and I downed it, waving to him to give me another one.

"No trouble." Woman troubles suggested that it was something that we could get over, but Analyn and I were done. Technically, we never really started. All we'd had were some spectacular sexual encounters. I thought there could be more, wanted there to be more, but as it turned out, I was an idiot.

"Shouldn't you be home with that beautiful wife and family of yours?" I said.

Max grinned, and I wondered why he got to be so lucky to marry a woman he clearly was over the moon for.

"Amelia is out with her girlfriends tonight, and my parents are in town, so they're watching the kids. I figured it was a good night for me to come in and make sure everything was running smoothly."

"Does it ever not run smoothly for you?" Max always seemed so smooth. Not like fake floor wax type of smooth. But legitimate happy, friendly, generous, with all the good luck that goes with that.

He shrugged. "For the most part, business runs pretty well. But every now and then we get some assholes in here." He paused for a moment. "Really, Reed, are you okay? You seem more than your normal grumpy self. Like you have more weighing on your mind tonight."

I shook my head. "I'm good. Nothing a few bourbons and waters won't take care of."

"We still haven't discussed that idea . . . but I see tonight isn't the night." Max stood and patted me on the back. "If you ever need anything, let me know."

"Thanks, man."

He ambled off, and I downed my second drink, ordering another. I wasn't sure how long I sat at the bar or even how many drinks I had when I finally decided to call it a night. I knew I had enough that I couldn't drive home. My brain felt foggy and my body felt like it was moving through syrup. But even with all that, Analyn's betrayal still stung as acutely as the moment I realized she'd played me for a fool. There was no escaping it.

I pulled out my phone, and after several tries, I was able to order a rideshare to go home. I made my way out front to wait for the car.

A dark sedan pulled up and the window came down. "Reed Hampton?"

I guess it looked like the car that was supposed to be coming, so I climbed into the back seat. A metal object jammed into my side, and when I turned, I realized I was sitting next to Gino.

"What the fuck, Gino?"

Gino smiled, but it was one of those sinister looking ones. "I am concerned that you have the wrong impression about the offer we made to you."

There was nothing like a gun in your side to sober you up. "I told you my people and I were going to look at it."

"Surely, you see how much money we can make together. It is the best thing for you and your company to accept the offer."

I stared at him, thinking I needed to be more afraid than I was. Mostly, I wondered if he was for real. It was like I was in a gangster movie.

"Here's the thing, Reed, there might be some room for negotiation, but there's no question that we'll be partnering together. We plan to expand in this territory, and you need to get on board or you're going to find yourself with some enemies that you do not want."

I kept quiet. There was no way I could join a partnership with Gino or Paradise Limited. But with a gun pointed at me, I couldn't very well tell him that unless I was ready to die.

"Now that I believe I've made myself clear, you have until next week to either accept the offer or, should you have any items you wish to negotiate, to let us know about that. I warn you that the longer you draw this out, the less compromising we're likely to be."

The door opened, and a hand reached in, grabbing my arm and yanking me out.

Gino leaned over so he could see me out of the open door. "Until next week." The door slammed shut, and the person who pulled me out climbed into the passenger seat. And then the driver drove them off.

"Mother fucker."

Another car pulled in front of me. The window came down. "Mr. Hampton?"

This time, I looked at the app and the driver to make sure this was the car I'd ordered. I climbed in, giving him my address.

During the whole ride home, I replayed Gino's encounter. I was well and truly fucked.

Not long ago, I wished for more excitement in my life. Something that made me feel. What was that old adage? Be careful what you wish for? I was feeling a lot right now. I was feeling like a fool at having been duped by Analyn. And I was pissed off that I was being squeezed by Gino.

I wondered if I could have a do-over. If I could go back in time, I'd go back to the night that Analyn walked into the Golden Oasis.

Only knowing what I know now, I would've pushed her away, just like I had with the big-bosomed blonde tonight.

That wouldn't solve my Gino problem, but at least I wouldn't be distracted. Had I been more focused, I might've been able to deal with Gino the first time he entered the office. He didn't strike me as the type who would simply walk away, but surely, if I hadn't been distracted by Analyn, I wouldn't be in the position I was in now. I'd have taken proactive action and gotten him the hell away from me and my company.

Jesus, I'd let two people fuck me over.

28

Analyn

I'd never really thought of myself as a brave person, but it had taken courage to leave my home in the Midwest and move to Las Vegas, even with my best friend here. I'd needed courage to go out by myself and walk up to a strange man the night that I met Reed.

But now I realized I was more of a coward. I wasn't brave enough to ask my supervisor, Clive, or anyone on my team why they'd said I'd been arrogant and not a team player. It wasn't true.

I hadn't had the courage to face Reed, either. It wasn't just that I didn't have the bravery to challenge my performance report to Reed. It was that I couldn't even face him. And of course, I still hadn't told Betts about Paul. Instead, I was buried in my work by day and letting Bo distract me in the evening.

I had to admit it was fun spending time with him. He was like an eight-year-old in a grown man's body. The guy could see fun in just about anything. His spontaneity and mischievous streak made life interesting. I'd even gone to another hockey game, this time sitting in the section reserved for wives and girlfriends. I had gotten over feeling like I was betraying Reed by hanging out with Bo, but going to one with Bo did feel a little bit wrong.

Tonight's activity was go-karting, another thing I had never done before. It wasn't something that had necessarily appealed to me, but like most things I had done with Bo, when they were over, I had to admit I'd had a good time.

When I arrived home after my fake date with Bo, I found Betts and Paul in full-blown wedding planning mode. I tried to go straight to my room with a quick goodnight to them, but Betts pulled me in. She wanted my opinion as her maid of honor.

I glanced at Paul, who smirked at me. Why couldn't I tell her what a sleazeball he was?

"This is your wedding, Betts. Whatever you want is going to be fine with me." I tried again to get away.

"You're the best, Analyn. But since this involves you, I'd love your feedback." She'd just pulled up some flowers when her phone rang. She looked at the caller ID. "It's a video call from my mom." She poked the button. "Hey, Mom, we're right in the middle of wedding plans."

"Then I called at the right time. Tell me all about it."

It was clear that Betts was going to continue with the call. So, I escaped into the kitchen to get a glass of water. I couldn't let this go on much longer. I shouldn't have let it go on as long as it had.

"I see you're putting out for the Las Vegas hockey star."

I tensed at Paul's voice.

"You know, men like that are all shine and no substance. You don't know what you're missing with me."

I whirled around on him. "You have no substance either, Paul. You're an idiot for doing this."

"Oh, come on. I know you want this. That's why you haven't told Betts."

"I haven't told Betts because I don't want to break her heart. But every time I see your smarmy face, my courage increases." I pushed past him, and as I did, his hand grabbed my ass.

I whirled around and ended up against him.

"I like it when they play hard to get."

The door opened, and Betts came into the kitchen, stopping short when she saw me and Paul. Paul quickly pulled his hand back, and I jumped away from him, shuddering at having been so close to him.

"What's going on?" Betts asked, her gaze going between me and Paul.

"It's nothing. We're just joking around. Isn't that right, Analyn?"

It was time to spill the beans. I was so angry at Paul but also at myself. "No, that's not right. Paul propositioned me, and just now, he was telling me what I was missing by not sleeping with him." I let out a breath, relief filling me at having finally gotten it out and at the same time fear that Betts wouldn't believe me.

Betts's jaw dropped. "What?"

Paul went to her, putting his hands on her shoulders. "That's not true, Betts. I would never do that to you. Analyn just misunderstood. You know what a jokester I am."

I studied her for a moment, trying to decide who she would believe.

"I have no reason to make something like that up, Betts. You deserve better than Paul."

Tears streamed down Betts's face. "I don't know which of you to believe."

I searched my brain for something I could say that would have her believe me. I understood that she loved Paul, and this had to be hard to hear. But what reason would I have to lie about this? None.

"I can't believe the two people that I love and trust most in the world have betrayed me." She turned and rushed out of the kitchen.

"I'm not going to let you ruin things for me," Paul said to me as he went after Betts.

I stood in the middle of the kitchen feeling truly alone now. I was going to go to my bedroom, but I heard Betts and Paul in the other room and didn't want to have to see either of them. I quietly made my way to the front door, grabbing my purse and coat and heading out.

I had a sense of déjà vu, but at least this time I wasn't in my pajamas. I also wouldn't be going to Reed's house, although deep down, I really wanted to.

He'd been so supportive of the situation before, but now he was distant, simmering with unexpressed anger. Anger toward me because he felt I'd been using him. His accusations refueled my anger toward him. That he could possibly believe that I was using sex to soften him up to get what I wanted at work. His logic made no sense considering every time we had sex, I told him how wrong it was and how important my reputation at work was to me. Somehow, he had turned it into my playing some sort of twisted game.

I went to my car deciding I would go to a hotel. It wouldn't be a fancy one, but my job paid well enough that I could afford something decent. Maybe I would spend the evening looking for a place of my own since it was possible Betts was going to kick me out. Then again, I also had to consider that I was on the verge of being fired. My life had become such a mess.

"Miss Watts."

I stopped short, whirling around holding my keys in a way that I could repel an attacker.

A strange, unsettling man stood several feet away from me. "I have a message for you, for your boss. The one you've been fucking."

I flinched at his words, not just that he said them but that he somehow knew my relationship with Reed. But it confirmed that it had gotten around. My staff did know, which was probably why they said what they did during my review.

"I'm not doing anything—"

"Tell your boss that Paradise Limited is considering a hostile takeover if he doesn't capitulate to their demands." The strange man turned and walked away into the night.

My mind was a whirl, wondering what he was talking about. What demands? And a hostile takeover? Was Reed in trouble?

I got my car door open, and I scrambled inside. I slammed the door shut, locking the doors, my heart beating hard and fast.

Reed's business involved gambling, but it had to be on the up and up, right? Were this man and Paradise Limited involved in shady deals? Was Reed involved in something shady? It was well known that organized crime and gambling were often linked together. I couldn't imagine that Reed would be involved in anything like that, but then I couldn't imagine him saying the things he had to me the other day. That proved that I didn't know him.

Just like with Betts, it was time I confronted Reed. I wasn't going to work for a company with ties to organized crime. I needed to find that same courage and confront Reed about this man as well as stand up for myself about my work. If he fired me, he fired me. I might've been helpless against the attraction I had to him, but it didn't diminish the importance my reputation held to me.

As I started my car and drove to a hotel, I determined that tomorrow, I was going to give Reed a piece of my mind. And just like tonight, where I didn't know where I stood with Betts, I'd take whatever came from standing up to Reed. It was time I took back my life.

29

Reed

I sat at my desk, feeling more miserable than I ever had in my whole life. The only other time I'd felt this rotten was when I was told I couldn't play hockey professionally anymore. But I knew that day was coming and had a contingency plan. But I had no contingency plan dealing with Analyn or Paradise Limited.

I wasn't getting any work done, and I wondered why I'd even bothered coming in. My phone buzzed, and Catherine told me that Clive was here to see me. I wondered if he was coming in personally to complain about Analyn. Maybe I should fire her, but I hadn't been able to bring myself to do it. Perhaps I was worried about what she'd do if I did fire her. Would she turn around and file a sexual harassment lawsuit? It was hard to imagine her doing that, but clearly, I didn't know this woman. How would I prove that she'd been an active, willing participant? Maybe Max Clarke could verify that she'd picked me up at the bar. What a shitshow this was.

"Let him in."

Clive entered, and I greeted him. He had been a marketing manager in a Silicon Valley tech company when I stole him away. His work, along with his team's, was what had put my company at the top of online gambling in a relatively short time. He wasn't just great at marketing, either. He was organized and a shrewd businessman. The few times I'd been away, I'd left him in charge, and he'd done a great job, even if Catherine wasn't as helpful to him as she was to me.

"Clive, hi. How can I help you?" I sat behind my desk as Clive took a seat in the chair in front of it.

"I was hoping to talk to you about Analyn Watts. There's been a change in her that I think may have occurred around the time she got her performance review."

I nodded. "I did talk to her about her performance review. To be honest, I was a little bit shocked by it. But hopefully, her attitude has improved."

Clive's brow furrowed. "Improved?"

"Yes. Her review suggested that she wasn't adequately listening to her team. That she was suggesting that she had special access or approval by me."

Clive shrugged. "Well, I wouldn't put it like that, necessarily. She did at one point tell us that you had approved an idea of hers that we weren't so sure about. Because of that, we're going forward with it."

I studied him for a moment. "You and everyone else who works in the marketing department should have input on ideas. Analyn isn't getting any special consideration from me. She needs to listen to her team and to you."

Clive frowned again. "I wouldn't say that she was dismissing or ignoring anyone on her team." He shook his head. "You know, it's one of the problems with submitting our performance reviews the way we do here. Not to be critical, and of course, you want to be involved, but the way we do them, I'm not so sure they're always interpreted the way we mean."

My gut clenched at the idea that I might have misinterpreted Analyn's report. The things I said to her. The accusations I'd made. They were vile, particularly if they weren't true.

"But you have my attention now. What did you mean?"

"We're all very happy with Analyn and her work. She's enthusiastic. And I suppose at some point, that enthusiasm can make it appear that she's not open to alternative ideas, but she and her team have connected very well. I haven't heard any complaints from them. There was just that one discussion in the beginning after the two of you apparently went to lunch. She had returned indicating you had given the thumbs up on the mythical creatures social media idea. Like I said, we weren't so sure about that. It's unclear to me whether people who like sports are also fantasy fans, but after a little bit of research, we thought maybe there was some overlap. And perhaps we could attract fantasy fans into sports gambling."

All this sounded very different from what had been in the report, and the thought that I was wrong about Analyn was making me sick. If that was the case, I was going to have to re-look at how performance reports were done.

"So, what's the issue with Analyn now?"

"She's been withdrawn, like she's avoiding us. Initially, I wondered if it was related to something personal. I think one of her team members indicated that she was having some issue with her roommate or something."

I nodded, knowing she was grappling with telling her roommate that her fiancé was a douchebag.

"Then, when I realized it was around her performance review, I thought her withdrawal was her hunkering down and wanting to make sure she corrected any of the issues we'd suggested she might work on."

That made sense. "You mean, except if her performance review said she was supposed to be listening to her team, avoiding them isn't the answer."

Clive nodded, but his face continued to be scrunched up in confusion. "True, but that really wasn't the biggest issue. I'm not quite sure why that came through on her performance report. As I said, she and her team seem to work well together. Or they did. And I suppose they still do. It's not that they don't communicate at all, it's that it's primarily done through email since the review. I haven't talked to her yet because I wanted to check with you on how her performance evaluation had gone. I wanted to get a sense of how she might have interpreted our feedback that had her withdrawing from us."

I sat back, not knowing what to think. "As I said, the report I received indicated that she was dismissive and ignoring her team. If she were fixing that, continuing to ignore them doesn't seem to be the right answer."

Clive stared at me, and it seemed to me that we were talking about two different people even though we weren't.

Finally, I asked, "Are you happy with Analyn's work?"

His head bobbed up and down. "Yes, of course. She's innovative and enthusiastic. Or she was. Like I said, I was planning to talk with her today about her recent change. I don't know. Maybe she's got something personal going on at home and that's what's happening. But I knew her performance review was recently, and I wanted to check with you. Are you happy with her work?"

"You're a better judge about whether or not Analyn is good at her job."

Clive stood. "I'll have a talk with her and explain my input on her performance review. I want to encourage her to get back involved with the team. I have been a little worried that she feels like we betrayed her in some way. It's another reason I feel like the review system should include department managers meeting with their staff."

He had a point.

"Thank you for your time."

I nodded and watched him as he left, wondering what the hell had happened. How had the performance review been so misinterpreted by me? I was getting ready to pull it up on the computer to read it again when Catherine buzzed.

"Analyn Watts is insisting on seeing you even though I have told her that you don't have time on your schedule."

As far as I knew, I didn't have anything specific on my schedule today. Catherine was just doing what she did best, gatekeeping. And up until I met with Clive, I might have let her send Analyn away. But something was off.

"Let her in."

I reminded myself that I needed to keep this discussion professional. I couldn't ask her about her relationship with Bo even though it consumed me day and night. I had to finally remove the social media apps for my phone because I was tired of seeing the two of them making goo-goo eyes at each other. I was even nearly to the point of accepting the fact that the two of them might be perfect for each other. They were closer in age, while I was so much older than her. Better yet, he wasn't her boss.

Analyn entered, her expression not revealing anything.

I held a hand out toward the chair in front of my desk. "Ms. Watts. Have a seat."

She walked up to the chair but remained standing. "I won't be here for long."

It was only then that I realized she looked a little pale, maybe even agitated. Like something had spooked her.

I sat down at my desk. "How can I help you?"

"After telling my roommate that her fiancé was a scumball, I ended up leaving my condo."

My eyes narrowed as I wondered why she was telling me a personal story. Especially since she was the one who had always been so adamant about keeping things professional.

"As I reached my car, a stranger confronted me. He told me he had a message for you."

I tensed. "What was it?"

"He said that Paradise Limited is considering a hostile takeover if you don't capitulate to their demands."

"Mother fucker." I said it under my breath, but there was no doubt that Analyn heard. I looked up at her. "Why are they telling you this?" I didn't really expect her to know. My question was more rhetorical. Why were Gino and his men targeting her?

"He prefaced his warning by saying he had a message for my boss, the one I was fucking."

I shot up from the desk. "He said that?" I wasn't sure what pissed me off more, that someone had approached her or that he would actually say those words to her. And how did they know about my relationship with Analyn? Had they staked out my home and made a guess when she showed up barely dressed the other night? Or had they seen us, maybe at the hockey game?

"Those were his exact words."

It was only then that I could tell that Analyn was trying to be strong and stoic, but underneath, she was rattled. I couldn't blame her. Gino—and I suspect anyone working for Gino—was the type of person to intimidate.

"What is Paradise Limited, and why are you working with them?" she asked.

I rounded my desk with the intention of touching her. Of wrapping my arms around her and comforting her. It was only when she tensed upon my approach that I realized what I was doing. It wasn't something I should be doing. It certainly wasn't something I was allowed to do. I stopped at the edge of the desk.

"I'm not working with Paradise Limited. They want that, but I've been blowing them off. But by approaching you, they've made a very costly mistake. One that I promise I'm going to take care of. I'm sorry that you've been put in the middle of this. It shouldn't have happened."

I realized I had another concern. If Gino knew about my hooking up with Analyn, who else knew? Had anyone at the office found out? Had Analyn's fears come true? Had the performance report meant that they believed Analyn was using her relationship with me to get what she wanted?

No. Surely, Clive would have hinted at it. And Catherine would've come right out and bluntly said something about it if she knew.

Analyn took in a deep breath as if shoring up her strength. Her dark eyes looked at me, and in that instant, the only thing I wanted was to hold her again.

"I don't know what my performance report said because I haven't gotten a copy of it."

Oh, shit. We always gave staff a copy of the report so that they could review it, and in particular, work on the areas that were suggested could be improved.

"But the things that you said to me about it are absolutely false. You probably think I told these Paradise Limited people about us, but I didn't. I don't want anyone to know what I've done with you, especially now. Especially knowing that you would think I would play you like that."

Jesus fuck. I'd been wrong. Somehow, I had misinterpreted that report. Maybe it was because my anger was clouding my judgment. Maybe it was my frustration at not having something I wanted so badly. And as result, I said heinous, horrible things to Analyn.

I dropped my head in shame. "Analyn, I'm sorry."

It now made sense why Analyn was acting the way she was at work. Yes, I told her she hadn't done a good job of working with her team, but I'd also accused her of using our relationship to get what she wanted at the office. By withdrawing and limiting her communication to email, she was trying to avoid looking like she was making a power play.

"I spoke with Clive this morning. He's concerned because apparently, you've become withdrawn."

She stared me in the eyes. "Are you going to fire me?"

"No. The quality of your work is good. Clive and your team are happy with your work. It appears that I misinterpreted their review. For that, I'm sorry."

She stared at me like she had expected me to push back harder. To argue with her. She gave a curt nod. "Thank you."

"I'm hoping that when you return to Clive and your team, things will go back to the way they were before your performance report. Clive says you and your team work together very well. He likes your ideas and your enthusiasm."

She blew out a breath. Clearly, she thought I was going to fire her. "Okay, then."

I leaned against the desk, trying to look relaxed even though what I wanted to do was take her in my arms and make her forget Bo.

"Does that mean you don't think I'm using sex to get what I want from you, while at the same time pushing you away so that I can look professional? You do know how crazy that sounds, right?"

My lips twitched up slightly. "When you say it like that, yes, it sounds a little crazy. But around you, Analyn, I'm ripe for manipulation."

Her eyes flashed with heat. "Manipulation? You think I'm manipulating you?"

I shrugged. "One minute, you and I are having spectacular sex, and a few minutes later, you're on the arm of Bo Tyler. And if social media is to be believed, you're his new woman. What is that all about?" I hoped that my voice sounded nonchalant, like I didn't care about the answer when in fact, the answer felt like it could be the end of the world for me.

She bit her lower lip. "The thing with me and Bo, that's not real."

I cocked my head to the side. "What do you mean, it's not real?"

She looked down, her fingers fidgeting. "It's fake. He wants to get his mama off his back. Apparently, she's about ready to send some woman out here for him to marry. If it looks like he's seeing someone, then she'll stop hassling him."

"And you agreed to that, even though you and I were . . ." I didn't know how to define what we were. We weren't in a true relationship, but we were fucking on a fairly regular basis.

"I figured if there was any question about you and me, seeing me with Bo would eliminate that. Clearly, with that Paradise Limited person, it didn't work." She lifted her head, and again, her eyes were clear as she stared at me. "I enjoy Bo's company, but we're just friends. That's all it is."

"What were we?"

She gave a little shrug. "I don't know. More than friends, but . . ." She didn't finish.

Even so, her words were like a balm to my tattered heart. I straightened from the desk and stepped toward her. I drew my finger down her cheek and was pleased when she tilted her head into it, into my touch. "I've missed you, Analyn."

She looked at me with wariness in her eyes. "How's that possible?

A couple of days ago, you were essentially suggesting I was pimping myself out—"

I covered her lips with my finger. "I'm sorry about that. I was wrong. Temporary insanity caused by jealousy." I watched her for a moment, wanting to see a sign that she might be softening to me. "In frustration."

"Frustration?"

"The back and forth with you. It's difficult to let something go when you want it so badly. And I want you."

I leaned in, moving slowly, though, giving her the chance to step away or stop me. But she didn't. As I drew closer, her head tilted up and her eyes drifted closed. I took that as a sign. A good sign. I pressed my mouth over hers, and sparks exploded, igniting liquid fuel in my blood.

"I missed you," I murmured again against her neck as I let my hands roam over her body. I wished we were anywhere but here. Actually, I wished we were at my home. In my big-ass king sized bed where I could strip her and take my time. I wanted to touch and taste every inch of her.

"Reed."

I loved the way my name sounded on her lips. Especially as a sigh. A sigh of surrender.

I considered lifting her skirt and taking her right there on my desk, fast and furious, but I didn't want our coming together to be so feral.

I maneuvered her to the couch, divesting her of her panties on the way. She pushed me back, and I bounced as my ass hit the couch. Then she straddled me and my heart sang. Up until that moment, I was working hard to distract her so she wouldn't say no. But now I knew she was with me.

I unbuttoned her blouse and buried my face in her perfect, round, soft tits. I sucked her lace-covered nipple, loving how she gasped and rubbed her pussy against my dick. Thank fuck, she undid my pants and freed him. She rose over me and sank down. Echoes of relief and satisfaction filled my office. Anyone outside my door would likely know what was going on. That alone should have had me stopping. Not that I gave a shit, but I knew Analyn did. But then she rocked over my cock, and all thought left my mind. I surrendered to feelings and sensations.

"Oh, God." Her fingers gripped my shoulders as she rode me.

I held her hips, helping her along. I licked her nipple, and her pussy contracted hard around me.

She buried her face in my neck. "I'm coming," she said in a harsh whisper. I realized she was trying to be quiet. Fuck, I wished we were in my bed so she could scream in ecstasy.

Her body tensed, she gripped my cock, and I knew she was there. I wanted to see her face. To see as pleasure cascaded through her, but it was still hidden against my neck.

As the pulsing of her body subsided, I pushed her back on the couch, withdrawing and sliding down her body.

"I'm thirsty for your juices, Analyn."

She didn't have time to respond before I was devouring her sweet juices. Only after she came again did I rise over her and re-enter her. I sank into her, feeling like here, with her, my world was right. Did she feel it? The inevitability of us?

30

Analyn

Here I go again. The words chanted in my brain as a reminder that I shouldn't be doing this. But like all the times before, I ignored it because I wanted him. Needed him.

And it wasn't just lust that was fueling my need. The sensations went beyond the erotic. Yes, he had hurt me with his terrible accusations, and for that alone I should have been pushing him away. But to a certain extent, I was complicit in the situation between us. How many times had I given in to him like this and then run away? Every time, including that first night over a month ago. It was no wonder he thought I was a tease.

The truth of the matter was that I wanted Reed. I wanted the interesting, sexy, lonely man I met at the bar. I wanted the sweet man who took me into his home and gave me the robe off his back when I'd gone to him after fleeing the encounter with Paul. I wanted the playful man I'd been with during the hockey game. I wanted him, heart and soul. And based on the fact that I couldn't stop this encounter, just like I hadn't been able to stop all the other ones in the past, it meant that it had always been like this.

There was so much at risk, but I pushed those thoughts out of my mind. I didn't want to think about it, not when I had the man I wanted touching me.

I'd been aware that we were in his office and did my best to keep quiet as I rode him and came hard. He hadn't come with me. Instead, he pushed me back and then used his mouth to push me up into the stratosphere again. I had bitten my fist to keep from screaming out in pleasure.

And then he rose over me, his blue eyes filled with desire and maybe something more as he thrust inside me. Perfection. That was what it felt like when he was inside me. It filled me physically but also emotionally. I'd never felt that with any other man. In moments like this, I wanted to quit my job, take away the one big issue between us. It would be stupid to change my life simply for the hope that a man would want me for more than sexual release. Luckily for me, when the orgasms were done, my common sense returned.

But right now, I perched on the edge of another orgasm. One that was promising to be as hard and pleasurable as the last two.

"Analyn."

I forced my eyes open to look into Reed's. "I want to watch you come."

Before Reed, the idea of a man watching as I succumb to an orgasm would have made me self-conscious. But with Reed, I wanted him to see what he did to me.

He continued to move, thrusting in and out, each time a little faster, a little harder. "Come, Analyn. I can't hold back much longer . . . fuck, I'm almost there." He lifted my thigh, opening me to him as he drove in deep. My orgasm peaked, stealing my breath. He pressed his lips over mine to muffle my cry, or maybe his, as he bucked and let his release carry him away.

Slowly, the high of orgasm drifted away, and all the old concerns returned.

Reed lifted his head to look down at me. His eyes searched my face, presumably trying to decide whether I was going to run again.

As if he knew all the thoughts running in my head, he said, "I know nothing has changed. I'm still your boss. I'm still too old. And what was the other issue? I still have too much money?"

My lips twitched up, but I didn't feel much humor in his comment. His expression didn't show a lot of humor, either.

"Don't forget you're being shaken down by a mobster."

"Oh, right." He stood up and began to straighten his clothes. I felt his absence deeply. Like all of a sudden, a chasm had opened up between us.

I sat up and straightened my clothes, not quite sure what to say.

He sat down on the couch next to me, his hands on his thighs. "Is your only objection to me that I'm your boss, I'm rich, and I'm older?"

"That's enough, isn't it?" I decided not to add the mobster bit. After all, he said he didn't want to do business with Paradise Limited.

His head turned to look at me, his expression filled with something I couldn't quite name, but it tugged at my heart. "Is it the totality of those three things?"

I continued to look at him, not sure what he was saying.

"I mean if it was only that I was rich, only that I was older than you, would that be something that could be overcome? Is this only because I'm your boss?"

I looked down at my hands clasped in my lap. I looked so prim and proper considering what I'd just done with him on the couch.

"What I'm asking, Analyn, is if none of those issues existed, would things change with you? I'm asking, is this just sex?"

My heart thundered loudly in my chest. He had to have been able to hear it. Did I tell him the truth? What good would that do? The fact remained that there was too much in the way. The biggest hurdle between us was that he was my boss and I didn't want to be the woman who moved up in the world because she was fucking the boss. Something that not long ago, he was accusing me of.

I turned to look at him because he deserved an answer, even if it wasn't the truth. But what I saw in his eyes made my heart stop and I was unable to fudge the truth.

"It's more than sex," I admitted. Now I felt guilty for his believing that was all that was between us. How could he think any differently when every time we had sex, I ran off?

He let out a breath, and it was only then I realized he'd been holding it. My answer mattered to him.

His fingers gently tugged a tendril of my hair. "I know that the situation hasn't changed. But considering the fact that we are helpless against this attraction between us, and that there are feelings here, maybe we need to find another solution."

"You mean that proposition where we indulge it until it burns out?" The memory of that had me rethinking admitting that I had feelings. After all, he believed we could have sex until the attraction died away. I knew that wasn't possible on my side. I'd simply fall deeper for him.

His jaw tightened. "That's one option. Another is I can walk out of here with you on my arm and announce to the world that you and I are together. And if anybody has a problem with it, they can go fuck off."

The tension in his face told me he wasn't joking, and yet there was something about his statement that released the tightness in my chest.

Not that I wanted him to go tell everybody to fuck off, because I didn't. "That still leaves people thinking that I'm sleeping my way up the ladder." Before he could respond to that by telling me they could all go fuck off, I pressed my hand to his chest. "It matters to me that people believe I'm in this job because I earned it."

He straightened and leaned forward, resting his forearms on his thighs. His head was down, and he looked defeated.

It tore my heart in two. "Do you have any other ideas?"

He let out a humorless laugh and sat back, letting his head drop onto the back of the couch. "Short of selling the company, no. Of course, if my financial status is a problem, I can give my money to charity. The age thing, though, Analyn, I can't change that."

"If the fact that my world is so different from yours doesn't bother you, or that I'm a lot younger than you—"

"Why would any of that matter to me? I wasn't born rich. And my interest in you has nothing to do with your age, background, or bank account. I don't give a shit what people think about it. Maybe I'm a cliché. I know I am. I'm the CEO who's fucking one of his employees, who's nearly twenty years younger than me. Anyone who was a problem with it can go—"

I gave him a wan smile. "Fuck off?"

He gave a curt nod. "Exactly."

"What about this threat about the hostile takeover?" I wasn't interested in being linked with mobsters or shady deals, either.

He gave me a hard look. "Are you suggesting I'd let them do it? It would solve the problem of my being your boss."

I shook my head vehemently. "No. Not at all. I don't want you to sell your company, and especially not to a bunch of mobsters, if that's what they are."

He pinched the bridge of his nose with his thumb and forefinger. "Yep, that's what they are."

We sat in silence, the weight of our predicament hanging heavily over us both.

He tilted his head toward me. "What if there is another alternative? Is being your boss a dealbreaker?"

I sucked in a breath and stared at him. He was asking me if I was willing to risk my work reputation to be with him. Inside my chest, my heart did a tug-of-war. My reputation, my integrity, meant something. But I yearned to be with this man. I couldn't find an answer.

"Your hesitation is the answer." He stood up, rolling his shoulders like he was letting the tension go . . . letting me go.

I opened my mouth to say something, although I didn't know what was going to come out, when the phone rang on his desk.

He looked at me, and in his expression, I saw a man who was also at a loss for what to say. Finally, he said, "I need to take this. And I'm sure you need to get back to work."

I stood up, straightening my clothes again. "Yes, of course." We stared at each other for a long moment, but still, neither of us could find words. Finally, I turned away and headed out of his office.

I didn't get very far when Catherine stepped into my path. "I know what's going on. Whatever you're trying to get from Reed, it's not going to work."

I stared at her, noting the fierceness in her eyes. I began to wonder if she was more than a gatekeeper and instead had a strange obsession with Reed. Maybe she was in love with him.

"I don't want anything from Reed." That wasn't exactly true, I realized as I said the words. I wanted his heart. I wanted his soul. And based on what Catherine said, it looked like maybe the secret was out. The man who'd stopped me yesterday clearly knew what I'd been doing with Reed. It was only a matter of time before everyone knew at work. It looked like maybe they already did if Catherine was confronting me and my team was questioning me. If that was the case, the effort to save my reputation was moot. The question now was, did I continue to prove them right by being with Reed?

Catherine's eyes flashed with a wild heat that had me stepping back. "You back off from Reed, or you're not going to like what happens next."

"Are you threatening me?" I couldn't decide if the answer was yes, did that mean my life was in danger, or just that work was going to become an unpleasant place to be?

"I'm not kidding, Analyn. Reed is off-limits. If you're smart, you won't test me on this." She brushed past me, heading toward Reed's office. I wanted to run over and press my ear to the door and eavesdrop, but I reminded myself that I was a better person.

I made my way back toward the marketing department, but the closer I got, the slower I walked. If Catherine knew about me and Reed, as well as the stranger on the street, my staff had to know. How could I face them?

"They can all go fuck off." Reed's words came back to me.

I liked the people I worked with, so I didn't plan on telling them to fuck off. But neither was I going to let their opinion of me scare me away. This was when I needed to be brave. I needed to have the courage I was lamenting I didn't have earlier. But I did have courage because I'd finally told Betts the truth, and I'd confronted Reed. And while I couldn't say my courage paid off for the positive, at least I didn't have the weight hanging over me anymore.

I walked into the department making a beeline to my office, but Clive stood at his door and called me over.

I took a breath to prepare myself for whatever he might say to me.

"Is everything all right?" I asked as I followed him into his office.

"Well, that's what I wanted to ask you, Analyn." He shut the door behind me. "Have a seat."

I sat in the chair by his desk as he rounded it and sat in his chair. "You've been distant lately. You've been doing your work, but me and your team have the feeling that you want to be left alone. I believe one of your team members mentioned there were some issues going on with your roommate, and we all thought that might be it. But then I realized that you had your first performance review, and I'm concerned that perhaps something in that report might have upset you."

You think? I worked to keep my face impassive. "There were some things for me to think about, for sure."

He nodded. "The thing is, I suspect that Mr. Hampton misread our comments. Or more accurately, I think Catherine misinterpreted what we reported to her."

"Catherine?"

He nodded. "Generally, Catherine talks to us all, and I talk to your team as well. Then I create a written report. My written work goes to Catherine, and she puts it all together into a single report for Reed to review. After I put two and two together that perhaps your behavior was related to the report, I went to talk to Reed. He seemed to believe things that we did not mean."

So, what did they mean?

"I went ahead and pulled up the report, and I know for sure that what we reported and what Catherine delivered was . . ." He tilted his head to his side and made a face like he couldn't find the right words.

In my mind, the words I came up with included lying and misrepresenting.

"They do not convey what we meant. So, I'm here to go over the review with you again and let you know what we meant. We think you're an excellent worker, Analyn, and we believe in you. To be honest, we were providing information about the review during the time you came up with that mythical creature idea. A few others and I had some doubts. But we went through with it because you indicated that you'd already talked to Mr. Hampton about it. There are some on the team who felt that you overstepped the line by doing that. There is a hierarchy here, and while we are all friendly, there's an expectation that you would respect it."

I swallowed the lump in my throat as I realized he was right. At the time, I was sharing the idea with Reed because he'd asked me about my day. I wanted to prove to him that I could come up with great ideas.

"I'm very sorry. That's not at all what I intended. Reed . . . ah . . . Mr. Hampton had asked me about my day, and I guess I thought I would impress him by sharing my unique idea. But it was not my intention to go above you."

He nodded. "I think we all understand that now. We all love your creativity and enthusiasm. I think sometimes, you try to dominate with your ideas, so all we ask is that you listen a little bit more to your team because they have great ideas too."

"Yes, of course." I never thought that I was shooting down ideas of my team, but I knew that I could get overly enthusiastic, and perhaps in doing so, I was inadvertently suggesting to my team that I wasn't open to new ideas. I'd definitely work on that.

I stared at him for a moment, waiting for him to say something about my relationship with Reed.

"So, knowing that, is everything all right now?" he asked.

"Ah . . . yes. Thank you for clearing that up. I will admit I was surprised by the report."

He stood, and so I rose from my chair as well. "I was afraid you were. Now, go out there and get with your team to finish up our mythical creatures campaign."

I smiled. "Absolutely. Thank you very much."

As I went to my office, I sank down in my chair, blowing out a breath at this crazy day I was having. I showed up, demanding to speak to Reed, fully expecting to be fired at the end of it. Instead, we had sex, and we each admitted that this thing between us was more than just lust. The confrontation with Catherine unsettled me, but now, meeting with Clive, I felt renewed energy. I was still stuck between a rock and a hard place when it came to my relationship with Reed, but deep inside, I had a little sense of hope. Like there would be a way for me to have my cake and eat it too.

31

Reed

I sat at my desk, unsure what the hell had just happened. I tried to let Analyn know that my feelings for her were more than just friendship or sex. And if I wasn't mistaken, she said it was the same for her as well. But it didn't change the fact that I was still her boss, and she still wanted to protect her reputation.

I hated the idea that two people wanting to be together would cause malicious gossip. I hired good, competent people to work for me, but human nature being what it was, it seemed likely that they would think badly of her. It killed me to know that some, if not all, of my staff would see her as not earning her position.

Jesus fuck, I was in love with her. I was sure of it now. All these years, I'd been looking for a woman I could love and cherish, to make a life with, to make babies with, and just my luck, she worked for me. I had to consider that while our relationship was more than sex, it didn't mean it included love on her end. If she loved me too, wouldn't she consider quitting her job?

I shook my head and let out a frustrated growl that my thoughts would go somewhere sexist like that. But being the owner and CEO, it wasn't like I could quit. At least not very easily.

A quick knock sounded on my door, and then it opened and Catherine strode in. Her expression was serious, bordering on anger. "I need to talk to you about Ms. Watts."

"I've got more important things I need to do." To be honest, I didn't know what they were, because once Analyn left I was having a difficult time getting myself focused on running my company. Maybe my distraction would cause it to tank, and it would solve my problem because I'd have no company to run anymore. Of course, if my company went out of business, Analyn wouldn't have a job, either.

"This is important too, Mr. Hampton." Her voice was sharp and clipped. I didn't much like the way she was speaking to me, and to be honest I was a little bit nervous about what she might tell me. Was she going to tell me something about Analyn that would blast a hole in my feelings for her as the performance review had?

I sat back in my chair, lacing my fingers together and resting them over my belly. I wanted her to see that I wasn't too interested in whatever she was about to tell me. "All right, then."

"Not only is Analyn's performance lacking, but she has the potential to ruin things for you. How long do you think it will be before the entire office knows what you did in here?"

Anger boiled deep down, but I tried to mask it. My response was an arched brow. "Careful, Catherine, you're about to overstep your bounds again."

Her jaw tightened. "It's my job to look out for you. She's a terrible worker, and people are going to wonder about your business sense that you would keep her on simply so you can—"

"Watch yourself."

"It will ruin morale. Everyone here earned their place, and it wasn't by sucking your dick."

I shot up from my chair. "I'm working really hard to remember how organized and dedicated you are to your job, but you're precariously close to being fired." In fact, the only reason I wasn't firing her at this moment was because she probably had a point. Not about Analyn's work ethic, but about the impact our affair could have on the morale of other workers. That tied in with Analyn's concern that they didn't believe she deserved her job.

"I will deal with the issue of Analyn. In the meantime, you are going to stay out of my private life. You're not my mother. You're not my babysitter. You're an administrative assistant, period."

She flinched, but her eyes narrowed even further. She wasn't happy with my response. Well, too bad, because I was the CEO of this company.

She turned brusquely and stalked to the door, slamming it behind her. What the fuck was up with her?

God, how could my life be on the verge of being so good, while actually being so fucked up?

I decided to give up on work and grabbed my coat, heading out of the office. I made my way to the rink where I knew Pierce would be working with the team on their upcoming game.

When I arrived, Pierce was off the ice, watching as the assistant coaches worked with the team on a variety of drills. I stepped up next to him when Bo performed a slapshot that could have possibly decapitated someone.

"Looks like Bo is out for blood."

Pierce looked at me and rolled his eyes. "Please don't tell me you're here to complain about him again. I told him to stay away from Analyn."

I put my hands in my pockets and shook my head. "That's not why I'm here. I just needed to get out of the office." I inhaled the cool, sweet scent of the ice. Not sweet like a bakery. Sweet as in how it brought back memories of when I was skating, not just for the fun of it, but for the thrill of it, the glory of it.

"So, you're alright with that little stunt they're pulling off?"

I cocked my head. "You knew it was fake?"

"Well, when I threatened to kick his ass and suspend him for the next three games, he told me what he was doing. Like all his other antics, it was stupid, but at least it wasn't going to get him arrested or hurt. Unless, of course, you're going to kick his ass."

I stared at him in shock. "And you didn't bother to tell me?"

He shrugged. "When you didn't show up to beat him up, I figured either you knew or you and Analyn were done."

I looked back over the ice. "I don't know what we are. But I know that I love her."

When Pierce didn't say anything, I turned my head to find him gaping at me.

"No shit? Like head over heels and a trip to the chapel type of love?"

I nodded, even though I was terrified of admitting it. "The thing is, while Analyn was willing to admit there was more than sex between us, I don't believe she loves me back. In fact, she still says the reason we can't be together is because I'm her boss."

"So fire her. Problem solved."

I gave him a hard stare. "I can't fire her. First of all, that is sexist. Second, I'm not so sure she'd see her newfound unemployment as an opportunity to fall for me. If that were the case, she'd quit."

Pierce scratched the back of his head. "So yeah, I guess she just isn't as into you as you are into her."

I turned back to the ice, not liking that answer. There had to be a way to work through this, but I'd be damned if I could figure it out.

"That's not the only shit I'm having to deal with. Paradise Limited is threatening a hostile takeover of my company."

"Jesus. That's one group of people you don't want to piss off. Why your company?"

"They've been pitching a partnership. For the most part, I've been blowing them off, and they're not happy about it. They even approached Analyn asking her to give me a message."

Pierce shook his head when something caught his eye on the ice. "Watch yourself, Lassiter. You had way too many fouls in your last game."

He turned back to me. "I suppose I'm not surprised to hear they're trying to get a company like yours. Rumor has it, they're looking into getting involved in teams as well."

"What do you mean? Like owning them?"

"What better way to control the outcome of the game than to have control over the players?"

It was my turn to gape. "Surely, a purchase like that by them would be investigated and prevented."

Pierce shrugged again. "These guys are shrewd and ruthless. They're looking at the Buckaroos here in Nevada. And they might get it because that owner is eager to sell."

The Buckaroos was the minor league hockey team here. Betting on minor league teams wasn't the same as the majors, but many sports organizations pulled players up from the minors. Even in hockey.

"We should buy it."

"What?" Pierce asked.

The words had left my mouth before I had fully formed the thought, but now that they were out, a spark of excitement burned deep in my gut. "We should buy the Buckaroos."

Pierce shook his head. "I've got my plate full coaching this bunch of assholes. I'm not going to coach—"

"You don't have to coach. We'll hire a coach. Or maybe I'll do it."

Pierce looked at me like I'd grown horns on my head. "Just like that? What about your company?"

I shrugged. "I'll find someone else to run it."

And then it struck like lightning that this was the answer. Granted, I'd still own the company, which technically made Analyn my employee, but if I wasn't there on the day-to-day, surely, that would help reduce the idea that she'd fucked her way into the job. Or maybe not. Either way, the idea of doing something different lit a fire inside me. I wondered if there was any conflict of interest for Pierce in owning the minor league team while coaching the major league one.

"What about Paradise Limited?" he asked.

"You mean could I sell it to them? That's not happening. No, I'm going to deal with them and get them out of my life and my company for good."

"How are you going to do that without you or someone you care about ending up at the bottom of Lake Mead?"

"I'll find a way." All of a sudden, I felt a new lift in my spirits that I hadn't felt since the first time I met Analyn. I was going to take this newfound energy and put everything in my life right. I'd get rid of Paradise Limited, and I would win Analyn's heart. You could bet on it.

32

Analyn

My job, at least with my team and department, was the best thing I had going for me right now. I'd like to say that Reed was too, but our relationship was up in the air. I wanted desperately to take what he was offering, but I just found it too difficult to sacrifice my integrity. What if it didn't work out?

I drove home feeling good about my work, but as I walked in the front door, I was faced with the new mess of my life. My friendship with Betts. I had no clue how she was going to be since I walked out last night.

I walked through the door. "Betts? Are you home?"

There was no response, but I heard movement in the kitchen. I took the shortcut from the door to the kitchen, the one I'd escaped through the night before.

"Betts?"

She had her back to me, pouring macaroni and cheese from a pot into a bowl. She set the pot back on the stove, picked up the bowl, and got a spoon from the drawer. She headed out the other side of the kitchen into the living room.

My heart dropped. She believed Paul and not me, hence the silent treatment. I blew out a breath and retreated to my bedroom. I'd showered at the hotel, but I'd had to wear the same clothes as I had yesterday, so I wanted to change. I put on a pair of sweatpants and an old college sweatshirt.

I took a moment to look at myself in the mirror, giving myself a pep talk. I needed to talk to her. I did it this morning with Reed. I could do it now too.

I walked back into the living room and sat on the overstuffed chair across from the couch where Betts sat watching something on her tablet.

"We need to talk."

"About what?" She kept her gaze on the tablet as she ate her macaroni and cheese.

"Don't be like this, Betts. You know what we need to talk about."

She lifted her gaze at me, and in her eyes I saw anger mixed with despair. "I figured the way you left last night that you were the one who was lying. Paul says you were the one hitting on him."

God, it was even worse than I thought. I should've stayed and stood my ground. But there was no going back, so I needed to make the most of this moment.

"I would never do that, Betts. You know that."

She arched a brow in challenge. "And he says he'd never cheat."

"Well, he's a liar."

"He says you are too. He says you propositioned him."

I shook my head. "Gag."

Her eyes narrowed, becoming even more incensed. "What does that mean?"

I looked her straight in the eyes, hating that I was going to have to hurt her, hating that it was very likely our friendship was over. But she needed to hear it all.

"Paul makes me sick. The night of your engagement, when you went out to get more champagne, he cornered me in the kitchen. He rubbed all over me, telling me how much I would really enjoy being with him. He basically said the same thing the other night, and when

I went to get away, he grabbed my ass. He grabbed me and pulled me to him. There isn't enough soap in the world to get him off me."

She stared at me, eyes wide in surprise. But in a blink, she returned to being skeptical of me. "If that's true, why didn't you tell me?"

I sighed as I sat back in the chair. "I wanted to. I started to so many times. But you were so happy, and I couldn't find it in my heart to take that away."

Her jaw tightened. "So you would let me marry someone who tried to hit on you?"

I shook my head. "No. I would've told you. Like I said, I started to, but then we'd get interrupted. Look, I know it's my word against his, but I have no reason to lie to you about this, Betts. Remember how happy I was for you when you told me about you and Paul getting back together? I helped you get dressed the night he was going to propose."

The tension in her body lessened some, but she still wasn't convinced. "Maybe you got jealous after that."

I shook my head. "I promise you. I've never ever had any interest in Paul, especially now. I don't think he's good enough for you. Of course he's going to turn things around to save face, but I've got my own man troubles. I don't want to be involved in yours."

She tilted her head to the side. "I've seen those pictures of you with that hockey player. He's not your boss, is he?"

I shook my head. "Bo is just a friend. We're hanging out because we both needed a friend. But that's it. My man troubles are still with my boss. And one thing that I've learned, Betts, is that the heart can want something really, really badly, but actually having it could be bad for you. I know you love Paul, and you have this whole life with him planned out, but he's not good for you. He's not good *to* you. I know that maybe you don't believe me, but—"

"I believe you." She scrubbed a hand over her face, so I wasn't sure I heard her right.

"What?"

She looked up at me and huffed out a breath. "I believe you. The signs were there, but I just didn't want to believe it."

"What signs?"

"The secret calls he would take. The business trips at all times. He doesn't think I notice, but I still see him looking at other women. And not in the way that anyone might look at an attractive person. He looks in a way like he's mentally taking note to get her number later. To be honest, the last big red flag came the night of our engagement when you stormed out of the house in your pajamas and slippers. You said you had to work, and Paul said he didn't know why you'd run off. And when you didn't say anything after that, I just figured it was my imagination."

Guilt burned like a boiling cauldron in my gut. I rose from the chair and went to the couch to sit next to her, taking her hand. "I am so sorry that I was such a coward. I've learned that about myself lately. I'm a big, fat coward."

She shrugged, leaning over and resting her head on my shoulder. "I get it. I suppose if it were reversed, I'd have a hard time telling you as well."

I shook my head. "No, you wouldn't."

She lifted her head, and for the first time, she smiled. "You're right, I would tell you. Next time I date a cheating jerk, I expect you to tell me."

I squeezed her hand. "I promise. Does that mean you forgive me?"

"Yes, I forgive you."

I put my arm around her, giving her a hug. "I don't know what I would do if I lost you as my friend."

"You'll never have to know."

I sat back on the couch. "So, where are things with you and Paul now? Did you break up last night?"

She shook her head. "No. I said I didn't want it to be true, and he spent the whole night saying all the right things. Making all the right promises. But I've had all day today to think about it, and if I'm honest with myself, I know you're the one telling the truth. Then I was peeved at you because you hadn't told me sooner. Because that was why you ran out the night of the engagement, right?"

I nodded, wondering how I could make this up to her. "So, what now?"

She pulled her phone out of her lounge pants pocket. "Now I call Paul and break up with him."

"Do you want me to leave the room?"

"You don't have to, but if you wanted to go get ice cream and wine to celebrate my newfound freedom, I wouldn't mind having that at the ready once I finish this call."

I grinned and patted her knee. "Ice cream and wine coming right up."

I hurried into the kitchen and opened the freezer. Two pints of ice cream sat unopened. I decided we didn't need bowls. I grabbed both containers and two spoons, setting them on a tray. Then I pulled out a bottle of wine from the refrigerator and two glasses.

I carried the tray into the living room just in time to hear Betts say, "You know, Paul, you're not as great as you think you are. I've had bigger dicks in my life. And I don't mean dick as in asshole. You win that contest. I mean I've had bigger penises. In fact, yours is the small-est." She poked the *Off* button and tossed the phone on the couch.

My brows were lifted as I set the tray on the coffee table.

"Asshole." She grabbed one of the containers of ice cream and a spoon.

"Is that true about his dick?"

She looked up and grinned. "Oh, yeah. It's true what they say, love is blind, because clearly, I decided his tiny dick wasn't important. I'd known from the start because his hands are pretty small."

I let out a laugh as I screwed the top off the wine and poured us each a large glass. "I always thought that was a myth. Now I know differently."

I sat on the couch next to her, and she looked at me with her head cocked to the side. "Do you have personal experience in debunking that myth?"

I couldn't hide my grin, and the way my cheeks warmed, I knew I was blushing. "Oh, yeah."

"I realize that in all this marriage excitement, I don't really know what's going on in your life, Analyn. If you have met a man with large hands, I need to know about it."

Betts and I spent the rest of the night eating ice cream and getting drunk on wine. We laughed and we cried, and our friendship was restored. To make up for my waiting so long to tell her about Paul, and knowing I would probably be hung over, I suggested we call in sick the next day and spend it together.

As I fell asleep that night, I was happy that at least two of three areas of my life were now back on track. But that third area, Reed, still weighed heavily on me. I began to wonder if I was going to have to be one of those people who settled for a good job and good friends but would never really know true love.

33

Reed

When I showed up at the office the next day, I went directly to see Clive. I went under the guise of making sure that everything with him and Analyn and the team was fine, but of course, the real reason I went was for a chance to see Analyn.

When she wasn't in her office, worry took root in my gut. Had she decided none of this was worth it and had taken off? Or worse, had Gino and his goons gotten to her again?

"I was stopping by to make sure everything with Analyn Watts was okay?" I said once I entered Clive's office.

Clive nodded from where he sat at his desk. "Yes. I brought her in yesterday and had a chat with her. For the rest of the day, it was business as usual. I can't tell you how happy we are to have the old Analyn back."

What I would do to have the old Analyn back. The one I met at the Golden Oasis. I nodded in the direction of her office. "I notice she's not in."

"Yes. She called in saying she needed to take a personal day. I know she's new, but I figured she's earned it."

I nodded in agreement even as that worry began to sprout. Why did she need a personal day? Was she thinking about me and our relationship? A part of me liked that idea. It suggested that she was taking me seriously. Then again, maybe she was making new plans that didn't have anything to do with me. Jesus, why was love so hard?

I left Clive to his work and nearly left the building to go find Analyn. If she was taking a personal day to think about us, I wanted to be there to plead my case. Instead, I headed back to my office. I told her what I felt and thought about us yesterday. If I went barging in, I might make things worse. Besides, I had other important things I needed to take care of, primarily, Gino and Paradise Limited.

I had already called my lawyer the night before to discuss my legal options. He indicated that it would be better for me to involve the Feds, but I wanted to get this thing over fast. I wanted Gino out of my life today. My lawyer acquiesced and said he'd put together papers and have them delivered to me this morning. As promised, the papers were on my desk when I arrived.

After looking over the documents, I stuffed them back in the envelope and headed out again. "I'm going to be gone for a little while."

Catherine looked up at me. Her expression held remnants of her annoyance from how I spoke to her yesterday. But she nodded.

I drove to the address that was on the papers Gino had given me. The building wasn't anything special, but it appeared professional. Then again, I didn't know what organized crime offices looked like.

I ignored the receptionist and walked right into Gino's office, tossing the envelope my lawyer had given me onto his desk.

Gino looked down at it and then up at me, a very satisfied smirk crossing his face as he leaned back in his chair. "I knew you'd come around. Have you accepted our offer? Or is this a counteroffer?"

"There's only one offer. You stop harassing me and my employees and walk away, or I will tie you up in court until you're old and gray and can only eat gruel to survive."

Gino arched a brow. "It's a pretty strong threat. What is gruel, anyway?"

"It's no threat. After talking with my lawyer, we've come up with a whole range of lawsuits, cease-and-desist orders, and restraining orders to stop you from stalking me. All that to say there will be no deals and no hostile takeovers."

Gino leaned forward, resting his forearms on his desk. His expression was dark. "I don't think you understand the picture. Paradise Limited is going to have a stake in your business. You should accept that now while our terms are favorable. If not, you're going to regret it."

"I guess I can add threatening to my list of lawsuits. The thing is, why would I want to work with a company that can't become successful on their own merits? If you have to bully and threaten to get what you want, you must be the worst sort of business people there are."

A vein on Gino's head throbbed, clearly not liking being told that he was a bad businessman.

"Me, I'm a good businessman. I have a lot of money, enough money to carry out lawsuits from now until the end of time. Trust me, going after me and my business isn't worth your time or effort. You'll lose."

"That's not very smart."

I leaned over, pressing my hands on the desk, getting close to his face. "And if you ever come near Analyn again, I will not be responsible for what happens next." Deciding I'd said enough, I turned and walked out.

Adrenaline pumped hard through my veins, and all I could think about was seeing Analyn. Once in my car, I drove over to her condo.

I knocked on Analyn's door, ready to drop to my knees and beg. I'd just stood up to a man with ties to organized crime. Surely, I could stand up to my own employees and tell them to give Analyn the respect she deserves, and she and I would be free to be together.

As I waited for her to answer, my mind was a whirl, wondering why she took the day off, hoping it wasn't to forget me, and trying to string together coherent words that would persuade her to give us a chance.

When the door opened, my heart filled with emotion. Analyn stood looking adorable in a pair of leggings and an old sweatshirt. Her dark hair was in a messy bun on top of her head. She was the most beautiful woman I'd ever seen.

I reached out, wrapping my arm around her, and tugged her close. "Do you want me to leave?" I only asked because I knew I couldn't just take her. I needed her consent.

"No."

"Thank fuck." My lips came down on hers, and I drank them in like a thirsty man finding an oasis in the desert. I maneuvered into her condo, shutting the door behind me. "Is your roommate here? If she is, she's about to get an eyeful."

"She just left. She had to run into work for something."

I scooped Analyn up into my arms. "I'd sure like to do this in a bed."

Her arms wrapped around my neck, and hope filled me. She pointed the way toward her bedroom. Once we were inside, I'd never gotten undressed so fast in my life. But when I was finally lying over Analyn, flesh to flesh, the world slowed down.

Too often for us, sex was a fast and furious romp. Now I had time. Time to show her how much I loved her. Time for her to see how good it could be with us, not just sexually, but as partners. Hell, partners in life, even. Of course, I couldn't blurt all that out now since I knew even as she was giving herself over to me at this moment, all the issues between us still existed.

But the forever I hoped to start with her could begin now, with me showing her through my touch that it was safe for her to risk her heart. That I was a safe bet.

My hands took their time as they explored every inch of her decadent body. I knew every spot that made her arch into my touch, that made her moan, that made her sigh. I followed that up with my lips, kissing and tasting every inch of her skin.

Could she feel it? Could she feel me handing my heart over to her? God, I hoped so.

34

Analyn

I couldn't fight it anymore. My love for Reed was too powerful to deny. So I gave in, even knowing the risk. Knowing it could ruin me at work. Knowing it could end and shatter me.

Reed's hands were magic on me. Everywhere he touched me, my body hummed with life and love. Then his lips caressed my skin, making me his. Whether he knew it or not, he was claiming me and I was willingly being claimed.

But I wanted a turn too. I wanted to claim him and so I pushed him back and used my hands and lips to discover his body, to learn what brought him pleasure. It wasn't like I didn't have an idea. It's not like we hadn't done this before. But this time, it wasn't a frenzied encounter set off by pent-up sexual need. Now I had the time and space and privacy to truly explore this man, and I took advantage of it.

I moved down his body, his abdominal muscles tightening under my lips.

"Analyn." His voice was a mixture of need and satisfaction.

I wrapped my hand around his dick, drawing my tongue around

his tip. I hadn't spent nearly enough time getting to know this part of his anatomy, and I intended to.

He groaned, his fingers lacing through my hair. "Yes, baby . . . more."

I smiled, loving the tone of his voice, the endearment *baby*. I rewarded him by sucking the tip of his dick into my mouth and swirling my tongue around the rim.

"Ah, fuck . . . that's good." His hips rose in response, so I took him in deeper. Massaging his balls, I slid my mouth up and down his shaft, loving how it thickened and pulsed with each slide. As much as I wanted to feel him inside me, I also wanted to bring him pleasure like this. To taste his cum.

But he had other ideas.

"Analyn." He gripped my arms and pulled me up until he could kiss me. His kiss was filled with need and burning desire. He rolled us until he was over me. "Open for me, baby."

I wrapped my legs around his hips. He thrust in, filling me in one move. Our cries of pleasure filled my tiny bedroom.

"Reed."

"Yes, baby." His lips suckled my neck as his hips rocked over me.

I wanted to tell him I loved him, but I couldn't quite get the words out. I couldn't stop my heart from opening fully, completely to him, but my brain still sought to protect itself. Instead of words, I moaned as he ground his hips against me.

"Do you feel me, Analyn?"

"Yes."

"Do you feel how good we are together?"

"Yes." I gripped his shoulders as I neared the edge. It was too soon coming, but I couldn't prevent it. I could only go with it. Go with Reed.

He must have felt the same as he levered up on his hands. "Look at me."

I opened my eyes and watched him watch me as our bodies moved together. As we drove toward pleasure together. As we reached the pinnacle together. My orgasm hit, and I cried out, arching into him, surrendering my heart, my soul to him.

"Yes . . . Analyn . . . yes . . ." He came with me, pistoning hard and fast until he collapsed over me.

I lay in Reed's arms, completely boneless. If the condo were on fire, I wouldn't have the energy to escape it. This was what I wanted in my life. Not just the sex, but the man who could make my body sing. Who could make me feel cherished, like there was nothing or no one else in the world but us two.

But of course, that was followed with the reality of our situation, and frustration filled me. This was the worst sort of torment.

Reed rolled onto his back, tugging me close to him. His hand rested on my head as I placed it on his shoulder. "We need to talk about where we go from here."

The muscles in his abs where my hand rested tensed. Like he was expecting me to respond the same way I had before, pushing him away . . . running off. I knew I should, and yet at the same time, I found I couldn't fight any longer.

"You're right."

His muscles relaxed. "I'd actually meant to talk to you first, but when I saw you at the door, I kinda lost it there."

I tilted my head up to see him giving me a sheepish smile.

"That's all right. Although I'm a little surprised, considering I must look like a mess. Especially next to you in your dark suit."

"I swear to God, when you opened the door, I saw the most beautiful woman I'd ever seen."

I gave his chest a light slap. "I know that's not true, but flattery will get you everywhere."

He looked at me, his blue eyes intense as his hand caressed my face. "It's true. You are beautiful and sexy, and smart and strong, and my world is a better place with you in it. I don't have any answers, but I'm not leaving here tonight until we figure it out."

"Okay." This wasn't the first time he'd sought to do this, but this time, his determination, his insistence that there was a solution, filled me with hope.

He studied me for a moment as if he was unsure of my response. "Okay, then."

"Will we be doing this here like this, or do you want to get up? We might have a little bit of wine left from last night. I could make you something to eat unless you want ice cream. Betts and I finished that off last night."

"I meant to ask why you had taken the day off. Does wine and ice cream have anything to do with it?"

I nodded, wondering if I could tell my boss the truth. But since my boss was naked in my bed, I figured I could. "Betts and I talked things out. She wasn't happy to hear what Paul had done, but the thing that bothered her the most was how long it took me to tell her about him. I should've said something sooner."

"But everything's okay now?"

"Yes. We did consume a little bit too much last night. Although to be honest, I'm not sure if it's the wine or the ice cream that I was hungover from this morning. We decided to spend the day together. Of course, she got called into work. You won't tell my boss I'm playing hooky, will you?"

Reed rolled us over until he was over me, his dick perched at my entrance. "I'm pretty sure your boss has no problem with you taking a day with your friend. He also has no problem with you taking some time with him." He thrust in, and for the next little while, we gave and took pleasure.

When we were done, we got out of bed and dressed. I went to the kitchen to fix something to eat, and then we were going to talk. I still didn't know how things were going to work out, but I was determined, just like he was, to find whatever the answer would be for us to be together.

I had just set out some cheese and crackers when his phone rang.

"Fuck."

"Who is it?"

"It's Catherine. I should take this."

I nodded. "Of course." The guy hadn't become a billionaire by shirking his duties.

I expected him to leave the kitchen, but he didn't. "Catherine, what's up?"

I couldn't hear the other side of the call, but Reed's expression darkened. "What do you mean? What's going on?"

Again, I watched him as he listened. His gaze drifted to me, and I saw a tug of war going on in his eyes. Something must be going on at the office.

"Fine." He hung up the call, putting the phone in his pocket. He walked over to me, his hands cradling my face. "There's something going on at the office. I have to go."

I nodded. "I understand. Really."

"We are going to talk and sort this out. You understand that, right?"

"I do. I'm going to hold you to it."

The tension in his face lessened, and a smile replaced his concern. "Good. How about this? Meet me at the Golden Oasis." He looked at his watch. "Say . . . in one hour."

I had no idea what time it was. Based on the light coming in the kitchen, I suspected it was after four, but it didn't matter what time it was. "I'll be there."

His smile was wide, his blue eyes bright, and I felt such happiness fill my chest.

"I'll be the guy at the end of the bar who needs someone to cheer him up."

I grinned. "I'll be there to do the cheering."

He leaned in and gave me a kiss. When he pulled back, he said, "One hour."

I nodded, feeling giddy like a teenage girl as I watched him leave. I hoped he'd be able to meet me in an hour and that whatever problem was at the office didn't take more time. But even if it did, I'd wait for him. He'd been right all along. There was no fighting what was between us. The only question was, how were we going to deal with the issues?

I took my time getting ready, vacillating between wearing a nice dress or jeans. Since Reed had mentioned re-creating the first time we met, I went with the red dress I'd worn that night. I combed my hair out, wearing it down in the soft waves I'd worn that night as well.

When Betts returned, she showed up in my bedroom doorway with a brown bag in each hand. "I've got more ice cream and wine." She arched a brow when she saw me preening in the mirror. "Or it looks like I'm going to help you get ready to go out."

I turned and looked at her. "Reed came by."

She glanced at my bed, and my cheeks inflamed. "I see it was a productive visit." Her gaze returned to me. "Does that mean the issue of his being your boss has been resolved?"

I shook my head. "Not exactly. But we are both determined to resolve it."

She gave me a concerned expression. "You're not going to be one of those women who quits her job for a man, though, are you?"

I shook my head. "But it's possible, even probable, that I'm going to have to deal with people wondering how I got my job. I hate that."

Betts looked at me in sympathy. "But you can't really go through life worrying about what other people think, right? I mean, that would suck if people thought you slept your way into your job, but you and Reed know the truth. And the quality of your work reveals the truth, right?"

She was right, of course, but it was still no easy feat trying to work in a place where you knew people questioned your ability, questioned whether or not you earned your spot.

Not wanting to think about it now, I asked, "How do I look?"

She grinned. "Confident. The poor guy is going to have a difficult time hiding how much he wants you."

I laughed. "Good."

I put on my coat, grabbed my purse, and headed out the door. Just as I was about to reach my car, a van pulled up, screeching to a halt. The door flew open, and as I turned, wondering what was going on, two arms wrapped around my shoulders and somebody else came around, grabbing my ankles, flipping me up until they were carrying me.

I screamed. "What's going on? Let me go." I tried to flail, but the two burly men had a strong hold on me. They tossed me into the side door of the van and climbed in behind me. I scrambled back into a corner trying to figure out how to escape.

"Your boyfriend really screwed up this time."

When I was able to focus on the man speaking, I realized it was the same person who'd given me the warning the other night. My heart raced and dread filled me as I realized what was going on. I was being kidnapped by people with ties to the mob.

35

Reed

I f my office wasn't on fire or otherwise erupting in chaos, I was going to fire Catherine. An emergency at work had come at the worst fucking time. I was on the cusp of creating something with Analyn when Catherine called in hysterics, telling me I needed to get to the office but not giving me any details about what was going on.

On the way to the office, I called the Golden Oasis to arrange flowers and a gourmet dinner for me and Analyn. No matter what was happening at the office, I was going to meet Analyn in an hour and woo her until she fell into my arms.

It was just after five in the evening when I exited the elevators and made my way toward my office. Everything around me was quiet. As I glanced over at the various departments, most were empty. The few employees who were still working were focused on their jobs. Goddammit, if Catherine brought me down here for no good reason . . .

I turned the corner into the space that made up the CEO's area, which included Catherine's desk and my office. When I walked in, I found Catherine standing in front of her desk as if she were waiting for me. But there were no hysterics in her expression. There was no fire, no emergency.

"What the fuck is going on?"

She lifted her chin at me defiantly. "I have served you faithfully for years. Women have come and gone in your life, but I'm still here."

"What the hell, Catherine?" She wasn't telling me anything I didn't know.

"I don't know how you can be one of the smartest men that I know and yet one of the dumbest."

My jaw tightened. "Watch yourself."

She stepped toward me, looking up into my eyes. "How could you not have seen after all these years how much I love you?"

My brain skidded to a halt. What did she just say? As her words filtered through my brain, much of her behavior started to make sense. I wasn't an idiot, as she seemed to suggest, but I definitely had missed the signs. Signs that started to make a little bit of sense.

Not wanting to be a total asshole, I tempered my anger. "I'm sorry, Catherine. I didn't notice. But if I did, it wouldn't have mattered. I admire and respect you, and I value you as my employee, but that's it."

She stared up at me, and I swore I could see her trying to decide what she wanted to say next. Was she going to lash out or continue to plead her case? Either way, it wouldn't matter.

"I don't know what you see in Analyn. I could give you so much more. I know you, Reed. I can make you happy." She pressed her hand on my chest.

Delicately, I wrapped my fingers around her wrist and pulled her hand off. "I love Analyn."

"No! That's impossible. If you gave me the chance, you would see . . ." She threw her arms around me, crushed her mouth against mine.

Shocked, I jerked away, stepping back, wiping her essence off my lips. "Catherine . . ." I didn't know what to say. I knew I needed to fire her, but it seemed too much to reject her love and take away her job in one breath.

"I'm sorry, but you and me, we're never going to be," I said as firmly, yet gently, as I could.

Her eyes fired with rage. Her hands fisted and her lips curled into a snarl. "All the things that I've done for you . . . all those women who were unworthy of you, I'm the one who saved you from them."

"What?"

She pressed her index finger into her chest as she leaned forward and raged at me. "I'm the one who got rid of them. And I tried to save you from Analyn too."

My hackles rose. "What does that mean?" Analyn's performance review came to mind. Had Catherine made changes to it knowing how I'd react? I realized I hadn't gone back and pulled it up to check the sources from which Catherine had pulled together the review.

"The only woman for you is me, Reed. She's making you look like a fool. For God's sake, I will—"

"What did I tell you about—" My phone rang, preventing me from finishing what I planned to say. Normally, I might've ignored the call, but on the chance it was Analyn, I pulled it out. The number was blocked, and my first instinct was to ignore it, but then a kernel of fear took root in my belly.

I swiped over the screen to answer. "Who is this?"

"It's your good friend Gino, Reed. I took a look at your coun-teroffer and it's totally unacceptable. So I've got a new offer for you."

There was a pause, and I was about to ask what he was talking about when in the background I heard a woman crying out. My heart stopped. "Analyn!"

"I figured my new bargaining chip might be something you'd pay attention to. I have to say, Reed, she's stunning in red."

"What the fuck, Gino. You'd better let her go or so help me, I will hunt you down and kill you like the dog that you are."

"Now, now, Reed, settle down. I'm going to text you an address. You meet me there in an hour ready to do business. If you do that, you can have your woman back. If you don't show up, or if you show up with cops, your woman doesn't stand a chance."

The line went dead before I could respond. "Holy Jesus fuck." I ran my hand over my head as I searched my brain for what to do. I'd overplayed my hand, and now Analyn was going to pay the price. The phone pinged. Checking the screen, the blocked number had sent a text of an address located in an area that would be deserted this time of night.

I looked up at Catherine all of a sudden, the perspective in my life changing. She and her deranged love for me meant nothing next to saving Analyn.

The look of horror on her face was the only thing that stopped me from running out of the room to take care of Analyn. I rounded on her. "What do you know about this?"

She shook her head. "Nothing, not much."

I wanted to throttle her.

She must've seen the murderous expression in my eyes as she said, "They just offered me a little something in exchange to help get in front of you."

"Did you tell them about me and Analyn?"

She shook her head. "I didn't have to. They had somebody following you."

I scowled. "And how would they know where I was going to be?"

She looked down.

"I trusted you, Catherine. You say you love me, and you did this to me?"

"I didn't know they would do something like this. I could see that you were miserable being the CEO, and I was just trying to help you." She stepped forward again, pressing her hands on my chest. "I did this out of love."

I slapped her hands away. "You're fired. As soon as I save Analyn, I'll decide whether you're going to jail as well." I hurried out of my office, rushing out to my car.

As soon as I was driving toward the warehouse, I called Pierce. "Those fucking bastards took Analyn."

"What fucking bastards? Oh, shit, not the Paradise Limited people?"

"Yes. They're holding her hostage. I'm going to have to agree to this partnership in order to save her." There was no question now that I would do whatever they wanted me to do. Once she was safe, I would figure out the next step, which would likely be calling the Feds and figuring out how to get rid of my part of the partnership. And then maybe tanking the company. I also had to figure out a way to save everyone on my staff from utter ruin. Everyone except Catherine, of course.

"You're not doing anything stupid, are you?" Pierce asked.

"If I call the cops, she's dead. If I show up willing to do this deal, they say they'll let her go."

"Can you trust them?"

"Not as far as I could throw them. But what choice do I have?" My tires squealed as I made a righthand turn onto the street that would take me out to the warehouse.

"You can't do this by yourself, Reed. Seriously, once you sign those papers, they could kill the both of you. You need help."

"No cops, Pierce."

The line was quiet for a moment. "Okay, no cops. But they didn't say anything about another kind of backup."

"What do you have in mind?"

"Come by the rink. I think I've got an idea."

36

Analyn

I was trembling, and I felt cold down to the marrow of my bones. But it wasn't the temperature that had me shaking. It was fear. I sat in a warehouse with boxes stacked twice as tall as me filling most of the space. In the open section, I sat in a chair with my hands tied behind my back. A man with a gun stood one side of me. On the other side of me was another man with a gun strapped to his side as he leaned against the wall scrolling through his phone and looking bored.

A third man, the one who'd given me the message for Reed, sat at a square card table with papers on it, talking on his phone. I got the feeling that while he oversaw the two men guarding me, he wasn't the one in charge of this entire operation.

"Hampton's on his way now. I'll get him to sign the paperwork, and you'll have a foothold in the most reputable online gambling site. After that, it's just a matter of investing in, buying sports teams, or just bribing players, and you have a way to fix games to make money. Plus, you'll have Hampton's company to launder money from all your other operations."

I was so dead. And Reed probably was too. I had no doubt that he was going to respond to this man's call and come to try and save me. Reed was a good man who cared for me. He wouldn't leave me here.

Anguish washed through me. How was it that life could be so unfair? Reed and I were on the verge of having something remarkable, and just like that, it was being ripped away. God! I thought of all the time I'd wasted being worried about my reputation when I could've done exactly as Reed said and told them all to fuck off and instead been with him. Loving him.

If we survived this, I wasn't going to let my fears keep me from living life. Yes, there were obstacles, but I loved Reed and I was thinking maybe he loved me too. The times when I allowed myself to be open to him, life was so good. It was fun and exciting. He was amazingly supportive of me and my goals. I hoped I had a chance to tell him everything I was thinking and feeling right now. About how amazing I thought he was. And how much I loved him.

There was a knock on the exterior door.

"He's here. I'll be in touch." The man at the table hung up the phone. "Marcus, get the door."

The guy with the phone nodded, putting it in his pocket as he strode toward the door. The man at the table rose, buttoning his coat as he walked over to me. He and the man with the gun stared at me with their backs to the door.

"Looks like lover boy is here," the head man said.

The other man opened the door and was immediately yanked out. I swallowed as I waited for the two men in front of me to realize what happened. But then, Reed strolled in through the door. It slammed behind him.

The head guy turned toward Reed. "Smart of you to come."

"You didn't give me much choice, Gino."

Then the man Reed called Gino looked toward the door. "Where's Marcus?"

"I guess he's guarding the door. Making sure I didn't call the cops," Reed said with a shrug. "Are you alright?" He spoke nonchalantly, but I saw worry and concern in his eyes.

I nodded to let him know I wasn't hurt.

Gino walked back to the table. "The paperwork is here. With all your antics, you forfeited any ability to negotiate the deal."

Reed walked over to the table but positioned himself so he could still see me.

"Let Analyn go, and I'll sign whatever you want."

Gino laughed. "You're in no position to negotiate. I just told you that."

"You let her go, and I'll sign whatever you want," Reed repeated. "Hell, I'll sign the whole company over to you."

My heart squeezed tight, hating that Reed was in a position to give up the company he'd worked so hard to build.

Gino shook his head. "You still don't get it, do you? Your company only has value to us with you running it. Your reputation is what's going to make this whole scheme work."

Reed gave him a hard look. "Getting in bed with a company like Paradise Limited is going to ruin my reputation more than my reputation is going to help Paradise Limited. Everything falls to the lowest denominator, which would be you."

Gino's eyes flashed with rage. He nodded toward the man next to me, and the man next to me lifted his gun, pointing it toward my head.

"You sign this now, or I kill her," Gino said.

"You mean your goon kills her because you and your boss are too pussy ass to do it yourself."

I flinched as a new wave of fear ran through me. Why was Reed antagonizing them?

"If you kill her, I still won't sign, which means you'll have to kill me, thereby ruining your plans to utilize my reputation. But I promise you if you hurt her, you will not leave this building alive. Neither will your goons."

Gino studied Reed for a moment, I suppose trying to get a feel of whether Reed was bluffing or not. Reed was an expert at gambling, and I had to believe that he knew what he was doing. I realized at that moment that I could believe in him. I could bet everything that I had, everything I was on him.

Gino looked toward the door, and I suspected he was wondering whether Marcus was really guarding things outside or if Reed had done something to him.

"Marcus!" Gino bellowed. There was a slight knock on the door, but it didn't open.

Reed shrugged. "It was locked when I tried to open it."

Gino looked at the man with the gun. "Go open the door for Marcus."

The man with the gun looked at me for a moment.

"She's not going anywhere," Gino said.

The man with the gun shrugged and walked over to the door. Reed moved, stepping in between me and Gino, keeping Gino facing me with the door to his back. Something was happening, and I knew at this moment, I was either going to be saved or be killed.

I looked at Reed, wishing I could see his eyes but still sending out all my love and faith in him.

The guy with the gun opened the door, and just like happened to the last guy, a hand came in, yanking him out. There was no sound to it, so whoever was on Reed's side was good at taking men down.

All of a sudden, I heard a commotion behind me and feared that Gino had more men. But Reed turned and rushed over to me, coming around behind me to undo my restraints.

"What are you doing?" Gino shouted. "Marcus, Anthony."

The door opened, and a man I didn't know came rushing in with a gun pointed at Gino's head. Behind him, another group of people filed in, and then more showed up behind me.

Two of them I recognized. "Bo? Pierce?"

Bo gave me his signature grin. "I'll tell you what, Analyn. Reed has me beat on creating excitement during a date."

In the next moment, my hands were free and I was pulled from the chair and held in Reed's arms.

"Tell me you're okay."

Realizing I was safe, I wrapped my arms around him. I would've wrapped my legs too except my dress prevented it.

He held me so tightly I was lifted off the ground. I pulled back enough that I could press my hands to his cheeks and look into his eyes. "I love you."

He blinked like he was in shock. "That's not just the adrenaline talking, is it?"

I shook my head. "No. I've known it for a long time, but I've been a coward for a long time too. But not anymore."

His grin was slow and sure, and happy. "That's good to hear, Analyn, because I love you too."

"Can you just kiss her already and we can get the hell out here?" Pierce's voice sounded across the warehouse.

Reed pressed his lips to mine, and I returned the kiss, pouring everything I had into it, hoping he could feel the truth of my feelings.

He lowered me down and slipped his arm around my waist, holding me close as we turned.

"Analyn, I think you know Bo and Pierce. These other men are the Las Vegas hockey team. Except for the man who's got Gino all tied up and ready to piss his pants. That's Dax Sheppard, from Saint security."

Dax saluted me and then pulled out his phone to make a call.

"Where are the other two guys?" I asked about Marcus and Anthony.

"Oh, my God Analyn, you should've seen it. Dax Sheppard is a fucking superhero. In one move, those guys were out for the count. They're tied up in the back of his van now." Bo spoke about Dax with the reverence of an eight-year-old.

I was happy that this ordeal was done, but I also knew our problems with Paradise Limited were not necessarily over. "Gino isn't the boss of the whole thing."

Reed turned to me, his hands rubbing my arms. "I know. But with Saint Security and the FBI involved, we should be safe."

"The Feds have just taken Carson Knowles and a bunch of his

men in. He's the head of the whole thing," Dax said, slipping his phone back into his pocket.

"Wow. That fast?" Pierce asked.

Dax nodded as he grabbed Gino. "That fast. How about it, Gino? You gonna go in easy?"

"I ain't saying nothing to any of you. I'll be out by the end of the night."

"We'll see about that. I'm your taxi to the FBI office."

I looked up at Reed. "So, it's over?"

He nodded. "For those guys, it is. But for you and me, Analyn, it's just the beginning, right?"

I launched myself into his arms, holding on tight. "Right."

37

Reed

I had never been so fucking scared in my life. But now, the whole ordeal was over. Analyn's rescue attempt had gone off without a hitch.

I was so thankful to have thought to call Pierce and let him know what was going on. I was ready to barge into the warehouse and probably get Analyn killed. I would've never been able to live with myself if that happened. But by reaching out to Pierce, he had the clarity of mind to come up with a plan.

The plan we executed wasn't a whole lot different from what we had come up with when I met him at the ice rink. It included me and Pierce and members of the hockey team who were willing to sacrifice themselves to save my woman. From then on, all of them had my eternal gratitude.

By chance, I got a call from Max at the Golden Oasis, asking why I wasn't there. I had forgotten that I had called to set up a romantic evening for me and Analyn. Of course, because my mind was scrambled, I blurted out everything that was going on.

"You can't go in there by yourself, Reed. Let me call my brother-in-law," Max said.

Brother-in-law? And then I remembered his sister had married a man who'd once worked as a mercenary and now was part of an elite security firm called Saint Security. I was running out of time, and at the same time, I knew having a security professional, ex-mercenary, no less, could be the difference between life and death for Analyn.

Several minutes later, Dax was on the phone with me, and I had relayed the plan we had set up so far. Dax met us up the street from the warehouse and made a few tweaks to the plan. Mostly, he was the one who yanked the two goons out, and Bo was right. With one move, those two guys were out cold. He'd also contacted other members of Saint Security and apparently, an entire team was mobilized to coordinate with the FBI to bring all of Paradise Limited down.

It felt like my life was about to end when I entered that warehouse, but now that it was all over, thanks to Dax and Bo and Pierce and the rest of the team, my life was just starting.

I swept Analyn up in my arms. She let out a squeak but grinned ear-to-ear.

"I want to thank all of you for what you did here tonight, but if you don't mind . . ."

"Please, leave now. We don't need to see what's going to happen next."

I hadn't realized how down Pierce was on love.

I strode to the door with Analyn in my arms.

"I guess our date for tomorrow's off?" Bo said, giving me a cheeky grin. If I were in a different kind of mood, I might've punched his lights out.

Analyn laughed. "I'm sorry, Bo. It's been fun, but—"

"I know, I know. What am I going to do once my mama realizes you've left me for another man?"

Pierce slapped Bo upside the head.

I'd already made it to the door, which I managed to get open, and I strode out to my car. I helped Analyn, surreptitiously taking in her body to make sure she wasn't hurt. It was only then I realized she was wearing the red dress she'd worn the night I met her. Tonight, our plans had been to meet at the Golden Oasis, where I hoped we could start over again. And as much as I wanted to do that, right now, what I needed more was to get Analyn home and hold her the entire night. Hell, my goal was to hold her forever.

As I drove, I held her hand, every now and then bringing it up to my lips and kissing it as if I needed a reminder that she was here and safe.

When I got home, I tugged her through the front door and shut it and then pulled her into my arms. "I can't tell you how fucking scared I was that I was going to lose you. I know there are still issues that need to be resolved—"

She pressed her finger over my lips. "There's nothing like being kidnapped and threatened with death to put things in perspective. If you really want to do this, I want to—"

"I've been telling you from the start that I want to do this. I want you. You're the only woman for me, past, present, and future." I watched her expression, hoping I wasn't saying too much, too soon.

"Well alright, then."

I took that as a sign that it was time to consummate this new part of our relationship. So, I scooped her up again and carried her to my bedroom. "I can't tell you how many times I've imagined having you in my bed."

"I've imagined being there."

I stumbled a moment and looked down at her in surprise. "Really?"

She laughed. "I must've done a really good job of hiding what I was really thinking and feeling."

I strode into my bedroom. "Must've been all the times you ran away."

Her eyes turned sad, and I hated that my words might be making her feel bad.

"I'm sorry for that, Reed. I was just—"

"I understand, Analyn. And if we need to talk more about all the other stuff, we can do it. But right now, I just want to get lost in you. Can we do that?"

"Absolutely."

I'd had wild sex with Analyn. I'd even had slow sex with her. But this felt like the first time. I suppose it was. The first time I made love to her, at least. What a difference it was to touch and taste her knowing she loved me. Knowing she was mine. The magnitude of that awed me. I vowed I'd never forget this gift.

When I moved to enter her, she pushed me back and rose over me. "I was so scared, Reed."

"I know, baby. I was too."

"But now, when I replay it . . . at least the part with you . . ." She bit her lower lip and gave me a flirty smile. "You were so strong and sexy."

"Yeah?" I rubbed my arms up and down her back as her pussy teased my cock. I wanted so badly to be inside her, and yet, I knew I had all the time in the world.

"Yeah. 'But I promise you if you hurt her, you will not leave this building alive.' When I remember you saying that, it makes me hot."

I levered up, pulling her close so I could lick her nipples. "I meant it too. You're everything to me."

She sank down on me like it was a reward. I pulled her to me, kissing her, completing the circuit of our bodies. We were one now. Not just two bodies joined in pleasure. We were two hearts, two souls, made one.

Soon, nature took over, and we moved in the most perfect harmony. She came first, nearly making my eyes roll back in my head as her body squeezed my cock.

I rolled us over, my hands clasping hers as I rocked in and out of her until she was climaxing again. This time, I let go and came with her, emptying my soul into her.

I held her in my arms, feeling like my life was finally as it should be. Or nearly.

I knew what she had said at the warehouse, but maybe that was just from all the adrenaline from being afraid and then being saved.

Maybe when all that settled down, the same concerns would rise, concerns that we still needed to deal with.

I kissed the top of her head, wanting one last loving gesture before I delved into the topic that could blow this all apart. "So, what happens next?"

She let out a satisfied sigh and nuzzled into me, her hand over my heart. Could she tell that it beat only for her?

"I don't know, but if I were the betting type, I'd lay odds on my staying the entire night here with you in this bed."

I smiled because I liked those words. But she'd only mentioned one night. She had said earlier that she had been a coward in not telling me how she was truly feeling.

It was my turn to work up the courage to tell her what I was feeling. "I will see that bet and raise you another."

She tilted her head up to me, her smile so sweet it made my heart pump even harder in my chest.

"You stay in this bed with me tonight, tomorrow night, the night after that, and all the other nights for the rest of our lives." I held my breath as she looked up at me, her eyes wide in shock.

Finally, she said, "I'll take that bet."

Happiness like I'd never felt before filled my chest. I pushed her back, hovering over her, staring into her dark eyes, wanting to make sure I heard her correctly. "You do understand that I'm proposing marriage, right?"

Her hand slid up, threading through my hair. "You'd better be proposing marriage because that's how I took it."

Another wave of happiness ran through me. "Analyn, you have put light back into my life."

I didn't let her say anything as my lips captured hers in a searing kiss filled with love and promise for our happily ever after. We were going to go the distance. We would last until our dying breaths. You could bet on it.

EPILOGUE

Analyn – One Year Later

I made my way to the offices of the Buckaroos minor league hockey team. Or, more likely, I should say I waddled, as I was just entering the fortieth week of my pregnancy.

The last year had been a whirlwind of changes, nearly all of them for the good. Being in Las Vegas, it was very easy to get married quickly. Reed and I didn't want to wait.

At first, Betts was worried about how quickly I jumped into marriage with Reed. After all, I didn't know him very well timewise. But I felt that I knew him soul to soul, and I knew I didn't want to wait a minute longer to discover all the things I would learn about him during our marriage.

Not too long after that, I was pregnant, and while we didn't set out to start our family so soon, we were both over the moon about it. In fact, Reed joked that his happiness had fortified his sperm, which had broken through any birth control effort. I don't know if it was super sperm or some sort of magic, but whatever it was, I couldn't have been happier.

During this year, Reed and Pierce bought a minor-league hockey team, which I thought was crazy considering they both had very demanding jobs. But while Reed still owned his fantasy sports empire, he had promoted Clive and hired new management to run the day-to-day operations, which allowed him all the time he wanted on his passion project.

Reed was no longer my boss, but it wasn't because I continued to work as the social media manager of his company. Now, I worked alongside him as a partner in the day-to-day operations of the hockey team.

It wasn't all totally smooth sailing this last year. Catherine raised a stink and even tried to sue Reed for sexual harassment. But luckily, Reed had a great deal of support around him and the best lawyers money could buy, and Catherine's efforts were squashed before they could get any traction. The last I heard, she'd left town to parts unknown.

During the case against Paradise Limited, I had a few moments of fear that someone might retaliate against us. But Reed made sure we had the finest security around us. And the people at Saint Security were not only very good at providing security, but also at assisting the FBI agents in their case that put most of the people working for Paradise Limited in jail.

I entered the office where Reed and Pierce were talking over something related to the team. When he saw me, Reed smiled, and even after a year of seeing it every day, it made my heart do flip-flops in my chest.

He strode to me, taking me in his arms and kissing me. "How are you feeling today?"

I looked up at him. "Very pregnant." He bent over and kissed my belly. "And how is our boy doing?"

I rubbed a hand over my belly. "I'm pretty sure he's a future hockey player because it feels like he's whacking pucks around inside me."

Both Reed and Pierce laughed. Pierce's phone pinged with a text, and after he looked at it, he said he had to take off. "Fortner and Kaplan are at it again on social media. I swear to God I'm gonna bang those two knuckleheads' heads together."

"Good luck with that," I called as he exited to deal with the two players on the team who had a social media feud going, apparently over a woman.

Reed took my hand and walked me over to the table where they had been talking. "What do you think of our new billboard design?"

I scanned it and felt it was pretty good. "It's not bad. But I hope you didn't finalize this. You know better than to finalize a campaign without my input."

He rolled his eyes. "Why do I keep having to remind you that you are on maternity leave? Which reminds me, I have a surprise for you." He walked over to a desk and opened a drawer, pulling out a package. It was wrapped in light blue paper with a big blue bow on it.

I eyed him, wondering what he was doing. I opened the box and pulled out a pale blue onesie with the hockey team's logo on it and a number one on the back.

I laughed and hugged him. "This is lovely. Oh, my God, it's so cute."

He grinned at me. "If you like that, I've got more." He went back to the desk and this time pulled out a slightly larger box. It was white, with a multicolored bow on the top.

I opened it up to find three more onesies in pastel colors, each with a number on the back from two to four.

I looked up at him, wondering if this meant what I thought it did.

He laughed. "We have four extra bedrooms in the house. I think we should fill it with our own little hockey team."

Tears of joy and happiness filled my eyes. "Can we get through number one first?"

His arms wrapped around me and his lips nuzzled against my neck. "Absolutely. I love you, Analyn." His lips captured mine and he kissed me.

My stomach cramped hard, and I gasped as I stepped back and a rush of liquid splashed on the floor.

Reed jumped back. "Oh, shit. Did I do that? Did I hurt you?"

I reached out, gripping his arms. "Reed, I think the baby is coming."

Reed grabbed his keys and his coat and ran out the door. I did my best to follow, but a contraction hit, and I had to stand for a moment to catch my breath.

He came rushing back into the room. "Analyn. We've gotta go."

I smiled despite the pain, realizing I had one of those husbands who was going to make our baby's birthday story humorous.

He finally got me to the car and then to the hospital. Six hours later, we were holding a baby boy in our arms.

"He's so beautiful, Analyn." The reverence in Reed's voice matched what I was feeling as I looked down into the sweet little face of my son.

Reed's hand cupped my cheek. "I had nearly given up hope on ever finding a woman I could love, who would love me and would want a family. And then one day, you walked in and picked me up at the bar. I am so fucking thankful for that."

"I am too. It's amazing what a little bravery and daring can get you in life."

He nodded. "All the gambles paid off."

"Absolutely."

He leaned in and kissed me. "You know, we haven't come up with a name for this little guy."

"We could call him Buckaroo."

Reed laughed.

"Or how about Puck? Slapshot?"

He rolled his eyes at me. "I think we should stick with gambling names. Roulette? Keno?"

I laughed. "Blackjack?"

We both stopped and stared at each other.

"Jack," we said at the same time.

"Jack, it is." Reed bent over, kissing baby Jack on the head, and then kissed me again. "Thank you for taking a gamble on me, Analyn."

Life came with ups and downs, but I knew with Reed, I'd always have a man who loved, respected, and cherished me. You could bet on it.

EXTENDED EPILOGUE

Bo Tyler

"Jump, jump, jump."

I stood on the roof of a low-rate Las Vegas motel overlooking groupies and hang-oners around the pool. I was drunk and buck naked. Yep, my cock was blowin' in the wind. I was on top of the world. The hockey season was set to start in two months, and I knew this year we'd make it to the Stanley Cup. We'd fucking win it, too. Women worshiped me. Men wanted to be me.

Little did they know, I was a fraud.

"Come on, Bo, get your naked ass down here. I want to see your cock up front and personal."

That came from the brunette in the white bikini . . . or was it the blonde in the red bikini? Hell, maybe it was the guy in the Speedo. Dudes loved me too.

I held my beer can up in salute to them. "Gotta finish my beer first. It would be a waste to waste it."

"Talk about wasted."

I was wasted. But even wasted, I felt empty. Why did I bother drinking? Or carousing? Or getting into mischief, as my mama called it? It never worked to fill the emptiness.

A shrink would have a field day with me. But I never went to one because I didn't need a therapist to tell me that I was drowning in booze and women because I was also drowning in guilt.

Everyone saw me as a boyish country boy who could play hockey like no one's business. They found my antics charming. My team's owners and manager liked how they filled the seats at the rink. Only my coach cared that I was one step away from self-destruction, but if I didn't care, why should he?

I knew the truth about me. I was the worst person possible. Ten years ago, I was responsible for my best friend's death. And then I fucked his girlfriend.

My stomach roiled, and I nearly hurled the contents of my booze-filled gut over the edge. That would surely clear out the fans who even now, knowing I was drunk, were encouraging me to jump off a roof and filming it for their TikTok and Instagram accounts. They didn't give a shit about me. But that was okay. I didn't give a shit about me, either.

"Jump, jump, jump."

I finished my beer, crushing the can and tossing it in the bushes. In the distance of the Las Vegas desert, I heard sirens. No doubt, someone called the cops. I wondered if Officer Henderson was on tonight. He was always gentle with the handcuffs.

"Are you ready?" I called down.

"Yes!"

I stood at the edge of the roof, holding my hands out and waggling my hips, making my dick flap.

And then I jumped.

I had a vague feeling of stinging as my body penetrated the water. My first thought was I didn't miss. But then I felt like I'd hit a wall and something inside my body popped.

I managed to stand up, only then realizing I'd landed closer to the shallow end and had hit the floor of the pool.

I went to raise my arms in victory, but my left arm felt like it had been shot and I couldn't lift it.

I walked to the steps and stumbled my way out to cheering fans.

"Hey, dude, something's wrong with your shoulder," some guy said.

"Huh?" I looked to my left shoulder, which was really starting to hurt like a motherfucker.

"He's right," the brunette in the white bikini said, making a face.

I was quickly sobering up,, and with it, realizing I'd dislocated my shoulder. If I'd just screwed up my hockey season, I was totally fucked.

"It's nothing," I said as I did my best to ignore the growing pain. "Where's my pants?" I didn't know how I managed it, but I finally got my ass covered and into my car. I dialed Pierce Jackson's number. He was the last person I wanted to call, but he was the only one I could think to contact through the fog of booze and growing pain. He was always the one I called because, as my coach, he was the only one who cared. I think I said that already.

"Jesus, you did what?" Pierce didn't sound mad as much as his tone was Christ-not-this-again.

"I dislocated my shoulder. I can't drive."

"Where are you?"

I gave him the best estimate of the address for the hotel I was at. Twenty minutes later, he pulled into the parking lot. I walked over to his car and got into the passenger seat.

"I'm not going to ask," he grumbled.

"Just as well."

He drove me to the hospital, not saying a word. What could he say? I might have just fucked up my chance at a Stanley Cup? I might have just ended my career? Sure, I was only twenty-nine, but not many hockey players made it through their thirties. All this I knew, and Pierce knew that I knew it.

He walked into the emergency room with me. When I was finally seen by the triage nurse, Pierce told me he'd wait. I didn't deserve to have his attention, but I appreciated it.

Hours later, after my shoulder was back in place and a sling was around my neck, I was let go.

"At least I didn't need surgery," I said to Pierce as he rose from the waiting room chair.

"How long?"

"Eight weeks." I gave him a sheepish grin. "I'll be better at the start of the season."

He wasn't buying my optimism. "I wish I knew what was riding your ass that you feel the need to act like an eight-year-old all the time."

I flinched.

"The thing is, Bo, I'm not going to be around next season to bail you out of jail or take you to the hospital."

"What?" His words hit me harder than the bottom of the pool had.

"While you were seeing the doctor, I got a text from Reed. Analyn had her baby tonight."

I smiled, happy for Analyn. And Reed, but mostly Analyn. I liked her. A lot. Not in a romantic or I-want-to-fuck-her way. As a friend. "That's great. But what does that have to do with you?"

"You know we bought the Buckaroos, and with the baby, Reed needs time. So I'm resigning as coach to take over duties."

"You're leaving as coach of an NHL team to coach a minor league team?" My gut clenched. I felt like I was losing my last tether to the world.

"I'm an owner of that team. Plus, they listen better." He gave me a sympathetic smile. "Bo, you really should think about getting your shit together. I'm willing to help, but you have to take the initiative."

A smart man would have taken the help Pierce offered. But I couldn't. I turned and walked out of the hospital.

"Bo. Come on, Son. Let me drive you home."

"You're not my coach anymore. I'll get myself home." Thankfully, he let me go. I managed to order a rideshare to get home. When I got there, I went looking for my bottle of JD. It would do just as good as any pain reliever to ease my shoulder pain.

The other pain? The guilt and self-loathing that came from losing my best friend and betraying him with his girl? I knew there was no relief from that.

Bo gets his own story soon. Meanwhile, **check out Max and Amelia Clarke's happily ever after here.**

It's true when they say that Las Vegas should be burned to the ground.
I'd burn it myself after ending up married to a woman and having no memory of it.
Was Amelia playing me?

DOWNLOAD MAX AND AMELIA'S STORY HERE

THE VEGAS BLUFF (SNEAK PEEK)

DESCRIPTION

I was right all along...
Amelia was just like *all* the other women I never wanted to see again after spending one night together.

In fact, she turned out to be worse than them.

Let me backup...

It's true when they say that Las Vegas should be burned to the ground.
I'd burn it myself after ending up married to a woman and having no memory of it.
Was Amelia playing me?
Judging by the way she was sweating and yelling in shock, I didn't think so.

My heart lied to me and begged me to believe in her authenticity.
You know, maybe she wasn't after my money or prestige, after all.
Maybe her gorgeous body contained a heart that I could actually love.

Boy was I wrong.

Instead of finding an honest heart, I discovered a nasty secret that made me want to rewind time and undo the moments I'd spent with her inside the bedroom.

She was a devil in human form.
A devil that was now wearing a wedding ring... *and* carrying my baby.
Could this Christmas bring me any more surprises?

PROLOGUE

Amelia

Slowly, I awoke from a heavy sleep. The fog in my brain was thick, making it difficult to fully come awake. At first, I was disoriented, not sure where I was. But then a heavy arm draped over my hip and a warm body spooned around me, bringing a memory and a smile back to my face.

Max.

Max with the large hands and an amazing expertise around a woman's body. Enough of the fog lifted that I was able to open my eyes. I frowned as I realized I was still dressed. Why was I sleeping in my clothes?

I scanned through my brain, trying to recall last night. Max had asked me out again, surprising me because I thought the night before had been a one-night thing. And while I wasn't interested in a relationship, I had to admit that I was happy to have another opportunity to spend the night with him. There was no danger of an entanglement because he was from New York and would leave today to return home.

I could recall a lovely dinner, and then a driver taking us through the city as we drank champagne. Had we drunk so much that when we got back to the hotel, we crashed out?

Max's large hand slid down my hip, over my thigh, and up again. His lips pressed to the back of my neck, nibbling, sending a delicious shiver through me.

"I think I drank too much last night," he murmured against my neck.

"Oh?"

"It's the only thing that can explain why we're in bed and still dressed. If I'd had my wits about me last night, we would be waking up naked."

"I was just thinking the same thing."

"Were you now?" His lips continued to trail kisses along my neck. "How do you feel about sleepy, slow sex in the morning?"

"I feel pretty good about it." Already, my body was flushed in anticipation. My nipples were hard and my pussy quivered, knowing the pleasure Max could bring.

He tugged the zipper of my dress down and pushed it from my shoulders. With him still spooned behind me, I shimmied out of my dress. He unclasped my bra, and I tossed that aside. Last, I divested myself of my panties.

He tugged me to him, his slacks-covered dick pressing against my ass as his hand slid over my belly and then down into my nest of curls.

"You're not going to join me?" I sighed against him.

His lips were on my neck again. "I will. But first, you." His fingers found my clit, gently rubbing it. I closed my eyes and sank into his touch, into the warmth of his firm body.

It didn't take long for my orgasm to wash over me. Only then did he undress. Naked, he spooned around me again, lifting my leg to make room for him. He slid inside me, and even though I'd just come, my body responded, my blood heating again.

Like he'd promised, he moved slowly and languidly. His lips kissed my neck and shoulder as he rocked in and out of me. It was sweet and lovely, and a part of me would miss him when he left. I'd never met a man like him. Oh, sure, there were plenty of good-looking, rich guys in Las Vegas. But Max was more than that. There was a down-to-earth feel about him that made me think he grew up in a good family, unlike mine. He wasn't necessarily open about his feelings, but that reservedness gave him a shy factor that was sweet. He was smart and interesting. And he knew how to have a good time.

He groaned against me. "I'm close." His whisper tickled along my neck. He reached over my body, pinching my nipple as he picked up the pace.

"Oh!" I cried out as my orgasm flowed through me, just like he'd described, sleepy and slow.

He thrust again, emptied, and then held me spooned against him as the last waves of pleasure flowed through us.

When our heart rates settled, he gave me one last kiss on the neck and rolled onto his back. I turned onto my back as well.

He slid his hands over his face as if he was still feeling foggy from last night. A flash of light from his hand caught my eye. A ring on his left hand.

In an instant, the languid warmth of my orgasm was gone, replaced by shock and anger. I scrambled out of the bed, grabbing the sheet and tugging it to cover my body as I stood next to the bed.

He brought his hands away from his face and looked at me with concern.

"You're married."

His expression morphed into confusion. "No, I'm not."

"You're wearing a wedding ring." How was it that I didn't notice that before? I wasn't against an occasional hookup with somebody from out of town, but I drew the line at married men.

He frowned and looked at his hand, the confusion remaining on his face. He looked over at me, his eyes squinting, hovering near where I clutched the sheet around my breasts.

I was about to take offense at his ogling me when his gaze returned to my eyes. "So are you."

"What?"

"You've got a ring too."

My head jerked down, looking at my left hand, and sure enough, there was a gold band around my finger. My brain ceased to function. It didn't make any sense. And then it did.

"Oh, my God." I turned and sank onto the bed. How did this happen?

"Care to fill me in?" Max's tone had gone from confused to suspicious.

I shook my head, still not believing I could've done something so stupid. "I've become a Las Vegas cliché."

The bed shifted, and I glanced back to see Max getting out of bed, finding his boxers and his pants and slipping them on. "What does that mean?"

"We must have gotten drunk-married last night."

His hands on his belt buckle stilled as his gaze jerked to me. "What?"

"It's the only thing that explains this."

He shook his head, finishing with his belt. "That doesn't explain this. First of all, no one in their right mind would marry two people who were incoherently drunk."

I arched a brow. "We're in Las Vegas, Max."

"Even so, there would have to be paperwork, right? A marriage license. Marriage certificate."

He pulled the ring from his finger and tossed it onto the pillow. I had no illusions that Max and I were going to have some great love affair. Still, it hurt a little bit the way he yanked the ring off and tossed it away.

Even so, he was right. I pulled the ring from my finger and leaned over to set it on the side table. That's when I saw the papers. I scooted closer to the side table and picked them up, studying them. "Oh, God."

"What?" Max rounded the bed, buttoning his shirt.

I held the papers up. "Marriage license and certificate."

He snatched the papers out of my hand, and again the force of it and the look on his face made me flinch.

His gaze moved from the paper to me. "Is this some sort of joke?"

He tossed the papers on the bed, much like he had done with the ring.

Incensed, I stood up, gripping the sheet around me even tighter. It was hard to believe that just a few minutes ago, I was wrapped up in this man. "You think I did this?"

"The proof is in the papers, sweetheart."

I was shocked at his derision. I wished I were fully dressed because I felt vulnerable in just the sheet. But maybe it was just as well because if my hands were free, I might've slapped him. "Your signature is on there as well, slick."

He reached over, picking up the papers again, looking at the signature line. For a moment, he stood, looking utterly confused. The anger and accusation dissipated as he sank down onto the bed. "We'll be able to get this annulled."

"Being drunk doesn't constitute being incapacitated to get an annulment in Las Vegas."

"Sounds like you have experience with this." A hint of his derision returned.

"This is Vegas, Max. I know about gambling and showgirls, but that doesn't mean I gamble and dance."

He set the paper on the bed and scraped his hand over his face again. "Not being able to read or understand what I was signing would be a reason to grant an annulment, wouldn't it?"

"I suppose, but I don't remember reading or signing it either, and I'm not so sure that being too drunk to read and sign will work."

He turned to look at me, and for the first time, I saw vulnerability in him. Like he was going to confess something he wanted to keep a secret. "I have dyslexia. It's often hard enough to read legal papers when I'm sober. I can't imagine I could do it drunk."

I was no lawyer, but his reasoning made sense to me. I sat on the bed next to him.

He looked at his watch. "Fuck." He turned to look at me. "I don't have a lot of time before I need to catch my flight." He shook his head. "I guess I could take a later flight. I can move my schedule around."

"I'm not sure how to go about this in the first place. Why don't you let me research and get whatever paperwork we need, and once it's together, I can let you know? Maybe we can do this long distance and you don't need to return to Las Vegas."

He nodded. "But if I do need to be here, I can come."

I hadn't thought much about being married since I left the romanticism of fairy tales behind me when I was a teenager. But I never could have imagined that on my wedding day, my husband would be eager to divorce me.

Keep Reading *THE VEGAS BLUFF*

Interested in Dax's story? Get it here.

ABOUT THE AUTHOR

Ajme Williams writes emotional, angsty contemporary romance. All her books can be enjoyed as full length, standalone romances and are FREE to read in Kindle Unlimited .

Books do not have to be read in order.

Heart of Hope Series
Our Last Chance | An Irish Affair | So Wrong | Imperfect Love | Eight Long Years | Friends to Lovers | The One and Only | Best Friend's Brother | Maybe It's Fate | Gone Too Far | Christmas with Brother's Best Friend | Fighting for US | Against All Odds | Hoping to Score | Thankful for Us | The Vegas Bluff | 365 Days

Billionaire Secrets
Twin Secrets | Just A Sham | Let's Start Over | The Baby Contract | Too Complicated

The Why Choose Haremland
Protecting Their Princess | Protecting Her Secret | Unwrapping Their Christmas Present

Dominant Bosses
His Rules | His Desires | His Needs | His Punishments | His Secret

Strong Brothers
Say Yes to Love | Giving In to Love | Wrong to Love You | Hate to Love You

Fake Marriage Series
Accidental Love | Accidental Baby | Accidental Affair | Accidental Meeting

Irresistible Billionaires
Admit You Miss Me | Admit You Love Me | Admit You Want Me | Admit You Need Me

The Why Choose Haremland (Reverse Harem Series)
Protecting Their Princess | Protecting Her Secret | Unwrapping their Christmas Present

Check out Ajme's full Amazon catalogue here.

Join her VIP NL here.

WANT MORE AJME WILLIAMS?

Join my no spam mailing list here.

You'll only be sent emails about my new releases, extended epilogues, deleted scenes and occasional FREE books.

v

Made in United States
Troutdale, OR
02/20/2024

17842073R00149